AMBI

Beyond THE *Streets*

D1483772

LOVE AND LOYALTY

PRESSURE

AND

EMPRESS

Copyright © 2018 by Pressure & Empress
Published by DMG DMA Publications

978-0-692-85433-4

All rights reserved. Except for use in any review, the reproduction
or utilization of this work in whole or in part in any form by any
electronic, mechanical or other means, now known or hereinafter
invented, including xerography, photocopying and recording, or
in any information storage or retrieval system, is forbidden without the written permission of the publisher.

This is a work of fiction. Names, characters, places and incidents
are either the product of the author's imagination or are used
fictitiously, and any resemblance to actual persons, living or dead,
business establishments, events or locales is entirely coincidental.

Printed in the USA.

DEDICATIONS

I am dedicating this book to two of the most inspirational and influential men in my life other than my father. These two men played a major role in my life that helped me Grow and Develop into the man God ordained me to be. Renardo Wade aka Hard Nard and Milas Black aka Mr. Black. Thank you for everything that you've both taught me and I hope and pray after reading this book you know without a doubt that your words were not spoken in vain. I love you both. Lastly, I want to thank my beautiful wife for sharing this wonderful experience with me. Not too many men can actually sit down with their woman and accomplish a project of this magnitude. It took a lot of Dedication, Determination and Discipline to finish this project, but we did it, and I love you dearly for this. As you already know this is just the beginning. My undying Love and Loyalty.

~ Pressure

And for love's sake each mistake made we forgave. If given the choice I'd rather die here in your screams of passion. To my husband – the most intriguing man I know. My eternal Sweetheart. I stay in love.

~ *Lady Pressure*

CHAPTER ONE

~ EMPRESS ~

"GIRL, YOU BETTER HURRY UP!" KRIS LITTLE'S DEEP voice yells out from the classroom door.

His name is Little, but nothing about him is small. He is a 6'4 burly, beefed up giant who I estimate weighs around 180 pounds. Little has a complete beard while most boys are strugglin' to grow a few chin hairs. Did I mention that he is the star defensive back of Brook High School's football team?

Little tackles his opponents with ease on the football field, but he does not know how to tackle his homework. Last year, I was his math tutor. I can't say he has improved much. To be honest, he could probably be in the top 10 of our class, but he just doesn't give a damn since he is banking on getting a full ride and going to the NFL. His prerogative didn't bother me not one bit as long as his parents paid me every week.

Even though he has a mean mug that rivals Ice Cube's icy stare, he knows how to keep people laughin' and he has a big heart. He's cool people. His pockets stay on chubby, so he's always buyin' his friends Flamin' Hot Cheetos, Big Texas Cinnamon Rolls, and Fruit Punch Gatorades out of the school's vending machines. He even buys us Krispy Kreme and Starbucks at least once a week. Not to mention, he played ball with my big brother Trapp, so that is another reason why he's always nice to me.

I learned early on that the "lil sis pass" has its advantages when I first started high school. For instance, when I was a freshman, three years ago, the other 9th graders feared being picked on or wished they could sit at the lunch table with the popular kids. But, I had the "lil sis pass" which made me unquestionably cool with my brother's upperclassman friends. The "lil sis pass" is no doubt nepotism at its finest and I would be a fool to decline its benefits.

"Empress, please can I get it for $20?" Chante says as I close my locker.

"Girl bye! You asked for an A+ paper and that's exactly what this is," I say in an annoyed tone while dangling the research paper in front of her face.

Chante is gettin' on my nerves, but I really need the money for the electric bill. The past due notice came yesterday and all I need is forty more dollars to go along with the money I have already. I cannot afford to go any lower than my asking price. I hate to be without any electricity. It is such a terrible feeling to come home and find that nothin' works.

One time when I was younger, my family spent two whole weeks powerless and in pitch-black. I hated every minute. There was a whole bunch of card playin' and candle lightin' to see through the darkness. It felt like we were living in the days of Little House on the Prairie and I was little Laura Ingalls just writing away all my thoughts in a spiral notebook. I vowed to myself then I would never be without if I could help it.

Not to mention, I spent my valuable time finding the appropriate sources to support the claims in this paper. If Chante doesn't wanna buy it, I'm sure someone else will, but I need the money today. ASAP!

It's not like she doesn't have the money. She drives a silver

BMW 128i, lives in a gated community full of mansions, and never wears the same outfit twice. Her dad owns a chain of AMC Theaters and her mom is a dentist with a private practice. They give Chante a weekly allowance of $300 on the condition she maintains her 2.5 grade point average. Ugh, I gotta get her to change her mind.

"$40. Take it or leave it. From the looks of your progress report, you need it to pass this semester. This paper is worth 50% of your grade and I know you do not have shit prepared in your book bag. Besides, you know your parents from the islands and they don't play. They will keep you back rather than pay for you to go to summer school. While we are all off partying at college, you're still gonna be here cheering at pep rallies," I say hoping that my threat will get Chante to budge.

"Dang, Empress, you don't have to be all loud and put my business out there," Chante whispers, embarrassed that a squad of underclass girls overheard my comment and are now laughing at her as they walk by.

"My bad, but it doesn't matter, because they will be your classmates next year anyways if you don't turn this paper in," I say with a slight giggle.

"Okay, okay," Chante says, looking in her Michael Kors wallet. "I don't have any cash. Do you take Venmo or PayPal?"

"Both. But Venmo me," I say after a second thought. "PayPal be trippin' and I would hate for them to lock my account."

"Cool," she says.

In less than a minute, I receive a notification alerting me that the cash is in my account. "Thank you, ma'am," I say with a bow. "This was all you had to do from the jump.

"Yeah, yeah," Chante playfully says. "Are you sure

this is an A+ paper?"

"Really, Chante?" I roll my eyes annoyed by her comment, but realizing she is joking, I add, "You know my work is always top-notch just like my clothes and hair."

We both giggle.

The hallway seems awfully quiet now. Looking down the hall, I no longer see Little's big shadow in the doorway. Looking up at the circular clock hanging from the wall, the time reads, "8:05 a.m."

Damn it! I'm late.

Glancing up the hall, I see Chante heading towards the gym for PE, her first-period class.

She is lucky because the coaches do not care what you do. They just want to flirt with all the pretty girls wearing tight gym shorts.

"If I get detention, you owe me an extra $10!" I scream at Chante just for the heck of it.

Man, I hope I don't get detention!

~ NARD ~

"YOOOOOO, NARD! YOU HEARD ABOUT JAZ takin' a hit last night?" Juke states like he knows all the facts.

I am in my zone completely ignoring everything around me and plottin' on my next move. So much has happened lately that it's stressing me out.

"My nigga, you hear me!?!" Juke says, becoming annoyed.

"Yeah, nigga, I hear you," I say with slight frustration. "That shit is irrelevant to me. If it ain't makin' no money, then I could care less who the fuck got hit. That's what's wrong with you. Stop that gossiping shit and get some money in your pocket."

"Man, shut the fuck up, nigga. I get money," Juke says, all in his feelings and shit as we get on the school bus.

Juke and his older brother, Larosa, may not be my biological brothers, but I feel like they are. We have been through many things together - the good, the bad, and the ugly. Plus, we are all DMG and this alone makes our bond unbreakable.

Dirty Money Gangstas are widely known as DMG. DMG is who I am and what I'm part of. Some call us a gang. Some call us a clique of niggas who get money. Others call us savages. Some of us build up our community and some of us help tear it down. This should not be, but the bottom line is no man can dictate how another man eats. At the end of the day we are a family that looks out for one another.

We originally started out local, but we branched off to other states. We even have a female branch called DMA, which stands for Dirty Money Angels. The founders of DMG are from my hood. These are the niggas who I looked up to grow-ing up because much money was runnin' thru their hands and they had respect from everyone. Right now, these same individuals keep us together and united. They have so many expectations from my generation, but sadly we've been letting them down with all this senseless beefin' with a crew known as YGC.

YGC stands for Young Gangsta Committee and was founded by former DMG member, Diesel, during OG Black's generation. Diesel thought he was bigger than the mob. Sad to say, but he took about a third of our members with him and has recruited many more. Because of this open betrayal, I hate them niggas with a passion and I'm not the only one that feels this way.

We hardly ever see Diesel these days, he's been MIA for the past two years. Some say he fled out of state, some say he sleepin' with the fishes, and others say he's found God and left the street life alone. Whatever it is, me nor my brothers fuck with them niggas which is the reason we were always fighting and killing each other until the OGs called a truce six months ago.

Back to Juke and what he said. What he doesn't know is that me and Larosa were the ones who hit Jaz last night. The way he's runnin' his damn mouth about the whole situation is only adding fuel to the fire.

Yeah, you read that right. Me and Larosa were the ones who hit Jaz last night. Let me tell you all about the night before.

———◆———

I HAD BOOSIE BLASTIN' THRU MY TWO 15 kickers as I drove from West Ave. back to the hood. If I did not look down and see my phone lighting up, I would have never known Larosa was calling.

"Say FAM, Jaz wants to fight his dog," he says.

"If it don't make money, it don't make sense," I thought. So, of course, my response was, "How much he talkin'?"

"He tryin' to flex on a nigga talmbout he got 5 bands," Larosa angrily answered.

I knew exactly what he was thinking. His pride always clouds his judgement which causes us to get into altercations with niggas and sometimes worse.

I had told myself a couple of months' prior I would give up on hittin' licks because I know the only future behind this is death or prison. Lately, my pockets been hurting because my job at Burger King isn't making ends meet. I'm definitely not planning to make Burger King a career.

Weighing the options out in my head, I thought to myself, "*Going legit is stressful, but I can't give in…but hell, I can use the money…it will catch me up too.*"

"What do you say, FAM? Let's get this nigga," Larosa asked as the light turned green.

The green light seemed to give me the answer I needed as I replied, "I'm on my way, FAM."

I later found out that the whole time I was talkin' to Larosa on the phone, he was already in the house socializing with Jaz and his crew.

Jaz came to Georgia, 7 months ago, from Baltimore to set up trap and he has been flexin' ever since. He immediately clicked up with those YGC niggas, our sworn enemies. But as I stated before the elders of both organizations agreed to a truce. Now he had pissed off the wrong nigga - Larosa.

The love I have for my brother is without measurement, so I am going to have his back in his right and in his wrong. That's the mentality we always had growing up together. Not saying it is right, but that is how we rock. We are all we got.

As I pulled into Harvest Grove, which is the hood I'm from, a million thoughts ran through my mind.

I was breaking one of my number one rules as a robber which is, 'don't never eat where you sleep'. And here I was about to rob this nigga out here where I stay.

Harvest Grove is a jackboy's paradise because of the many paths and cuts that run through it. There's almost a 0% chance of 12 catching you if you are familiar with the lay-out. It may not be the most up kept hood with broken down shingles in the front of the buildings and paint chipping from the weather, but it's where I've been all my life and I'll never forget where I come from. I say this to say, I don't plan to stay here forever.

"*Fuck it,*" I said to myself as I jumped out my all white, double burgundy striped '84 Monte Carlo SS with my .40 in my hand.

I crept up to the apartment and immediately heard music and laughin'. Questions raced through my mind, *"How many niggas are in there?" "How the fuck am I going to pull this off?"*

My mind deliberated on the questions and I called Larosa back.

"What's poppin', FAM?" He answered.

"How many niggas are in there? Cause it sounds like y'all havin' a party," I asked.

"Where you at, FAM?" He asked through the noise.

"I'm outside," I responded.

"Bet. Just knock on the door and do your thing."

Click.

Now, had this been anyone else, I would have been furious. My question never got answered. I still didn't know how many niggas were in there. I don't like doing shit in the blind, but I knew Larosa would never send me on a death wish. Then again, the more I thought about the situation, I realized that this was all this shit was. Especially since I did not know how many people were in the apartment.

My phone lit up again.

"Wat's good?" I asked.

"Mannnnnnnn, knock on the damn door," Larosa said, clearly irritated.

"Aight, nigga."

Click.

I walked up to the apartment door, covered my face with my black bandanna and knocked.

"Hold on!" Someone yelled through the door.

As the locks turned, and the door opened, I became stuck for a split-second due to the beauty of the woman who was standing at the entrance.

She had a golden-brown complexion, with a blonde

straight weave. Her curves fit her tall model body just right. She had a nice round ass with nice plump breasts to match. The catsuit she wore left little to my imagination. She was sexy as fuck.

After staring at her for a minute, I snapped out of my lust because I realized she was about to scream due to me having a black bandanna around my face. I immediately jumped into action, grabbing her by the throat, placing my .40 to her gut.

The trap music loudly pumped into everyone's ears, so no one heard the hard thump of her falling to the floor and her cries of, "Please, don't hurt me!"

I walked her to the kitchen where everyone was either standing or sitting at the wooden table which looked as though it was infected by termites. By the time they realized what was happening, it was too late. Larosa had pulled his .40 out and demanded all five niggas take a seat at the table.

Following his lead, I ordered them to place their hands out on top of the table as he ranned their pockets. While he was doin' that, I gave the woman a bag and told her to put everything on the table in it.

As I yelled, "Where's the safe?!?" I noticed two things – Jaz dropping his head knowing he was about to get cleaned out, and the woman, who by this point had collected everything off the table, had somehow slipped away.

I quickly found her in the laundry room with her phone. I grabbed the bag and grabbed her by the throat, pointing my gun at her gut once again.

Just as I whispered in her ear, "I'm not going to hurt you," I noticed she had called 911. I snatched the phone out of her hand and quickly hung up.

"Let's go!!!" I yelled to Larosa.

We started hearing sirens as we backed out the apartment door with our guns aimed at them niggas.

Now, shit had gotten real.

Good thing they lived on the first floor because we could hop in my ride quickly. As I whipped out the hood, three police cars pulled in with their lights and sirens off. We got away, but the plan was never to leave them niggas alive because they knew who FAM was.

"Nigga, how hard was it to let me know how many niggas was in there!?!" I screamed at Larosa knowing that was a close call.

He is the type of nigga who gets a rush from living a fast life, oblivious, and not givin' a fuck about consequences.

"Bruh, it wasn't even goin' to matter. We still was goin' to go thru with it!" He screamed back. "Plus, that nigga, Jaz, disrespectful as fuck. Now, I gotta figure out a way on how I'm goin' to dead that nigga before he try to dead me. How the fuck you let that bitch call 12, FAM!?!"

"I didn't even see her slip in that laundry room cause I had my eye on Jaz and 'em, tryin' to make sure they didn't pull a stunt on your ass," I angrily responded.

"But, that bitch was sexy as fuck," I said changing the direction of the conversation, seeing we wouldn't see eye to eye on the situation because we both can be hard-headed and stubborn. "Who broad that was?"

"Heard's," replied Larosa.

"Awwww shit, once that nigga find out we had sumthin to do with that shit, he is going to be pissed." Thinking once more, I added, "Hold up, Heard wasn't even in there, so what the fuck was shawty doin' at that trap?"

"She got caught up," Larosa said with a chuckle because he knew she was fuckin' with Jaz on the low.

"She had just gotten there."

"So, wat the hell we gonna do about her and those niggas?" I asked.

"First, let me call Heard to see where his mind at," Larosa responded, looking out the rearview mirror to make sure 12 wasn't tailing us. "Then we goin' to lay on these other niggas," he continued. "Call Danielle and let her know we pullin' up so we can count this money and split it."

———◆———

AND THAT'S HOW SHIT WENT DOWN. NOW, I'M stuck dealing with this bullshit because me and Larosa reignited a beef that was once deaded between two rival crews.

Chapter Two

"SAY FAM, WAT'S GOOD?" LAROSA ASKS HEARD over the phone as he rolls a blunt in bed.

"I was wondering the same thing when my wife came home last night talkin' bout she was held at gunpoint. So, wat's up with that Larosa?" Heard aggressively asks.

"Did she get robbed though? That's the question?" Larosa fires back.

"That ain't the muthafuckin question, Larosa, and you know that shit wasn't right. You and Nard could've done y'all thing at a later time and you know that," Heard states with even more aggression.

"What are you sayin'?" Larosa questions, every muscle in his body tensing as he stretches out in bed. He has a bad temper and the smallest of things can set him off. "If you got sumthin on your chest, let me know. I'm not about to argue," he adds.

"That's my woman, nigga, and you knew that before you put her in harm's way, so I am highly offended," Heard replies, matching the hostility.

"This shit comes with the territory, so do what you feel is necessary to appease your spirit," Larosa says.

Completely fed up by Larosa's blatant disrespect, Heard takes an understated deep breath.

"Say less. May God grant you and Nard mercy once you reach the afterlife and teach you both that there is a time and a place for everything," Heard says ending the call.

The conversation with Heard replays in Larosa's mind as he lays back in bed and looks up at the ceiling. Anger travels in his veins and uncertainty looms in his mind.

Heard is no one to take lightly. At 36, he has built a solid rep as a known shooter. Murder is his profession, and he is good at it. He has never killed anyone in Rockdale because that is where he's from and where he rests his head. Still, niggas in the area know not to cross him. With that said, Larosa knows Heard is a patient killer and strikes when least expected.

~ EMPRESS ~

HAVE YOU EVER WISHED YOU WERE INVISIBLE? Well, I don't wish I were invisible altogether, just invisible long enough to teleport into a desk in Mrs. Rozier's classroom. I know it's wishful thinking, but I really do not feel like hearin' this woman's mouth.

Mrs. Rozier is an old-school teacher who has been teaching at Brook High for 20 years - longer than I have been alive. She's a tall, slim woman that dresses nice every day. I don't think I've ever seen her wear the same thing twice. She's tough, but I know how to get on her good side.

"Lord, please soften this woman's heart, so I won't get detention. I can't afford to be late to work," I silently pray before entering the classroom.

Slowly, I open the heavy wooden door with the intention of creeping in. Not to my surprise, Mrs. Rozier is writing something on the dry-erase board.

I'm annoyed someone is sittin' in my usual seat on the third row behind my friend Olivia, so I scope out the classroom to see where are the open seats. Shocked that Mrs. Rozier has not noticed my entrance, I smile thinking I have gotten away with being late until Byron Walker opens his big ass mouth.

"Pssst...Empress, come sit your fine ass right here."

"Do I hear profanity in my classroom?" Mrs. Rozier suspiciously asks the class as she writes on the dry-erase board.

"OMG! Thanks a lot, dumbass," I say, rolling my eyes at Byron causing all twenty students to laugh.

"You're too cute to be mean, girl," Byron says. "A nigga just tryin' -"

"Who keeps using that profane language?!" Mrs. Rozier asks again as she turns to face the class.

Byron is cute, but he talks entirely too much. This is the main reason I have not and will not give him the time of day. Not to mention he has dreads - which I hate. I bet Mrs. Rozier will surely give me detention now and it will be all his fault.

"Why Empress, you have decided to join us today," she sarcastically says while pulling off her designer eye-glasses.

"Yes, Mrs. Rozier, I have," I reply in the sweetest voice with an innocent smile.

"You're late again, Empress," she tiredly says.

"Fashionably late, though," I joke, garnering laughs from the class, but unfortunately, not from Mrs. Rozier.

"Yeah girl," Kimani agrees. "You do look cute today. I love that MCM backpack. Did you just get it?"

"Thanks," I reply, loving the compliment. "Yeah, I got it -"

"Excuse me, ladies, this is not a fashion show," Mrs.

Rozier interrupts. "Empress, you've disrupted enough class time. Find a seat. I will see you in detention."

"Detention? Mrs. Rozier please, I have to be at work today by 2pm and I'm only here for two periods. I can't stay late," I sincerely say.

"Well, you should have made it a priority to be on time to my class," Mrs. Rozier responds without budging.

As I make my way to the empty seat, on the front row, Little makes it a point to tell me he tried to keep the door open. Apparently, Mrs. Rozier made him close the door.

"It's cool," I softly say, appreciating him lookin' out for me.

"Class, I am disappointed that I heard the 'N-word' being used," Mrs. Rozier says as she walks to the center of the class.

"We are all black, so it doesn't matter," Little says as he daps another member of the football team.

"It does matter," Mrs. Rozier sternly says, putting emphasis on the word 'does' which causes the class to become eerily silent.

"Now, I know this is not history class, but don't you all realize that 'nigga' was the last word some black people heard before they were lynched, shot, or tormented by racist," she passionately continues, placing vivid images of past monstrosities in our minds.

"Have you all ever heard of Margaret Garner?" She asks.

"No," the class replies simultaneously.

"Well, she was born a slave, and in 1856 she decided to escape to Cincinnati where she and her three children would be free. They were not even free for an entire day when the federal marshals stormed the

Underground Railroad safe house they were at for no longer than a day with warrants for her arrest. Determined not to return to slavery, Margaret decided to take the lives of herself and the children. When the marshals found Margaret in a back room, she had killed her two-year-old daughter by slitting her throat with a butcher knife. The other children laid on the floor wounded, but still alive. Can you all imagine knowing your entire existence would be to pick cotton on a plantation and never being considered a human, but a nigga?"

"Wow," I say aloud, unable to fathom what it must have felt like to never know freedom.

"Don't let me get started on the East St. Louis Massacres of 1917 or Black Wall Street," Mrs. Rozier says, ready to delve further in the discussion.

"Tell us about it!" Olivia excitedly says, eager to know more.

"I would if we had enough time," Mrs. Rozier says, wishing she could give us a full-fledged history lesson.

"I challenge you all to Google these terrorist attacks against blacks and maybe your perspectives may change," she continues. "I don't like policing your conversations, but I will not allow you all to utter that word in my classroom. The 'N-word' was created to strip people of their humanity. Even though you all may not admit it, words have power. You all are better than calling yourselves a word that was systematically used to deny our ancestors human rights and privileges."

"Dang, I never really thought about it like that," Little says.

"Me either," Byron chimes. "You know you my favorite teacher, so I didn't mean to make you mad,

Mrs. Rozier."

"I'm not mad, Byron. You all just need to be informed. It is my responsibility as your teacher to educate and this is a perfect moment. This is something for you all to think about."

"Dang, this was so deep! I see you, Mrs. Rozier," Kimani says with a smile.

"Okay, moving along with today's lesson. No one got the brain teaser correct," Mrs. Rozier says as she flips through the papers.

"Can I try to answer it?" I ask.

"Sure, but I doubt if you will get it correct seeing that your classmates did not," she responds.

"What celebrity mansion is in Grassland?" I read the written question aloud.

"I bet she doesn't get it," I hear someone behind me say.

"Elvis," I answer, with a broad smile.

"Who is that?" Someone in the back of the class says.

"Excellent job, Empress!" Mrs. Rozier smiles, Unable to control her excitement because I got the answer right

"Could you possibly retract my detention since I'm the only one who got the answer right?" I ask.

"Deal," Mrs. Rozier says, without a second passing.

Whew! I'm so glad she has a heart. Thank you, God.

"Empress, can you explain to the class how you got the answer?" Mrs. Rozier asks.

"Yeah, pay attention you imbeciles," I jokingly say. "Soooo, Elvis' house was called Graceland, and the question says grassland, so it is sort of a play on words."

"Huh? How do you know that?" Olivia questions.

"Don't let the pretty face fool you," I say in all fun. "This girl does know some things."

~ NARD ~

AS THE SCHOOL BUS APPROACHES THE FRONT entrance, I wish that I was back at regular school. Even though I have a car, the school does not permit students to drive. We're also not allowed to wear normal clothes. All students must wear khakis with a polo style shirt that has the school's logo stitched on it. The administration tries to stop individuality anyway they can. I hate the dumb rules, but what can I do?

Alpha Alternative is one ugly ass school. It looks like an ancient dungeon with holes for windows and doors. The resemblance to a county jail is uncanny. I'm not sure if the janitors clean every night because spider webs fill the ceilings and the floors are dirty as hell. But, I digress, I'm here and I gotta deal with this shit, just like I do everything else in life.

Getting off the school bus, I mentally prepare myself for schoolwork, especially after a night like last night. I don't carry my gun when I'm at school because there is no need to bring unwanted attention to myself. Some dumbass young nigga got caught last week going through the metal detector with a 9-millimeter handgun and two clips. What the nigga was planning on doin' with it? I don't know, but I know nobody here is dumb enough to try me.

As I wait to go through the metal detector, my phone starts vibrating like crazy in my pocket. I step aside and let the other students move up in line, so I can answer the call.

"Wat up, bruh? Wat you doin' up so early?" I ask Larosa because he hasn't been up this early since he dropped out of high school last year.

"Maaaan, shit is crazy!" Larosa loudly replies, causing

me to turn my phone volume down. "We got problems with Heard now."

"So, you are telling me we've got problems with Heard now?" I ask, confused.

"That's what I just said, bruh," Larosa replies, sounding defeated.

"That's bad business, Family, but we got in this mess so we must clean it up," I say, shaking my head. "Wat's up with him, tho?"

"He feels disrespected because we robbed Jaz and his crew while his girl was present," Larosa explains.

Walking away from the building to ensure I have complete privacy, I shake my head.

Something told me I should've spoke to Heard myself because Larosa's communication skills are on the floor.

"FAM, just know once this is over, I'm hangin' up my guns for good, no exceptions," I say in all earnestness. "I will be one of the few who make it out."

"I hear you, FAM, and I respect your decision. Just remember old habits are hard to break, especially if this is all you know," Larosa says without a hint of optimism.

"I'm strong-minded so breaking this habit won't be a problem," I firmly say. "I will strive to make a better way for the betterment of my family, but this isn't it."

"I will miss you, but I'm in the game for life," Larosa replies.

"You will get tired one day or God forbids something worse happens," I counter. "I will be praying for you."

"It is what it is, Family. This is sumthin I chose and I have no regrets," Larosa shoots back.

"That's right. I'm glad you know that, but enough of

this. My class is about to start. Meet me at Black's spot later so we can let the others know what's goin' on."

"Love," we both say ending the call.

CHAPTER THREE

~ EMPRESS ~

EVEN THOUGH I WAS LATE, SCIENCE CLASS IS STILL going by slow. I've read all the shade there was to read on The Shade Room and now my battery is low. Hopefully, I can catch a charge from someone before I get to work.

The bell finally rings.

"Empress, you have no respect for time," Mrs. Rozier walks over to my desk and says as I pack up my things. "You're one of my brightest students. I would like for you to be a positive example and not a negative one," she genuinely adds. "Please attempt to get to class on time."

"Okay, Mrs. Rozier. I will try. Thanks again," I say as I exit the class.

I understand what she is saying and I recognize that she is coming from a good place, but really, I have other concerns and problems to face.

Money for the electric bill – Check
No detention – Check
A ride to work – Uncheck

Problem number three - how am I going to get to work?

Getting here is always a challenge since I go to school out of district. Not to mention, the family vehicle is unreliable. This happens to be one of those unreliable days. Trapp dropped me off this morning, but he texted me during class to tell me that the alternator has gone out.

If it isn't one thing, it is always something else. I've been trying to put aside money to buy a cash car, but it's hard to save when money is constantly going out and everyone is depending on me. MARTA does not run in the suburbs and I do not want to spend the little money I have on an Uber or a cab. Ugh, now I have to figure out how the hell I will get to work in the next 2 hours.

"Young Empress! What you got goin' on today?" Olivia asks as we walk to our lockers which are by each other.

"Nothin' much. I have to go to work soon. Why didn't you save me a seat in class?"

"Oh, girl. Deshun had started talkin' to me and you know I like him."

"And I know how your brain goes on dumb whenever you're around him," I say in a playful manner.

"He's so fine, girl. He wants me to come over to his house tomorrow night!" Olivia excitedly says.

"Are you going?"

"Hell yeah, he is too fine! I can't say no."

"You know you're not going to be his girlfriend, right?" I comment, shaking my head.

"Well, it's a start," Olivia says, her voice trailing off.

"A start to thot-ness," I say laughing.

"Somebody has jokes, eh?" Olivia responds, annoyed by my opinion. "What kinda action are you gettin' into?"

"None. I don't want none of these little boys at

Brook High. Besides you know I don't chase no boys. I chase my money and the dream of getting a record deal," I say with a grin.

As we're talking, Church Williams sneaks up from behind and places his arm around my shoulder.

Church's real name is Tony, but he got the nickname Church due to his father being a reverend at one of the popular mega churches in Georgia. Church is in the twelfth grade, same as me. He is our star point guard and a lot of college recruiters are visiting our school just to convince him to commit to their university.

He is dark-skinned with deep dimples that compliment his great smile. He also has a nice low fade with deep waves. Church is fine, but I am not interested. I am probably the only girl in school who feels this way. He is at the top of the "school food chain." He has been with nearly every popular girl at school. How do I know this, you ask? Well, most of the girls who he hooks up with brag about fuckin' him just for props.

"What's up wit you, girl?" He says with a goofy, yet cute smile on his face.

"Um, I do have a name," I reply, making sure not to make eye contact with him.

"My bad, my bad, Miss Empress. How are you doing?"

"That's better," I say with a smile. "Aren't you going to say hi to my friend?"

"Oh, yeah. What's her name?" He asks.

"Olivia," I whisper in his ear.

"Hey, Olivia," he says with a smirk.

Olivia is sooo thirsty to return the "hey" that she nearly trips over her feet as we cruise the hallway. Looking at her out of the corner of my eye, I can tell she wants to say more, but she doesn't know what to say.

"Church, what do you want with me?" I ask.

"Whisper in my ear again and I'll tell you," he says with a devilish grin. "You know what I want from you, gurl."

"You wish," I say, playfully hitting him on the stomach.

"Forreal, forreal tho, I'm havin' a kickback at my house this weekend and I want to see you there," Church confidently says.

"I can't make it," I say.

"Dang, you gonna leave me hangin' like that? I know you are a boujee girl, so I promise it won't be nothin' ratchet."

"I'm good, Church. Maybe next time," I say.

"Bet," he says as he hands me a sheet of paper.

"What's this?" I ask.

"Just some notes I jotted down for you before you made it to class," he responds.

"Gee, thanks," I say, taken by surprise.

"I see you studying in the library from time to time. You know I got a library in my house, right?" He asks, wrapping his arm around my waist. "Not to mention, you know I ace all our science tests so I can give you a few pointers on a whole lot of things, starting with anatomy. You know what they say, studying is more fun with a buddy," he adds with a wink.

"The school library is just fine and I like to study alone," I say, mocking the wink he gave me as I remove his hand from my waist.

"Hahaha. Be like that then. When you're ready to cash in that coupon I just offered you, hit me up," he says with a sly smile.

"That nigga Byron is right, your ass is fine," he adds as he walks away.

Finding what happened to be completely ridiculous, Olivia can barely finish entering her combination to open her locker.

"You're crazy! How can you turn down Church Williams?!? He is the cutest and most popular boy at the school," she cries.

"Ah, he's alrite. Besides, I have to work both of my jobs on Saturday," I reply.

"Girl, if I were you, I would be like, 'Church let's go to your house right now!'" she says while getting her books for the next period.

"Olivia, you're crazy," I say with a laugh.

"You can't be Snow White Jr. forever. All these fine ass boys tryna talk to you and you turn them all down. You don't give none of them play. You don't realize how lucky you are," Olivia says in an almost lecturing manner.

"Just because you've been giving it up since 8th grade doesn't mean shit. Everyone is not deserving of your time, let alone your body, Olivia. The first time I made a mistake by listening to you telling me it was time and how I couldn't graduate as a virgin. This time, I'm waiting for the right guy. If he even exists. All these boys are only interested in sex and I want more than that," I say, closing my locker.

"Aw, Empress please," Olivia says with a laugh. "Boys don't fuck with girls who not givin' it up and I mean that literally. Anyways, that's how you get popular."

"Not true," I fire back. "I'm popular and it's not because I've slept with alot of guys. Is sex the only thing you think about?

"Um, duh!" She says with a laugh. "C'mon let's get to class before you get caught up and get detention again."

~ NARD ~

"SHIT CRAZY OUT HERE IN THE HOOD. 12 HOT as fuck," I explain to Danielle as we walk down the hallway of Alpha Alternative. "Jaz got a hit out for Larosa and is paying double if they take out the other nigga who was with him,"

"Cut the bullshit, Nard. Everybody knows who the second nigga was, and that was you," she says, pointing her long acrylic nail into my polo shirt.

Danielle is coffee brown, 5'6, and feisty. She thinks she's the baddest bitch out here cause she's thick. The only way she can stand out in a crowd is by dressing like a hoe. She's the type of girl who drives around town blastin' her music just as loud as any nigga and she loves drama. It's nothin' for her to bust a bitch in they shit. Fighting is why her ass at this school. Hell, she even done dirt with me before - set up niggas and everything. She reps DMA, the female branch of DMG, to the fullest.

Even though Danielle is hard on the outside, I know another side of her that most don't see. She is extremely emotional and insecure on the inside which makes her unstable. This is why I never tell her about anything she isn't tied to personally. Don't get me wrong, I trust her to an extent, but I can't have her gettin' angry with me because she caught feels for me during a fling we had last year.

She believes in her heart I will make her my woman if she ride for a nigga when needed. I will never give anyone that type of ammunition against me because you never know who will fold on you. I trust no one.

"You can fool everybody else, but you can't fool me," she says, smacking her lips. "I know you, nigga. And if you so called didn't do it, why you call me at midnight talkin' about y'all pullin' up and shit?" Danielle asks, looking me dead in the eyes. "Had I'd been there, I would've known the truth, but a bitch had to handle her business, ya dig?"

"Nigga, I told you, I had nothin' to do with that shit because I've cleaned up," I reply, becoming upset. "So, stop saying that shit before the wrong ears hear it and run wild wit it."

"Bullshit," she says as we walk into Mr. Boston's math class. "Just know the truth shall set you free and you ain't gotta lie to me."

We both take a seat and she rushes to finish homework that Mr. Boston will collect in 5 minutes.

"Damn, nigga. Why the fuck did we do that shit?" I ask myself, thinking about the night before. *That shit wasn't worth no $7,500, especially having to split it down the middle. I realize this shit ain't about to blow over and I may be forced to pick up my guns again.*

While I'm in my thoughts, it feels like someone is staring at me. Turning my head to the right, it is my brother from another mother, Juke, looking back at me.

He had to be reading my mind because he whispers, "Ain't nothin' good going to come out of this, so there is no need of stressin' about this shit. BOSS up or get BOSS'd around...make a decision."

"There ain't no decision to make because it's already been made," I defensively reply. "I'm just plottin', my nigga. My only concern now is gettin' to work and makin' legit money."

"And you think that's safe?" Juke asks. "Like them

niggas don't know you work at Burger King."

"Them niggas ain't stupid," I confidently say. "But, if they are, I got my piece."

Growing tired of our conversation, I get up from the desk to sharpen my pencil.

"Ima holla at you when I get off," I tell Juke before walking away.

CHAPTER FOUR

~ EMPRESS ~

MAN, I STILL DO NOT KNOW HOW THE HELL I'm getting to work, let alone home. I'm not paying attention to anything Frau Isleigh is teaching in German class. This class is so boring and annoying much like the dated German soap opera from the 1980s we are watching. I wish I could say, 'Auf Wiedersehen' to this course, but I am required to take a language class and this is the only one open this semester. Meanings and spellings of words, I know, but pronunciation is another thing. I am not looking forward to the oral examine I have to take in a few minutes.

My mind is so cluttered and focused on everything besides German. I can't think. Trapp hasn't texted back, so for the last 45 minutes I have been trying to think of someone who will drive 30 minutes away to drop me off at work.

Since Brook High is the best school in DeKalb County for academics and sports, it was determined by my mother that this would be the school Trapp and I would attend, even though it is out of district. The high schools near my neighborhood in Rockdale have less than stellar reviews. The schools are poor and the teachers do not care.

Brook High is different. One major reason is because it is a prep school. Students and teachers are expected to adhere to the highest academic standards in the state of Georgia. The coursework is no doubt rigorous. On average, I probably spend 2 to 3 hours a night on homework. A B- average is required for admittance and a C- average has to be maintained to continue attending. For the last three years, I have worked very hard to maintain my A- average.

Olivia talks a lot about college, especially now since we are seniors. She's been trying to get me to apply to the same colleges she has, but I have not found the need to. I'm a pretty, good singer, rapper, and songwriter and music is my passion. I've posted a few videos on YouTube and some tracks on SoundCloud, which has gotten about 180,000 views and downloads.

Mostly good reviews, I may add. If I get my views up to the millions, not only would it be easier for me to get discovered, but I can get paid from YouTube. Imagine that. Post a video every week, sit back and collect my check. Au revoir crummy jobs and haters!

I'm already a YouTube partner, so I'm one step closer. I even have my own girl group called Da Girls. Well, we were a group, a quartet to be exact, but we broke up. You know, typical girl group drama - jealousy, pettiness, and lies. Music and the sense of purpose it afforded was really the only element of compatibility that Da Girls shared. Now, I am a solo act which does not surprise me because the only person I can always depend on is myself.

I am thinking of singing a song I wrote for the spring talent show, but I'm not sure just yet. Hopefully, I am off work the night of the talent show. Once I get a record deal, I won't have to worry about none of this bullshit.

Music has always been a part of my life since I can remember. It is my escape and allows me to express myself. Even with that being said, my mom has been nagging me to apply *to colleges. She taught me to always have a Plan B, so I guess I will apply to a university Trapp mentioned he liked in Florida when he went on a college tour a few years back. I can see myself chillin' on the beach and enjoying life in Florida. Besides, I don't want to work an hourly, uniform-required job my whole life.*

As class is ending, Trapp finally texts me back:

Trapp: I got you a ride to work. Carlos from the hood on his way now.
Empress: Who?
Trapp: Lo, you met him before. He's Courtney's brother.
Empress: Oh okay. I don't want just anybody picking me up.
Trapp: Beggars can't be choosers. Anyways, he knows not to try nothin'.
Empress: Okay.

W.E.B. Dubois had a concept of "two-ness" or what he called "double consciousness" meaning that a person's identity is divided into several parts making it difficult or impossible to have one unified identity. I feel like this concept applies to me.

After all, here I am living two lives, inhabiting two paradoxical worlds. Boujee girl with no worries at school during the day and barely keeping my family's head above water by night. Guess it's true what they say - looks are quite deceiving. My clothes may be nice, but they don't come easy. I work my fingers to the bone with a 4-hour school shift and an 8-hour work shift.

With two little sisters, my mom does not make enough money to buy the clothes I like to wear and I don't want to be a burden on her, so I bust my ass at both of my part-time jobs. Besides, fashion runs Brook High. Everything is so superficial here. Whoever said it is not on the outside what counts, but what's in the inside, lied. If I came to school wearing cheap clothes, I would never hear the end of it.

I feel like I live two different existences between being a prep school girl in an affluent neighborhood and being raised by a single mother in the hood. The hardships I face daily are hidden from my prep school world. Once school is over I always have to wonder what is going on in my alternate universe.

Unlike most girls my age, I am not boy-crazy. Boys… who needs them? Don't get me wrong, I like being someone's girl, but boys do not rule my world. Besides, they are all the same - only looking out for themselves. So, I will look out for myself because I can trust no man. I do not know if I will ever find a guy I can trust, but I know this guy, Lo, better not try anything funny.

———◆———

"THANKS AGAIN FOR THE RIDE," I SAY TO LO, hopping out of his ol' skool '90 Caprice on 30" For-giato's.

His wax job makes the candy teal paint glisten. The wheels are a little too big for my liking, but it is a nice car.

In Rockdale, cars, especially ol' skool cars, are a big thing for guys. They all try to outdo each other. The fact is a guy's car is an aspect of his identity. It may be a subtle statement, but it is a statement. Guys are so competitive to the point where it is silly. All of them want to be the alpha male and that is apparent in the cars they invest in. They all seem to love loud, big, and dangerous cars. You couldn't pay a guy from Rockdale to drive an electric car like the Fiat 500e.

"No problem, shawty," he responds, cranking the music back up which makes the nearby parked cars shake.

Ugh, I hate when guys call me "shawty." It is so annoying, but growing up in Atlanta, it is something that a girl gets used to.

As I walk into Krystal's, I see Miss Mable at one of the front register's counting down the drawer to make sure the money is right before my shift starts.

Miss Mable is a feisty, heavy set, thinning hair, elderly lady. She has been working at Krystal's for nearly 30 years. The limp in her walk proves how tired she is and her few missing bottom teeth prove how hard of a life she has lived. Since she is so old and has mostly gray hair, I call her grandma.

"Hey, grandma!" I say with a smile.

"Empress, don't come in here with all that playin' today," Miss Mable says as she puts the difference from the till in a clear deposit slip.

"Dang, I can't even say hey to my grandma," I say with a giggle.

"Who that was that dropped you off, Empress? Your man?" Enrique asks as he clocks back in from his break.

Enrique has been crushin' on me since my first day on the job, two years ago. He is extremely jealous of any guy that flirts with me, but I think he understands that he is strictly friend-zoned.

"Enrique, why you all up in my business?" I ask as I stand at the front counter.

He may be nosey, but Enrique is a blast to work with. He is a year younger than me and is extremely funny, especially once his Latin accent grows stronger. At times, he sounds like a bootleg Tony Montana. He keeps me laughing regularly on this shitty job, which causes Miss Mable to constantly yell, "Empress, stop all that laughin'!" I take things seriously when I need to, but this isn't my career path. So, I don't mind laughing now and then. Besides, life is too short to be so uptight.

Since I got promoted to master cashier, some of the older people hate on me, which I don't mind. As they say, if you don't have haters, you're doing something wrong. I don't want to be like these people - grown and working a child's job.

Being master cashier means that out of all the cashiers at the restaurant, I have the fastest time in the drive-thru and I follow all proper protocol and processes for cashing out orders and bagging food. I was very appreciative to receive the promotion as it came with a $4 raise that God knows my family and I need. Too bad it also came with a bright ass yellow button-down shirt that is too big for me and makes me look like I belong on Sesame Street with Big Bird. I am waiting on Jake, the store manager, to put in a new order for a smaller shirt for me. Hopefully, it will come soon.

After changing into my uniform, I walk over to the second front register to clock-in. As I press the green punch-in button, on the screen, a man that looks to be in his mid-thirties, possibly forties, approaches the front counter to look at the huge menu that hangs above it.

He looks like he is either going or coming from the gym. Either way, I think eating greasy fast food is a poor decision on his end.

Miss Mable and Vanessa, the shift leader, tell me to take the man's order.

"But, I haven't counted down a drawer yet," I complain.

"Just use mine," Vanessa says.

"Okay."

"Hi, welcome to Krystal's. Would you like to try our

number one combo with cheese?" I ask the man who has been checkin' me out since he entered the building.

"I'll take the number one without cheese - for now," he says with a creepy smile.

Taking his money, I explain I will bring his food to his table when the order is complete.

His order is up in 5 minutes. Placing four boxed Krystal's and a cup of fresh, hot fries on our famous red plastic trays, I take the man his food.

Once I arrive at his table he looks at my stitched, red name tag, and says, "Empress," as if he knows me. Taking a long pause and staring at me intently he adds, "You're pretty."

"Thanks," I dryly say.

"Seems like you heard that too many times before," he coolly replies.

Without a response from me and seeing I am not amused by him, he asks, "How old are you?"

"I'm seventeen," I reply.

"Damn, you gotta fat ass for such a little girl," he laughs. "If you were mine, you wouldn't be working in a place like this. I know you probably gotta little boyfriend, but I want to call you sometimes."

He reaches for my hand, but I quickly snatch it back.

I could be this man's daughter! What is he thinking? He must be an R. Kelly fan. Working at Krystal's has taught me that older men are often sexually inappropriate with teenage girls. Just last year, I realized after reading an article about sexual harassment that I had faced countless incidents since being employed here.

The guy makes a disgusting smacking sound with his lips as I roll my eyes and respond, "Not interested."

It is one thing to fight off little boys, but grown men...that's another story. They are relentless!

"Empress! C'mon and count this drawer. I need you in drive-thru," Vanessa calls out.

Vanessa's timing could not be better. I need to get away from this old creep immediately!

I walk over to the tiny drive-thru space and count the drawer to make sure that it is $100.

"That's why we put you in the drive-thru. You are too much in the front," Vanessa says, implying that I had started the conversation with the guy.

"It's not me. I came here to do my job," I indignantly say.

"Hi, I'm Empress!" I say introducing myself to the new hire that is about to leave.

"Were you smilin' like that when you took that man's order?" Vanessa asks.

"Yeah, I always smile when I greet customers. It's the first rule in that dumbass employee handbook y'all gave me to study when I first started," I reply.

"That smile is too much...too flirtatious," she comments.

"How is my natural born smile too much?" I ask, offended by her comment. Not waiting for her to supply an answer, I say, "It's these guys that are too much. It doesn't matter where y'all put me. They will all act the same way."

"I don't know what they see in you. It has to be that soft squeaky ass voice," April, the other and much older cashier on my shift mumbles, thinking I don't hear her.

"Ah, don't be a hater April. I'm sure when you were younger, you had plenty of boys tryin' to holla at you," I say with a smile, shaking my head from the shade she tried to throw my way.

Staring at her for a brief second, I add, "Well, maybe

not," with a laugh which causes Vanessa to also laugh.

Vanessa is a cool manager. She is a little on the heavy side, but very easy to get along with, which makes working my eight-hour shift a breeze. Whenever we are experiencing what the fast food world would consider a "rush", she does not sit in the office and let the crew suffer. She joins in and helps, which I respect. Vanessa is thirty-five, married, and has two toddler-aged sons. She gives me rides home when I need them without charging gas money. Plus, she lets me do my homework on the clock if we are really slow.

Before I clock out for my thirty-minute break, I always change back into my regular clothes, which today is black skinny jeans and a plain V-neck white tee. I consider this my model look minus the bomber jacket and heels I had on at school. A little much I know, but if I am not at Krystal's I don't wanna be seen in this tacky uniform with ugly black slip resistant shoes. Even though boys seem to like me with the uniform on, I think it is hideous. Especially when I have to put on the stupid red visor. I try all the time not to put the visor on, but that usually results in threats from senior management saying things like, "Empress, if you don't put on the visor, you're gonna get a write up!" I don't want to be written up or docked for pay, so I just cooperate.

Making my way to the coat hanger rack in the back of the store to put my uniform in my MCM backpack, I get distracted when I see two of my co-workers, Egypt and Shay, sitting at the round high tables. The conversation looks to be tense.

"Hey, y'all. What's going on?" I stop and ask, genuinely concerned.

"Shay is pregnant, again," Egypt answers without confirming with Shay whether it is okay to tell me, which causes Shay to shoot her a look that says it all.

Shay is eighteen, a year older than me. Pregnancy seems to be a recurring theme in her life. She has been pregnant twice since I have been working at Krystal's. Both pregnancies were terminated. Now, here she goes on her third abortion. I didn't even know abortions were this common until I started working here. These girls make abortions sound as easy as poppin' Plan B.

Egypt, 26, had explained to me that the recovery took no time and the procedure is safe. At least safer than when she almost killed herself by taking a pain pill and cough syrup concoction when she was 15 and pregnant for the first time. Egypt has had several other abortions that I am aware of even after she had her 2-year-old son. I once asked why she had so many abortions and her answer of the timing being bad every single time shocked me. I still wonder why these girls just don't use protection.

Even though I've just entered the conversation, it is already too deep for me. I really feel that there is nothing more I can say to Shay about this touchy issue.

Gently placing my hand on Shay's hand, I say, "I'm going on break."

In the midst of her tears, Shay looks up and laughs at me. "Girl, you are such a hot tamale," she says. "I don't know nobody who changes their clothes just to go on break."

"Chile, she thinks she is a fashion model. She thinks this is America's Next Top Model," Vanessa says with a chuckle.

"Ah, whatever," I respond as I walk towards the door giving my best imitation of Naomi Campbell on the catwalk. Before exiting, I add, "You never know who you might meet."

I am not really hungry and there are not that many restaurants to choose from that are within walking distance. After a minute of pondering, I decide to go to Burger King which is in the shopping center besides Krystal. The line seems to be semi-long, but I am in no rush. Plus, I still have not decided on what to eat. As my eyes search for something appealing on the fast food menu, I stumble upon something new, something that is quite enticing, mouthwatering even, something that is not on the menu.

If this was a movie, everything would slow down and a heavenly light would shine upon the beautiful guy who is putting together the burgers. God had to create this beautiful creature to spoil my eyes. He has me completely enamored, and he has my undivided attention. Even while fixing burgers and dressed in a work uniform, I can clearly see that this guy is fine! I can't help but gaze.

Tall, dark, and handsome is an understatement. He looks lean and strong. Toned, but not too toned. His physique is without a doubt nice. I bet he is an athlete. He probably plays football or maybe basketball. His body language exudes confidence as he moves faster than the other guy making burgers with him. Clearly, he's the alpha male and there is no doubt about it.

Not only is his body on point, but he has beautiful caramel brown skin. His bone structure is perfectly symmetrical. Tiny, fine black hairs cover his chin. A hair net shields his medium length black dreads, which lay perfectly under his black visor. I hate dreads, but I love them on him. Damn, he is fine! If my mom could read my mind right now, she would surely lock me up. I have got to know this boy!

I want him to look my way. My eyes zero in on him. I bite my bottom lip and wonder if I stare harder will he feel my eyes and energy. An indescribable feeling has come over me. It is a feeling that not too many people experience in a lifetime. Unfortunately, some people never experience this burst of euphoria that I have right now at this moment. It is as though my circle of fantasy is complete.

Peace, desire, and excitement comes over me. I have never experienced this magical feeling before. An unsaid bond between me and this nameless guy, who has not made eye contact with me, seems to form at this very moment. I have got to know him! He's so focused on looking at the order ticket on the monitor and making those damn Whoppers that his eyes have not roamed. Ugh! why doesn't he look my way? Some guys tell me that I have bedroom eyes…I hope this is true and they don't fail me now.

Should I ask someone to get his attention? Na, that would be doing too much. What would the divas I admire so much do? For sure, they would remain calm and collected. So, I have to keep it subtle and be extra cool and extra smooth.

The rest of the world seems to vanish as I look at this incredibly beautiful boy. I'm so caught up in his rapture of beauty that I do not notice the cashier waiting to take my order. As I am brought back to my reality, I order a vanilla shake and fries.

Oh no! Where did he go? He seems to have vanished into thin air. After my shake and fries are ready, I wait around an extra five minutes just to see if my mystery man will reappear.

Still, nothing.

Finally, I head back to Krystal's with one priority on my mind which is finding out who this guy is.

"OMG! VANESSA, I HAVE JUST SEEN THE FINEST BOY at Burger King. When I say fine, I mean fine! He is soooo cute! He has -"

"Whoa! Whoa! Girl, sloooow down!" Vanessa says as she tries to make out what I said in my high-pitched, excited voice.

"Why is this chile jumpin' up and down now?" Miss Mable asks Vanessa as she scratches off the lottery scratch-offs I brought her back from the Shell gas station.

"Sumthin 'bout some boy, Miss Mable," Vanessa says in the laziest of tones as she hands me my MCM backpack so I can change back into my uniform.

"Oh Lawd! I swear that's all this chile thinks about," Miss Mable says, causing me to side-eye her because she has me pegged all wrong. But whatever, she is just an old lady who thinks she knows everything.

"For sure!" April quickly adds, her Jamaican accent as present as ever.

Who was even asking April? She can shut up too.

Continuing to talk for no reason at all, April adds, "Empress, all these boys come through here every day giving you their number. What makes this boy so special?"

"I don't know...it's just something about him," I answer with the biggest Cheshire grin on my face; quite sure I look like the biggest cornball on the planet.

"Okay, Empress, you are soundin' like those white girls in those teen movies right now," Vanessa says as she puts her hand on my forehead.

"Um, what are you doin'?" I ask, looking confused.

"I'm just checkin' to make sure you're not sick. Cause this is not the Empress I know," Vanessa says loudly, making a scene which cause me to burst out laughing.

She is absolutely right. Normally I am chill and nonchalant, but the boy from Burger King is breakin' me out of character. My thoughts are chasing after a boy that didn't even see me. I'm trippin! I better snap out of this fast.

"Yeah, you're right, but I may just have to take my break over there tomorrow. They have some really good fries," I say with a smile. Still smiling, I add, "Plus, I've never seen him before."

"I just gotta know him! I just gotta, I tell ya!" I say in an overly animated voice.

"Something is wrong with that girl," I hear Miss Mable say as I walk off to the bathroom to change back into my uniform.

"I heard that Grandma!" I yell from the dining area because there are not any customers inside.

———◆———

AS THE EVENING TRANSITIONS INTO NIGHT, I begin to fall under the weather. My head is hot and my throat is scratchy with a slight burn. I am in no mood to work, especially with such a high volume of customers. Taking off my headset, I ask Vanessa if I can work one of the front counter registers instead of drive-thru because there is hardly anyone coming inside the restaurant to order food.

"Empress, you know corporate is comin' in a couple of days. We need your drive- thru time for the store stats. Our restaurant sales need to be the highest in the region and we need to have the fastest drive-thru speed. You're the only one who can get an order out in 60 seconds or less," she responds, annoying me because she is more worried about looking good for corporate rather than being concerned about my health.

"I understand that, but I think this fall air is gettin' to me, Vanessa. My throat is scratchy and my head feels heavy," I plea.

"You have been quiet these past few hours," she says as she looks at me with suspicious eyes. "Alrite, tell April to switch. You will work the front and she will work drive-thru. Since we lock the doors at 11 p.m. and it's about 10:30 p.m. now, you won't have to worry about customers," she informs me.

"But, I'm not tryin' to clean those dirty ass bathrooms or mop these nasty floors. What do I look like?" I quip.

"You look like a lil girl who is about to either switch out with April or go home," Vanessa shoots back.

Go home? She is crazy. I need all the money I can get.

"Ugh, alrite, just tell me y' all have changed the mop head. Where are the gloves? I need some gloves," I say with a soft cough.

Vanessa looks like she is so over me as she points to the cleaning supply closet.

The bathrooms only contain one toilet, but I pray the customers have not messed each bathroom up to the point of no return.

This is some bullshit.

Chapter Five

~ NARD ~

"UM, LEMME GET A NUMBER ONE WITH cheese, no onions, light mayo, and extra ketchup," is all I hear coming through the black headset I wear to hear orders from the drive-thru. Every cook does not wear a headset, but I do because I want the food to be done or almost ready once customers pull up to the second window.

Working at Burger King is becoming annoyin' as hell. These people literally work you like a slave and barely pay you. Then they got a nigga working in the back which stays humid because the grill and deep fryer are always on. The only way to cool down is to slide in the walk-in deep freezer whenever there aren't any customers. When I question myself about why I got this job, I remind myself that I'm tryna go legit.

"Yo, Stacy, that order ready and I'm 'bout to clock out," I say, placing the headset on the counter.

Stacy is my manager and she's cool as hell, but is very unattractive. To make matters worse, I believe she knows this because she practically throws her body at every new nigga that is hired at Burger king. I'm sure she causes her mother, the hiring manager, embarrassment, but a mother's love is never ending.

"Hold up, wait, you have got to help me close," Stacy whines.

"Hell naw, I'm scheduled to work from 4 p.m. to 10 p.m. tonight because it's a school night," I reply.

"But, I don't have no one else to close the restaurant. Besides, you act like you 'bout to go straight home," she retorts with a slight attitude.

"It ain't 'bout that. I'm tired and I'm ready to go," I snap, my words becoming shorter because I really want to leave.

"Well, look, work 'til close and take the day off tomorrow," she suggests, making a compromise.

She doesn't have to say that twice. Plus, this gives me time to meditate and think of a plan to resolve the situation me and Larosa got ourselves into with Jaz and Heard.

"OK, you got a deal," I say with a smile. "But, let me take a 15-minute break."

"OK, just 15 minutes cause I don't want a rush to come," Stacy says.

If you have ever worked fast food, you know a rush is the worst thing that can happen, especially when a restaurant is understaffed. Customers become ruder and employees tend to snap on one another because nobody is ever moving fast enough to get the orders out of the window.

Now, what am I going to eat during my break? I'm so sick and tired of eating Whoppers and Chicken Fries. Chilli cheese pups from Krystal's sound good though. Plus, it's close - walking distance. I think I'll go there.

~ EMPRESS ~

"EMPRESS, GET UP AND GET OFF THAT PHONE AND lock the front door and the two side doors," Vanessa tells me as she pulls my drawer to count the register down to $100. "You can start cleaning the dining area and bathrooms now."

"Ugh, do I have to?"

"Don't play," Vanessa says in a playful tone as she picks up a handful of pennies. "Do you need a ride home?"

"Yes," I reply. "But, I'll probably need for you to pick me up tomorrow if that's cool?"

"I gotcha."

"Cool, thanks," I say, getting up from the high table. "I knew I liked you for a reason."

We both giggle.

"Man, this mop head smells!" I exclaim to Vanessa as I wheel the mop bucket out from the back.

"Well, Jake didn't order one this week, so you just gon' have to deal," she replies.

"How does the General Manager forget to do that?" I rhetorically ask out loud knowing there is no answer.

This is definitely not wat's up.

~ NARD ~

I TUG THE FRONT DOOR OF KRYSTAL'S, BUT to my surprise, it is locked. Seeing my failed attempt, the manager yells through the clear, thick Plexiglass door that the dining area is closed and I need to go through the drive-thru.

For a moment, I hesitate because I do not want to look like a complete idiot standing at the drive-thru window.

What the hell...I don't have time to walk back to Burger king to get my whip and who the hell am I tryin' to impress, anyway? Besides, at first glance inside the restaurant them hoes looked busted, so I wish they would try to clown me. I will give them the business.

~ EMPRESS ~

WHILE MOPPING THE DISGUSTING MEN'S bathroom, with its strong permanent piss stench, I overhear Vanessa talking unusually loud to someone.

I hope it is not an unruly customer or another attempted robbery again. I really don't have time for that. I just want to go home and lay down. Each minute that passes, I feel weaker.

With the mop still in my hand, I peek my head outside the bathroom door to see what is going on.

Instantly, I drop the mop.

"*It's him! It's him!*" I scream out loud to myself full of excitement.

"Who are you talkin' about, Empress?" Vanessa responds, clearly annoyed by my childlike behavior.

"The guy from Burger King that I was telling you about earlier!" I blush, embarrassed that she heard me.

"Oh wow! Was he just in here? Dang!" I quickly and excitedly say in a high-pitched tone.

"You sure that was him?" Vanessa questions with a chuckle. "Because if it was, he sure is slow. He walked around the drive-thru to order food since we closed the inside."

"*Drive-thru? Is he still here?*" I think to myself, my mind processes everything rapidly.

Led by Vanessa's words, I run behind the counter to catch him in the drive-thru.

Oh! I hope he's still here.

From the bagging station, I squint my eyes to see if he is still standing at the window.

Yes! My mystery man is still here!

"Have you taken his order?" I coolly ask April who is stirring the chili pot.

"What are you talking about," she asks, looking at me as though I was a Martian.

"The guy over there," I say, nodding my head at the window, trying to remain low-key.

"No," she sluggishly replies. "I didn't even know someone was standing there. I guess the beep didn't go off because he's not in a car."

"Well, uh, let me take it," I slyly suggest.

"Why?" She suspiciously questions.

"Oh, no reason," I reply.

"Okay," she says with a smirk and look of skepticism.

~ NARD ~

SO, HERE I AM STANDING OUTSIDE OF Krystal's drive-thru window waiting to place my order. I wish these folks would hurry up cause it's kinda cold out here.

Finally, it looks like a girl is coming over to take my order. I can't believe it.

Why the hell is she working here?

She's beautiful - gorgeous. I guess I am doing a little stereotyping because all the females that work in the fast food industry usually be busted or thots. Every now and then, you might find a beautiful woman workin' at a place like this, but not for long because beautiful women can never handle being told what to do. I guess these simp ass niggas got them used to gettin' their way.

"Hi, welcome to Krystal's. May I take your order?"

Her sweet voice asks, abruptly interrupting my thoughts of her.

"Uh…. yeah," I say, still admiring her beauty.

My eyes must be deceiving me, she is a goddess.

"Lemme get 3 chili cheese hot dogs and a medium fry."

She has the kind of face that leaves you dumbfounded. I bet she's probably used to men reacting this way over her. She's bad, and she knows it.

"That will be $5.64," she sweetly says.

Quickly, I hand her a $20 bill and she closes the drive-thru window.

Noticing that it is pitch black outside, I refocus on my surroundings.

I must always stay on point regardless of the situation.

"*I'm trippin',*" I say to myself. "*Or paranoid, hell might as well be safe than sorry.*"

The drive-thru window re-opens, interrupting my thoughts again.

"Here you go. Thank you for coming to Krystal's," she says handing me the bag of food.

"By the way, you're cute," she says confidently with a beautiful white smile.

"Thank you," I reply, before she turns away in shyness.

Chapter Six

ASHES AND WEED ROACHES FILL THE SQUARE GLASS ashtray that sits on Jaz's patio furniture. His traphouse may be in the hood where everything is poppin', but he lives in virtual privacy on a beautiful $1.6 million, 30-acre estate off Lennox Drive. He may only be 26, but solely judging his 9,529 square foot home, many assume that he has done well for himself.

The home captures the serene views of a spring fed lake. It features four bedrooms with ensuite baths, two master suites, a chef's kitchen, gym, enclosed water-front pool house & pavilion, a detached workshop garage+studio apartment plus a greenhouse.

For the last two days, he's been chillin' at his property, enjoying the company of beautiful hoes and retracing in his mind how the hit went down at the traphouse. He isn't hurting for cash, but it's the principal and his reputation. How can he show his face on the streets if this problem is not rectified? The more he thinks about the incident the angrier he becomes. A lil young nigga from the south had plotted on him.

KG, his top shooter, has come over to get all the details since he was not present during the robbery. KG was big bruh to Larosa, Nard and other DMG members until he walked away with Diesel. He's been unstable from the beginning.

Some believe it came from all the dope he put in his nose. Rumor has it that he upgraded to crack cocaine, but few have ever seen him do it, nor does he have the symptoms of a junkie. Never would the DMG crew have thought KG would abandon the set, but he did and now he's enemies with his brothers.

"I can't believe that nigga Larosa had the courage to rob me," Jaz says before inhaling. He feels the smoke travel down his windpipe and fill his lungs.

"That nigga is as good as dead!!!" He grisly adds, stomping his blunt out in the ashtray.

"Why the fuck y'all haven't found that nigga yet?!?!"

"My nigga, we tryin' but we ain't seen that nigga. But, best believe he is a dead nigga once I find him," KG says in an assertive tone.

"I told Bianca I'll take care of this shit," Jaz says, as he stands in front of his 20 x 40 rectangle in-ground pool watching his reflection.

"Why the fuck did that bitch call the police knowing what the fuck you had goin' on?" KG asks. "She could've jammed you up, man."

"I dunno know," Jaz answers. "She panicked. Talkin' 'bout if she hadn't called 12, we all would have been dead."

"Dumbass hoe," KG says while shaking his head.

"That's the reason why I bounced out the back door," Jaz continues. "I told that bitch she was goin' to have to make this shit right. I told her, 'when 12 knock on the door, tell them folks what happened. Tell 'em that they snatched your phone and that's why you hung up, but don't give no names and no descriptions.'"

"Damn, bruh," KG says as he continues to shake his

head. "I would've never thought Larosa would try to pull some shit like this. Especially, since we go so far back. You would think he would've loved that we've reached a truce. He was once my younger brother, and I played a major role in his life."

"Do you not understand? We got EA'd! It's in the game," Jaz reminds KG.

KG pours a shot of Cîroc at the outdoor bar as he reminisces about the past life he shared with his DMG brothers. The hot vodka stings his throat even more than usual because he dreads what he must do.

"You know what?" Jaz asks slowly as he stares out into the woods that surround his home. "Fuck findin' that nigga!"

"What???" KG says, not comprehending Jaz's statement.

"We goin' to force that nigga to come out of hidin'."

"And how do you expect to do that???" KG questions.

"Think Nigga!!! And stop acting like a fuckin' amateur," Jaz yells, before he whistles to signal his favorite large Rottweiler to come to him. "You are supposed to be my right-hand man and you haven't advised me of shit - just sittin' here lookin' dumb as fuck."

"Well, I thought lookin' for Larosa was a brilliant idea since he was the one who robbed us, nigga. But since you have a better idea, go ahead and shoot," KG fires back.

"That smart-ass mouth is goin' to get you fucked up, so I suggest you shut up and listen," Jaz says with an intimidating look in his eyes. "Snatch up that nigga, CJ, also known as C, and call me when you do. Meet me at the spot in Covington. Once we make this statement, that nigga Larosa will know we ain't playin' and will show his face."

"What makes you so sure this will make Larosa come out of hidin'???"

"Because that's his first cousin, and he loves him dearly," Jaz replies.

"Aite, man, I gotta bounce," KG says after taking another shot, knowing his brotherly ties to Larosa have officially come to an end

~ EMPRESS ~

STARTING THE SCHOOL DAY OFF REQUIRES A trip to the girl's bathroom which feels more like a beauty shop in the morning. In the bathroom you can find girl's contouring their faces, or at least trying to imitate some YouTube tutorial. You can also find girls flat ironing their hair, spritzing their natural hair or making sure their sew-in is intact. I am no stranger to the bathroom as I always want to look my best.

"Olivia, do you think I'm getting ugly?" I ask while lining my lips with my NYX brown lip liner.

"No. Why would you say a stupid thing like that?" Olivia says, puzzled by my question.

"Cause I've got to be losing my looks or sumthin," I answer as I apply my Gerard Cosmetics Adam & Eve liquid lipstick and ColourPop Tight Fit lip gloss.

"Empress, I'm not understanding why you are saying all this dumb-ass shit," Olivia says, annoyed not only by me, but by all the girls that continue to fill the bathroom and hog the mirror before the bell rings.

Looking at Olivia through the large square bathroom mirror that I'm staring in, I respond, "Because I do not understand why this totally cute boy didn't ask me for my number - especially after I gave him a compliment. Now that's some dumb-ass shit."

"Boo hoo! Sounds like someone's ego is hurt," Olivia says in a mocking tone, irritating me.

"This may sound crazy," I say, after rolling my eyes at Olivia. "But, I felt some kinda connection with him…I can't even describe it to you."

"Coming from you, Empress, yeah that does sound crazy," Olivia says as we walk out of the bathroom into the crowded hallway.

"Well, I guess I'm not meant to know him," I say with a sigh.

~ NARD ~

IT'S 8:20 A.M., BUT CLASS DOES NOT START UNTIL 8:30 a.m. Mr. Boston has 30 students on his roster, but only has 17 seats in his classroom. I'm here early because I'm not 'bout to stand up the entire period.

The constant loud hum from the old air vent prevents no one from doing their thing. You've got niggas shooting craps in one corner of the classroom, girls gossiping in another corner of the classroom, and niggas getting their macc on, putting their bid in with the hoes for when school lets out spread throughout the classroom. So, pretty much this shit is lit while we wait on Mr. Boston to start class.

Sometimes I believe Mr. Boston be wanting to say, 'fuck it' and walk out and never return because he be lookin' so tired as he waits for the national anthem to start. I can't lie, we do give him a hard time, but hell this is what happens when you have a school full of delinquents.

"FAM!" I loudly say, so Juke can hear me as I motion for him to take out his earbuds. "I saw the most beautiful woman I've ever seen last night. She works at Krystal's."

"Nigga, did you even get that math???" He asks.

"No," I respond, feeling stupid.

"What do you mean no???" Juke questions, making me feel even worse.

Not wanting to repeat myself, I shake my head.

"So, you mean to tell me you saw the most beautiful woman in your life and you didn't even attempt to get her math???" Juke asks yet another question because he still does not understand how I could let such a fine woman get away. "Did she at least speak to you, bruh?"

"Yeah nigga, she said I was cute," I respond aggravated.

"Awwww look at you, you're sooooo cute," Juke says, tryin' to clown.

"Don't get beat up nigga," I say in a serious, yet joking manner.

"Aight, Aight, but why the hell you didn't say shit?"

"Hell, I got tongue-tied."

"No fucking way, Nard gets tongue-tied," Juke laughs, yet again adding more fuel to the fire. "Nigga, you losing your touch."

"Did I just hear wrong or did Nard just say he got tongue-tied tryin' to talk to a bitch?" Danielle jumps in our conversation, after eavesdropping for a few minutes.

"No," Juke clarifies, without a second passing. "He didn't even attempt. Hahahaha."

"Oh shit, yeah you losing your fuckin' touch, boo," Danielle says, loving every minute of this, relishing in my embarrassment even further. "What the hell juvenile did to you?"

She knows exactly what to say to get under my skin.

"I'm not losing my touch, my nigga. So, you can go ahead and cut that shit out. And juve didn't do shit to me, cause I had a bitch in there. Ain't a nigga in the city fuckin' with me when it comes to these hoes. Real nigga shit."

"Then why you didn't get her math???" Juke says, still laughing.

"Nigga, shut the fuck up. I'm goin' back up there today," I respond.

"Yeah, yeah, we will see," Juke says. "I gotta see how she looks, anyway. This goin' to be interesting."

CHAPTER SEVEN

~ EMPRESS ~

"WORKIN' HERE IS PUTTING A DAMPER ON MY social life," I complain as I hand my friends, Olivia, Chante, Fallon, and Alexis the Krystal's burgers and fries they ordered.

Since the start of senior year, three months ago, we have all become more interested in social activities rather than academics. The girls traveled to Rockdale after school to visit Sneakerheadz. It is the Eastside's version of Walter's, a popular shoe store in Atlanta that has all the hottest sneakers. Before heading back to the Stone Mountain/Lithonia area in DeKalb county, they dropped by to give me the fifth degree about going to prom.

While we talk, I pretend to wipe down the tables so none of the managers tell me I had better get back to work.

"Yeah, it sure is," Fallon says agreeing with my statement. "You missed a really good game last night."

"Who did we play again?" I ask.

"Stephenson," Alexis says as she dips her fries into the square of ketchup pouch. "And you know those Stephenson boys are so fine," Fallon adds as she sips her soda. "Little Miss A got mad at me cause I kept missing count. I know she's our cheer coach, but I couldn't help it though cause #21 kept staring at me. I think they call him AR."

"Yeah, I know who you're talking about," Chante chimes. "He had them waves on swim and he was scoring all the points. He was lookin' good out there. I think you would've liked him Empress."

"Oh yeah?" I amusingly reply.

"Yeah," Chante responds.

"Didn't he look like her type, Fallon?" Chante asks trying to back up her claim.

"For sure," Fallon agrees.

"You know who else was lookin' good out there?" Olivia asks as she finishes her first Krystal burger.

"Who?" All the girls except me ask because I'm not interested.

"Church, with those big broad shoulders and those chiseled arms," Olivia says with a Cheshire grin on her face, trying to get a reaction out of me.

"Um…Empress, you should totally see if they can switch around your schedule here. Little Miss A said she would be open to letting you try out for the cheer squad. You'd be the perfect cheerleader and of course I'd be there to show you the ropes," Fallon says in a sincere attempt to change the subject as she senses that things are getting a little weird.

"Thanks, Fallon. But, no thanks," I reply. "Cheerleading isn't really my thing."

"Are you kidding? You'd be perfect!" Fallon exclaims.

"I'm straight. Besides, I really can't free up my schedule."

"Empress, Church is having another party at his house this weekend –" Olivia eagerly says.

"Yeah, it's going to be a pool party," Alexis chimes in,

interrupting Olivia.

"So?" I dryly reply, not caring about the subject.

"So!?!" They both say in unison.

"Yeah, so? How can someone have a pool party in the dead of fall?" I ask.

"It's going to be indoors," Olivia says.

"So?" I reply again.

"Empress, girl you are trippin'. Olivia already told me how you turned down his invitation to his kick-back yesterday," Alexis says.

"Yeah," Olivia adds. "We've all been doing the thirty-minute ab challenge for two months now. This is the best time to show off your abs."

When I was around ten, I became inspired to get abs after seeing a promo poster for Janet Jackson's Live in Hawaii Concert. I vowed then I would grow up and have washboard abs and I am well on my way. Having a small frame and inheriting a fast metabolism from my mother, it is easy for me to do a half hour worth of crunches and see fast results.

"True," I say as I think about how I can show off my newly pierced belly button. "Let me think about it."

"What is there to think about? The hottest party of the fall is happenin' and everyone will be there - including every fine ass boy that goes to Brook, Stephenson, and Lithonia," Alexis says, tryin' to talk some sense into me.

"I heard people from Miller Grove and Redan supposed to be coming through, too," Chante adds.

"Ugh, I hope not," Fallon comments. "Those niggas and bitches are so ratchet. They are always looking to fight. They don't know the meaning of the word chill."

"I'm just not feelin' it," I remark.

"Not feeling it?" Olivia questions, still tryin' to talk sense into me. "You know Church is feelin' you.

Besides, prom will be here before we know it and you need to start choosin' your date now. Who better to go with than Church? You'd be a bona fide shoo-in to win prom queen because you know he will automatically win prom king. Plus, y'all will be so fly. You know he is going to ballout."

"It would be nice to be the prom queen. With a name like Empress, that's only fitting, right?" I say with a smile.

"Finally, our girl is comin' around!" Alexis says as she high fives Olivia.

"Not too fast," I say. "I do not know about prom or Church. I need to think this over."

"Huh??? Empress you're trippin'," Alexis states, shaking her head.

"She probably got that mystery guy from Burger King on her mind because she definitely isn't making sense," Olivia says.

"Aw, please!" I say rolling my eyes. "I am not thinkin' about him."

I just lied through my teeth. All day I have been thinking about a guy I will probably never see again.

"Oh no! We've gotta go, y'all. My mom is going to kill me, I was supposed to pick up my little brother from soccer practice," Alexis says.

"See ya Empress! We'll call you when you get off."

"Bye."

~ NARD ~

I HAVE NOT BEEN ABLE TO THINK STRAIGHT since last night. The drop-dead beauty who works at Krystal's has been on my mind all day. I had to come back here and see her again. She has me in a trance. I keep thinkin' about that soft, relaxed smile she gave me and the alluring shape of her almond eyes. Last night, in less than six minutes she managed to overwhelm and impress me. In less than six minutes! I wonder if she will remember me when she sees me.

"Damn, my nigga, you let that get by you last night?" Juke remarks as he sees my mystery woman emerge from the tiny drive-thru space to Krystal's front counter where we are standing in line.

"I know, right? She's gorgeous, isn't she?" I say, my eyes following her every step and turn. "She's even more beautiful than last night."

"Well, are you gonna stand here and tell me that shit or you goin' to tell her that shit and get her number?"

"Shut up, nigga. Here she comes," I tell Juke as my eyes connect with the girl I have been thinkin' about all day. "Get the fuck on."

"Hi, may I help you?" She asks, hypnotizing me with her sweet voice. I know she has asked this mandatory question a million times today, but right now it feels like this question was meant especially for me.

"Will your order be for dine-in or carryout?" She adds with a natural smile on her face.

"I believe I will have a Sprite and your name because I forgot to get it last night," I say, quickly glancing at her name tag. "Empress," I proudly add with a smile, without giving her a chance to answer.

"Why are you smiling?" She asks, her voice sounding softer than rose petals and clearer than a bell.

"Because your parents gave you a name that fits you perfectly," I reply, causing her to blush and give me a super sexy smile.

Long, black eyelashes, frame her hazel eyes, which are so beautiful. They are a remarkable color, a mix of light and dark. I can see her face clearly because her hair is styled in a ponytail. She has a mole above her right eyebrow and a blemish free complexion.

For a moment, we stare at each other without saying a word.

"So, what's your name?" She inquires.

"My name is Renardo."

"Renardo...what???" She curiously asks.

"That's privy information," I say with a smile. "I don't tell just anyone my full government. Hell, you might be a spy," I jokingly add, my smile growing wider.

"A spy?" Empress playfully questions.

"Yeah. I've never seen you in my city. It's like you're an angel that has appeared overnight, just for me," I explain, causing Empress to blush.

"I can assure you that I'm no spy, so you can stop your paranoia," she says in the most seductive way.

"*This woman is enchanting,*" I say to myself as I stare deep into her beautiful eyes, trying to read her.

"Well," I say, with my mind's sole focus being getting to know her better. "Since I'm drawn to your aura, I'll tell you. It's Wade."

"Well, it's nice to meet you, Renardo Wade," she says as she shakes my hand.

"C'mon now, this has gotta be a two-way street. If I told you mine, you've got to tell me yours," I say, our hands intertwining, her skin being the softest I have ever felt.

"It's the same as my mother and father," she replies with a sly grin.

"And what's that?" I ask, still spellbound.

"Cunningham," she says as our hands slowly slip apart.

"Are you about to take a break soon so we can sit and talk? Because I know you don't want nothin' to eat from the place you work. Hell, that's why I came down here last night because I'm so sick and tired of eating damn Burger king, it's ridiculous. I need something different.

"Yes, you are correct. You need something different," she says with a smirk. "No one wants nasty Krystal's. Oooops! Did I say that out loud?" She asks.

"Yes, you most definitely said that out loud," I say with a chuckle.

"Well, I don't think anyone heard me, but I can't today because we are semi-busy, plus I already took my break."

"Well, can I at least get your number and call you at a later time?"

"Yes, you can," she says, with a smile that could melt the coldest man's heart. "Let me see your phone."

~ EMPRESS ~

"GUESS WHAT?!!!" I SAY TO VANESSA AS I ENTER THE small Krystal's manager's office.

"Oh boy, it must be good news judging from the huge smile on your face," Vanessa says as she fills out the inventory sheet.

"It is!" I excitedly say, unable to control my excitement and the pitch of my voice from rising. "Renardo said my name fits me perfectly and he asked for my number!"

"Who is a Renardo?" She asks, staring at me blankly.

"The guy from Burger King…" I reply, trying to refresh her memory.

Vanessa continues to stare at me blankly.

"You know, the fine ass guy that walked through the drive-thru last night," I say, still trying to jog her memory.

"Oh, that lil boy? Chile, please," she says, rolling her eyes.

Even Vanessa's dull response cannot deter my excitement.

"Renardo, isn't that such a beautiful name?" I comment thinking out loud and talking to Vanessa at the same time.

"Wow, Empress, I've never seen you act like this before."

"Vanessa, he is soooo cute! He knows how to dress. You should've seen him. He looked so sexy in his G-Star leather letterman jacket."

"And you're talkin' 'bout that dread head that came through here last night???"

"Yes!"

"I didn't see nothin' special. Now, I can see if Idris Elba fine self came in here or Ghost sexy ass from Power," Vanessa says as she laughs and high fives Shay and April.

"Vanessa, don't you understand? He makes me nervous - ME!!!" I say.

Following her into the giant freezer to count the frozen inventory, I continue, "The way he looked right into my eyes, it was like he knew what I was thinking, like he knew what I was feeling. It's like I'm out of control! Like without saying anything at all, we have this unsaid understanding."

The side eye Vanessa is giving me is so shady; she should be on a meme.

"You don't understand," I say, seeing she is not respecting nor comprehending my perspective. "It's hard to explain. I can't even explain it to myself." With a smile, I add, "That's what makes this even more exciting."

"So, are you sayin' this is love at first sight?" She asks as we exit the giant freezer.

"I don't know…maybe…or sumthin like it. I can't tell you. I've never been in love," I reply.

"Lil girl, lil girl, what are we goin' to do with you?" She says, walking towards the stock area to count the bread, condiments, napkins, etc. "Just tell me that you were not actin' this nutty when you were talkin' to Ricardo."

"It's Renardo!" I respond in a playful defensive way. "And of course not! You know I kept it playa pimp."

We both laugh at my silliness.

"One thing I know is, I can't let him know how much I like him. He must respect me first. He may be fine, but he's not goin' to play me like a fool. Look at me. We haven't even -"

Beep.

Beep.

Beep.

My headset sounds off because someone has pulled up to have their order taken in the middle of my romantic fairy tale. It is back to my slangin' burgers and French fry grease reality.

"Welcome to Krystal's! Would you like to try our number three combo with a large Coke?"

~ NARD ~

WALKING OUT OF KRYSTAL'S, I SEE JUKE POSTED on my car, blasting my 15-inch speakers.

"If I get a ticket you paying for it, my nigga," I say to him as I open the driver's door.

Rockdale County doesn't play when it comes to music. They give out fines, like the NFL does Cam Newton every time he gives a football to a fan.

"Sooooo, tell me how that went?" Juke asks, ignoring my statement.

"There isn't shit to tell you," I reply. "I got her number and I'm goin' to call her later. The rest is my business so stop tryin' to be nosy."

"Nigga, you trippin' with all that cuffin'."

"I ain't trippin' nigga - she different."

"What you mean by different???" Juke questions, looking perplexed.

"I want to get to know her mentally. She's a mystery to me," I explain. "I've never seen her around and I want to know why. I practically know everyone from the hood, but not her. She can't be from down here and she can't be a hoe because her name would be familiar to me. I've never heard of her and that's a good thing."

"Yeah, you trippin'," Juke says while shaking his head. "The only thing you need to be doing is tryin' to see how good that pussy is in bed."

"Introduction to manhood. Boys chase hoes, but a man finds a woman," I explain. "I'm tired of chasin' hoes, my nigga. It's too much shit out there and I'm definitely not tryin' to go out like Easy-E."

"You jokin' right??? How the fuck you goin' to get tired of chasin' pussy????"

Juke's childish comment makes me smile.

"I see now that you didn't hear or understand what I just said, but it's okay," I reply with a laugh. "I understand you are not competent enough."

"Nigga, fuck you," Juke grumbles, not liking my insult.

Continuing to laugh at him, I drive-off and make a right onto Highway 138.

"Look, Larosa wants me to meet him at Black's house, you comin'?" I ask.

"Yeah, let's ride," Juke says, still all in his feelings.

———◆———

LIL KIDS JUMP ROPE AND RIDE SCOOTERS ON THE sidewalks as I turn into Black's neighborhood. Being that it is almost 6 o'clock and it is almost getting dark, I'm sure all their mama's will be hollering for them to come in the house soon. I would love to be so carefree again just like them. Honestly, I can't remember how that feels because I never really had a childhood. It seems like I've always been focused on surviving and gettin' money.

I put on my blinker to indicate to the car behind me that I am about to turn into Black's driveways.

Black and his wife, Tanesha, have a very nice two-story house with a beautiful manicured lawn. Cedar shakes mixed with siding and stone make up the exterior of their home. I swear he has the greenest grass I have ever seen. But, hell, his house and grass should look the best in the neighborhood considering that he owns a lawn care business and his wife is a real estate agent.

"Ay, man, me and Juke in the driveway. Let us in," I call and tell Larosa.

"Aight."

"Where is Black?" Juke asks, as Larosa opens the privacy fence and we walk onto the deck

"He went with his wife to go show some houses in Valdosta to an interested buyer cause he don't like when she work at night or go far out," Larosa replies as he chugs down some beer. "They won't be back for a couple of days, so he told me to keep an eye out on the house."

"Damn that's far out," Juke says as he sits on the beige outdoor furniture. "I know that nigga ain't gonna give a muthafucka the chance to try nothin' with his wife."

"Damn right," Larosa says with a chuckle.

"You know we are going to have to deal with this situation before it gets out of hand," I say to Larosa, wiping the smile off his face.

"I know," he says after taking a deep breathe. "I'm just tryin' to see if this shit will blow over."

"Well, I'm going to tell you now, you'll be better off chasin' ghosts. First of all, we made one major mistake by robbin' a nigga in our hood," I matter-of-factly say. "Not only did we rob a nigga from the hood, but you know that nigga run with them YGC niggas. I noticed the mistake before we did this shit, but I wanted the money and I needed the money."

"I know what mistake we made nigga!" Larosa claps back. "Fuck them YGC niggas! I don't even know why we have a truce with them niggas anyways. My question is, how the hell we goin' to fix it?"

"Oh, so now you have questions that need answers, but when I had a very simple question the other night, that shit fell on deaf ears. Ha! This shit hilarious," I say, pissed off by Larosa.

"Are you goin' to live in the past or are you goin' to help me fix this problem?" Larosa asks.

"Nigga, what kind of dumbass question is that? You already know we gonna take care of these niggas, but all I'm sayin' is that it's goin' to be difficult to just dead these niggas when they stay in the same hood as us. Them niggas end up dead, there will be questions and we will be the prime suspects."

"No," Larosa says while pointing at himself. "I'm

going to be the prime suspect because they don't know who you are."

"Nigga, you act like people don't know who you run with, because you damn sure don't fuck with just anybody unless I'm in the joint. And by the way, you gotta stop doin' that shit. People are already talkin' and my name is in the mix."

"Nigga, you do the same shit, so I ain't tryin' to hear it. But what do you suggest?" Larosa asks.

"I suggest we take a trip to go see the sister Karen in Baltimore," I reply.

Karen is a sister from OG Black's generation, who has eternal love for our organization. She is also the wife of the Legend OG Forte. Even though she is no longer in the street life, she is always aiding and assisting whenever it is needed. We give her the utmost respect because of who she is and how she has stayed down with big bruh, who is serving a life sentence, this whole time.

"Man, we can enjoy ourselves for a few months," I add. "And let the brother Tmoe handle that business for us. We are clean. We come back in about 6 months and we will return the favor to FAM when needed."

"What about your job, FAM?" Larosa asks.

"I'm about to quit."

"Damn bruh… I got you into all this shit… I should've never called you that night because I know you tryin' to keep your hands clean… I'm sorry FAM, real shit."

"That's what brothers are for, right? I'm my brother's keeper always," I say, assuring Larosa.

"Always," Larosa says with a smile.

My phone rings.

"Hello?" I answer.

"They got CJ… they got CJ!" Amanda, CJ's older

sister, wails into the phone.

"What the fuck you mean they got CJ... who got him?" I ask.

"KG!!!" She fearfully screams.

"How do you know KG got him?!" I ask, trippin' off what she just said.

"Cause," she replies, barely able to talk through her tears. "He called me from CJ's phone and told me if I want to see my brother alive I had better tell Larosa to stop hiding!!! I tried callin' him but he changed his number!! You've got to do sumthin!! Do you know where he's at??"

"Everything will be fine, just don't call 12. I'm going to get your brother back."

"Do you know where Larosa at!??!!"

"Bye, Amanda." I quickly say, having heard enough. *Click.*

"How much worse could it possibly get?" I wonder to myself.

"What the fuck was that all about?" Larosa and Juke both ask, lookin' every bit as confused as I am.

"It looks like we have to devise a new plan," I reply, unsure of what the future holds.

CHAPTER EIGHT

"YOOOO! GO LIFT THE GARAGE UP FOR JAZ!"
KG yells out to the YGC crew.

After parking his car, Jaz steps into the dimly lit garage and finds a beaten down CJ, tied down to an aluminum folding chair. He is beyond recognition. The only way Jaz can tell that he is alive is from his heavy breathing through the duct tape around his mouth.

Even though CJ is fourteen, KG and his niggas did not spare him as they beat him mercilessly.

Without saying a word, Jaz walks up to CJ and hits him with a blow hard enough to cause a concussion. CJ quickly blinks his swollen black eyes in an attempt to regain his blurry vision. His ears ring as he grows drowsy.

Walking in circles around CJ, Jaz stares at him with menacing eyes.

"You do know how we ended up in this situation right?" Jaz calmly says with a smirk.

"When I ask a question, I'm expecting an answer!" He shouts, growing angrier by the minute.

Realizing that CJ is gagged, Jaz sarcastically says, "Damn, let me help you out with your gag. How rude am I to expect a man that is gagged to speak?"

Jaz removes the gag and immediately hits CJ with another hard blow knocking him unconscious.

"No, no, no, no, no, no, wake your bitch ass up!!! You still haven't answered my fuckin' question!!!" Jaz says growing irate with each word he speaks as he slaps CJ in the face.

"Go get him some water and wake this bitch up!!!" Jaz yells at his crew who all stand silently against the walls, witnessing Jaz's fury.

~ NARD ~

ME AND LAROSA HAVE BEEN CHILLIN' AT Johnson Park since droppin' Juke off at their apartment. We've been sittin' on the hood of my Monte Carlo playing music all night. *I guess it is our form of relaxation or meditation.* We manage to make small talk, *but nothing can hide the elephant in the room or should I say the elephant in the streets - our partna CJ is missing.*

"Fuuuuuckkkk!!!! God knows I never meant for this shit to happen like this," Larosa howls out into the cool night air. "I can assure you I'm goin' to fix this shit, Nard."

"No, we are goin' to fix this shit," I reassure Larosa. "For right now, we gotta go to the spot and get more guns."

The spot is a condo that we all pitch in for whenever we need a place to rest our head or whenever we decide to have a kickback. It's in Hunting Creek, another hood in DMG territory.

"Call Congo and Black," I instruct Larosa. "Let them know we're on the way. Give them brothers a summary of what's goin' on, but leave out the incident that caused all this shit."

"You don't think those brothers already know about the other night?" Larosa questions.

"They most likely have heard rumors and have made assumptions, but don't admit to shit," I say. "It will only make the situation worse if all this comes out. We will be the ones in violation for puttin' a brother's life in jeopardy and breaking the truce. So, just handle the business just as I said."

"That's the business, Family," Larosa replies.

"*It's about to be bodies coming up missing,*" I mumble to myself.

"Congo, we're on the way to the spot. Is Black with you?" Larosa calls and asks with the phone on speaker.

"I've been waiting on this call for two days now. And yes, he's here. We'll be waiting," Congo replies sternly.

"Give us ten minutes," Larosa says, matching Congo's tone.

Click.

"Well, from the sounds of it, Congo has been waitin' on us to pull up for the past two days", Larosa says with a chuckle.

"Don't worry because that's what we are gonna do," I reply.

———◆———

CONGO IS A BROTHER ORIGINALLY FROM AFRICA, who has been putting in work since he laid foot on American soil. He is stern, but fair. I know if he knows the truth about this situation, it won't go well for me nor Larosa. I've got a better chance with telling Black the truth due to the fact of him being my teacher. Since he taught me everything about

DMG, I know he will be understanding.

Once we arrive at the spot, we give Congo and Black a summary of the events that have occurred in the past 48 hours. Afterwards, I inform them of me and Larosa's plan to defuse the situation.

"Jaz has a nephew named Roc who goes to Prime-time every Friday," I explain. "We need leverage to be able to bargain to get CJ back or else they ain't budgin,' my nigga. So, we are goin' to snatch him up then."

Pacing the hardwood floor, I continue, "As of now, they have the upper hand and I hate that with a passion. We believe this is the only way to get CJ back alive."

"I want everyone to leave the room except Nard," Black instructs.

Closing the door behind Larosa and Congo, Black turns to me with a distrustful look in his eyes and says, "What's really going on, lil bruh? Because I'm not buyin' that story you gave. Ain't no way in hell Jaz is crazy enough to snatch up a brother knowin' the mob behind him. What the hell did you and Larosa do? I'm coming to you as a brother, so what you tell me will never be repeated."

"Bruh, now you know I can't tell you what actually went on that night. Just know I fucked up and I wish I can turn back the hands of time, but if I waste time dwelling on the past then I'm stagnating my future," I firmly reply.

"Did y'all have something to do with Jaz getting robbed?"

The sly smirk that comes across my face tells him everything he needs to know which causes him to shake his head.

When Black was a young man, that was his M.O., so he

*understands, but he has grown and developed from that life-
style. Deep down, he prays that me and Larosa do the same.
But when we were children, we both looked up to him and
learned from him. This is one thing he regrets in life.*

"Say less, lil bruh. Just clean this shit up before it gets
messy. We don't have until Friday. Its Tuesday and that
nigga has to be found within the next 48 hours and
that's a directive. After all this is over, you, Larosa, and I
need to have a sit down. God forbids something happens to that brother because of your actions."

"I haven't admitted to nothin', FAM," I adamantly
say. "And I never implicated Larosa in shit, so after I
clean this shit up, everything will go back to normal."

"And you are absolutely correct," Black says with
a light chuckle. "That's why I love you, because you
know how to keep your mouth closed and sealed. But,
I still have to drop some knowledge on you for future
references."

"Well, drop them on me now," I sarcastically respond.

"There is a time and a place for everything, lil bruh,"
Black says, walking out the room.

CHAPTER NINE

~ NARD ~

BLACK'S WORDS HAUNT MY MIND AS I DRIVE back to the crib. Beyond everything, Black is an elder brother, my teacher, who has put in a lot of work. He has high expectations for all the young brothers, but he really wants to see me succeed. Words can't describe the love and loyalty I have for this man. That's big bruh and I know he will never lead me wrong in nothin'. But, what did he mean when he said there is a time and a place for everything? Speaking to a man like Black, you always have to decipher riddles and shit. I guess that's where I get it from because people tell me that I speak in riddles. After all this is over, I need to take a vacation.

My mind drifts to the beauty I saw last night as I put the convo with Black outta my mind.

"What time is it?" I think to myself.

After looking at the car clock I see that it is 12 o'clock midnight.

I wonder if it is too late to call her and if she will get upset because it's so late.

After dwelling on the thought for a few seconds, I say, *"Fuck it."*

I've got to get my mind off everything that's goin' on. I feel like she's the one to do just that.

Ring.

Ring.

Ring.

"Hello, may I speak with Empress?"

"Speaking, may I ask who is this?"

"This is Renardo, and I hope I didn't wake you up."

"Re-Nardo???"

"Yeah, Renardo…from Burger King. We met last night… in the drive-thru at Krystal's."

"I don't recall meeting someone named Re-Nar-Do," She coldly replies, breaking down every syllable of my name.

Puzzled, I pull the phone from my ear and stare at it for a few seconds to make sure I called the right number. Yes, this definitely is the right number because she put the number in my phone and she just told me her name is Empress.

"OK, I apologize for calling at such a late time. Rest easy."

Click.

Now that was weird as fuck. Did I just meet the girl from the movie 50 First Dates? The girl who had short-term memory loss and every night all memories of the present day erased. You have got to be kiddin' me! Maybe I misjudged her. Maybe she is a hoe. Hell, I'm foolish to think I'm the only nigga that approached her yesterday. She probably gave her number out to every decent lookin' nigga that came through the drive-thru.

Feeling like a fool I simultaneously laugh lightly at the situation; my phone starts ringing. It's Empress!

"Hello? Hi, Renardo. I do remember meeting you yesterday," she says in a much more pleasant tone than our prior conversation.

She has gotta be kiddin' me. So, now she remembers me? I want to ask her what caused this amnesia, but I will hold back.

"Soooo, I hope I didn't interrupt your sleep?" I reply as I pull up to my apartment building and park.

"No, you didn't. I stay up late almost every night. I literally don't go to bed until 2 or 3 every night - or morning if you want to be technical."

"Shit, I don't see how you do it because workin' and goin' to school has me exhausted."

"Hold on, how old are you, Renardo?" She says, sounding astonished.

"Seventeen," I reply.

"Really??? I mean, I thought you were at least 20."

"Naw, I'm just mature for my age, but enough about me, tell me about yourself - like why have I never seen you around the city. I practically know everybody or everybody knows me."

"Well, I am seventeen also, but I don't go to school in this district because my mother thought it would be best if I finish out the school year at Brook High in DeKalb County since this is my senior year. I definitely don't know you, but I would love to get to know you."

"I would love that, too," I say with a slight grin on my face. "I must warn you that I'm a mystery, so beware."

"Mystery, huh? Well, I never read a mystery book I didn't like."

"Where do you live?"

"I stay in a neighborhood called Field Stone. Have you heard of it?"

"No fuckin' way!" I say in disbelief, shocked that such a beautiful and articulate young lady lives in a place I frequently visit.

"Yes, I do. Why do you say that?" She innocently

asks.

"Because I practically be in the hood at least twice a week. My people got a spot out there. Matter of fact I'm just coming from down there."

I can't believe Empress lives in Field Stone because it is known to be YGC headquarters. Ever since the truce, DMG got a spot out there to keep an eye on them YGC niggas.

I purposefully added the last part about comin' from the hood to test her and to see what type of female she really is. If she tells me she wants me to turn around, so she can see me then I know she a hoe and I will be all in that pussy tonight. But if she completely disregards my statement, she is a woman I want to get to know.

"Oh really? Well, I am barely home because if I'm not at school, I'm working at one of my jobs," she responds.

"Yes! My woman!" I say to myself with a smile.

"So, you have two jobs?" I ask.

"Yes."

"Damn. How do you do that? Not being physically drained and tired."

"Well, I've got no choice. I'm a family-oriented person and I will look out for my family no matter what. I have this drive in me that won't quit. I just keep pushing forward."

"I know what you mean. I've gone through a struggle practically my whole life, too. I've basically been takin' care of myself since I was 14, so believe me I understand what you mean."

"Yes, but I'm really not trying to talk about that," she responds, tryin' to avoid our current conversation.

"That's respectable… we all have memories we try to erase out of our minds. Just know you are not alone."

"If I ever decide to tell you some of those memories,

can I trust you?"

"Yes, you can trust me. I'm not one to gossip."

"Good, because I'm very secretive. What is it that Lil Wayne says? 'Real Gs move in silence like lasagna.'"

We both laugh at her recital of the rapper's lyrics.

"Soooo, when are you goin' to allow me to take your beautiful self out on a date?"

"Well, considering the limited time I have on my hands, I will have to talk with my managers and take a Saturday off, so, you can do that soon."

"That's a bet," I reply, pleased with her answer.

"I guess I'm about to let you get some sleep before morning and go inside my apartment, so that I can do the same thing."

"You're not in the house?"

"Well, I've been parked in front of my apartment for the past thirty minutes. I've just been sittin' in my car talkin' to you."

We both laugh.

"Well, I'm glad you called," she says.

"I'm glad I called as well. You really took a lot off my mind tonight and you don't even know it. Thank you."

"Really??? Well, you're welcome. I'm glad I could assist you with your stress," she says in such a sweet manner that I can picture her smiling through the phone. "I guess it's good night."

"Yes, this is good night. Sweet dreams."

"Same to you."

Chapter Ten

~ EMPRESS ~

SINCE MY TRANSPORTATION OPTIONS ARE unreliable or nonexistent, I hung around school today and decided to crash at Chante's house after school. Surprisingly, I am not scheduled to work today at either of my jobs. I work so much that it feels abnormal not working. What would I do with the free time? My grandmother always says idle time is the devil's playground. Maybe she is right. Perhaps, working has prevented me from getting caught up in the pitfalls and temptations in life. I do not know for sure, but I know I have this undying drive inside of me. I have got to stay focused. Tunnelvision. Even though we are a little too old to be having a slumber party, Chante invited Olivia, Alexis, and Fallon. It is different being at Chante's home. The worries of my household do not seem to impact this gated mansion, not one bit. Here, Chante comfortably enjoys the lap of luxury while I try not to fall off the bony knee of poverty. I am among them, but I am not like them.

They don't know the struggle of watching an old ass show like the Golden Girls from nearly 30 years ago and wishing that you could have a piece of that cheesecake they're always eating or drinking some of that orange juice they are always drinking because you look inside your refrigerator and see only a box of baking soda and a tube of butter.

Things they think are major seem minor to me. The chips are definitely piling on my tiny shoulders, but I have to keep movin' forward. When am I going to get discovered by a major dope producer? After all, I do live in Atlanta, the capital of trap beats and trap music. It has always been a dream of mines to record at PatchWerk Studios with Zaytoven or Metro Boomin. How much will it cost to book studio time? It has to be expensive because they have financing options. Am I going to stay here and support my family or go to college? God knows there is a much better life than this and I want it. Is that a bad thing? If I am not here to contribute, will my family make it? Am I going to see Renardo soon? I enjoyed our conversation last night. Hopefully, he will call me back. Will I ever be able to save enough money to buy a car? Will I get an A+ in science? What color polish will I get on my nails when I go to the nail shop? Where in the world is Carmen Sandiego? So many questions on my mind.

Maybe one of life's test is to make what we are given good. After all, they say there's always a light at the end of every tunnel. At night, my friends sleep and dream about Prince Charming, while I'm awake, calculating my next move to propel me to the next level because I know I do not have a Daddy Warbucks and I'm not looking for a Prince Charming to save me. I have to save myself. I do not want any man to ever think that I owe him anything or that he owns me. I have seen how my mom, aunts, co-workers, friends, and so many women in my life have gotten played by men and I have vowed to myself that I will never allow that to happen to me. I have too much self-respect. I do not have time to play around because my actions not only affect my future, but also my family.

Here I am though… the hardest workin' girl in the twelfth

*grade acting as though I am unbothered by the possibility
of my family being put out of our duplex if we can't come
up with the rest of the rent money. In this very moment, I
seemingly have no worries. But, that's what life is all about
right? Moments.*

"Stop hoggin' all the popcorn, Empress," Chante says
as she flops onto the couch.

"Ooops, my bad," I reply with a chuckle.

"What do you guys want to watch on Netflix?" Fallon asks.

"What about a classic film?" I suggest.

"Do you mean those boring black and white movies?" Olivia asks as she pops open her can soda.

"Um, they aren't boring," I say, shielding the wonderful movies of the past from Olivia's insult.

"Empress, we're not watchin' that old shit," Chante
says as she stuffs popcorn in her mouth.

"Whatever. Y'all don't know what you're missing.
Great story lines, glamour, glitz, and galore," I say, still
defending the honor of the classic black and white
films that I love so much.

"Nobody not tryin' to watch ghosts and cobwebs,
Empress," Alexis says as she scrolls through Instagram.

"Yeah, yeah," I grumble. "One day I'm going to be
sittin' on the TCM couch talkin' to Robert Osborne
about my top five favorite classic films on *The Essentials* and then you all will be sayin', 'Dang, we should
have listened to Empress.'"

"First off, who the hell is Robert Osborne? Second,
nobody ain't gon be sayin' that because nobody will
see you. We don't watch that channel," Chante says,
making us laugh.

*I pick up my phone to check the time. I see that I have three
unread messages. One is probably from my mother checking*

if I have eaten dinner. The other two texts are probably from Trapp just checkin' up on me. Opening the messages, I am elated to see that they are from Renardo.

Renardo: Hope you got a good night's rest. I really enjoyed our convo.

Renardo: Btw, this is Renardo just in case your memory fails you. :)

Renardo: Wyd?

Wow! It is Renardo! He enjoyed our convo too... this is great! Shit! He texted this ten minutes ago. Hopefully, he's not busy doing something else.

Me: LOL. Funny. Having a slumber party with my girls. What about you?

I'm getting butterflies just thinking about what his response will be.

Renardo: Slumber party? Aren't y'all a little too old for that? LOL.

Me: Ikr. We're just doing girlie things like painting nails and talking about fashion.

Renardo: I thought you had forgot about a nigga.

Renardo: Were you able to get Saturday off at both of your jobs?

Yes! Just the question I was waiting for to answer with an instant yes.

Me: Yes.

Dang, did I just text too fast? Was I too short? Should I

have added a little more?

Renardo: Cool. I already know your dress game is on point, so I don't have to tell   you to wear sumthin nice.

"Wear sumthin nice…" Oh wow, I wonder what Renardo has in mind.

Me: Where are we going?
Renardo: Don't worry your pretty little head about that. Just make sure you look fly.

A man full of surprises! I think I'm falling for him already. I hate when boys ask me where I want to go on our first date. I think that should always be up to the man because he asked to take me out.

Me: Okie dokie :)
Renardo: Can you send me a pic? I would love to see that beautiful face of yours.

Chante has turned the lights off, so I will have to go to the bathroom to take a few pictures in decent light. I want to make sure that I look extra cute.

Me: Only if you send me one too.
Renardo: Deal.
Renardo: I have to take care of some business.
Renardo: Can I expect to talk to you later tonight?
Me: Okay. I'll be expecting your call.

~ NARD ~

I RECLINE BACK IN MY LA-Z-BOY, EXCITED about the possibility of taking Empress out on a date. I can't wait to talk to her later tonight. I love the sound of her voice. I know I've got to impress her and take her somewhere super nice. I've gotta think of sumthin, but right now I'm forced to deal with this bullshit between Larosa and Jaz.

"OK, where are we goin' to start lookin' for this nigga, Roc?" Larosa wonders as he paces my apartment floor. "This nigga seems to be a ghost and whenever we do see this nigga, he with a crowd of niggas."

"Well this nigga, Roc, likes to trick off a lot, and it just so happens Danielle fucks around with him on the regular. She was with the nigga the night all this shit went down," I inform Larosa.

"So, you telling me she down with settin' up her nigga?" Larosa asks, puzzled.

"Business is business, Family. Her loyalty lies with the Family, not some nigga that is only temporary," I reply.

"Ooooo, that bitch cold," Larosa says with a grin.

"I know. I raised and molded her to be just that, Gangsta. And my meaning of Gangsta is Family first, willing to make any sacrifice to protect your Family. At the end of the day, we love and care for her, no one else. That's why I didn't mind quitting my job and going to war for you because I know you would do the same thing for me if the situation was reversed."

"Already know and that's facts. Love, FAM," Larosa says as we dap each other up.

"Without measure, Family," I reply.

"So, when all this supposed to go down?" Larosa asks.

"Tonight. He is taking her out and after that they are goin' back to her spot to do they thing."

"What's the plan nigga?" Larosa asks, yet another question.

"We are goin' to take the nigga at her spot and we are goin' to make sure Danielle is put up somewhere after all this shit goes down."

"So, you goin' to keep her put up at your spot?" Without a doubt, Larosa is asking more questions than usual today.

"Can't do that."

"Why not nigga?"

"I met this girl and I'm thinkin' about settling down. I don't need her thinkin' I'm tryin' to play her."

"What my nigga???" Larosa says staring at me as if I have two heads. Seeing that my stern facial expression won't budge, he adds, "Oh, you dead serious? I noticed you were textin' on your phone, but I ain't no it was some girl. Sometimes I worry about you."

"What for?" I ask.

"Cause you are seventeen and you act like you are fifty," Larosa says shaking his head. "Nigga enjoy life. Fuck these hoes and get money, my nigga."

"That's what you don't understand. I've done all that, FAM. I don't believe there's a nigga out there who's done the shit I've done at my age. Hoes, I've ranned through the city and by God's grace I don't got shit. Money, you know that shit comes and goes, especially with the lifestyle we live. I'm tryin' to live, my nigga. This might be living to you, but not me, FAM. There has to be more to life. Plus, this girl brings me peace. I've never had a female that makes me feel the way she makes me feel and that's real nigga shit."

"Man, shut up with all that mushy shit!"

"Hahaha," I cannot help but laugh. "Aight nigga, but on the real, I'm goin' to make her my Queen. She has goals and wants something for herself in life. I love that about her."

"Aight, nigga, I got you," Larosa says shaking his head and laughing. "Well, nigga I plan on being a free agent until kingdom comes. Me and these hoes have an understanding. I will never sign no fuckin' contract with no team. I'm not a team player."

"One day you will get tired of that shit."

"But, I was thinking about puttin' her up at Congo's spot until we take care of everything," I say, getting back to the question of where Danielle will stay once everything goes down.

"That's the business," Larosa says, pleased with this option.

"Already know," I nod in agreement.

———◆———

"WELL, WELL, WELL…SLEEPING BEAUTY HAS finally awakened," Jaz taunts CJ as his swollen black eyes open. "It's not lookin' good for you baby boy because my niggas still haven't found that nigga Larosa. You know your cousin is a fool, right?"

"I don't even know why you got me here!" CJ pleads, as his eyes search the dim garage. With little to eat or drink in the last twenty-four hours, he is extremely dehydrated, cold, and exhausted.

Hearing these words makes Jaz extremely angry. If steam could blow out of his ears, it would. He is furious.

"Oh, so you don't know your cousin robbed me???" Jaz angrily asks. "He only hit me for $7,500 but it's the principle. He tried the fuck out of me after I embraced him as a friend. I don't have too many of them, you know."

"But it's OK, he'll be a dead issue in the next few days. If he doesn't show up in the next twenty-four hours, then you will be no use to me and a dead issue too," Jaz says with a loud laugh. "But, until then, tell me every muthafuckin' thing you know about the second man who robbed me and I will consider letting you live. The streets tell me his name is Renardo aka Hard Nard."

"Nigga, fuck you," he yells out spitting directly in Jaz's face. CJ would never sell out his FAM.

Like a chain reaction, Jaz reflexes and backhands CJ, flippin' him out of the chair.

"Bitch nigga, you just cut your time to live in half. You've got twelve hours now. I'm going to personally put a bullet in your head and enjoy every fuckin' millisecond."

Chapter Eleven

~ NARD ~

"NARD, WE JUST GOT TO MY SPOT," DANIELLE whispers into her phone, trying to be discreet. "I left the back door open. Give me like twenty minutes before you come in."

"Also, I need every dollar in this nigga pocket - I believe I deserve it," she adds with a mischievous laugh.

"OK, OK, you can keep that shit," I hurriedly say because the last thing I care about is the few dollars he may have in his pockets.

"Is that nigga holdin'?" I ask.

"He left it in the car," she quickly replies.

"Bet. Go ahead and do your thing," I respond as I make a sharp right turn en route to her apartment.

"You owe me, nigga. You know that, right?" She says.

"The only thing I owe you is loyalty and I expect the same," I state firmly. "Bye, Danielle. I will see you in a few."

Ending the phone call with Danielle, I turn to Larosa and ask, "You ready my nigga?"

"Is that a question? I'm always ready. This is what I do..." Pausing In mid- sentence Larosa says, "This is all I know."

For a split second, it appears he is in pain from life itself.

"Believe me, I feel you bruh. I feel you," I say in acknowledgment of his unsaid sorrow.

"I know you do. That's why I trust you with all my secrets."

We both hop out the car with our Glocks cocked and creep to Danielle's apartment. I slowly turn the knob making the littlest amount of noise as possible. I know this duplex better than my own apartment.

With Larosa a few steps behind me, we gradually and softly walk directly to Danielle's bedroom where we hear noise of her fuckin' Roc. Looking back at Larosa, I smile because I knew my plan would work. He grins from ear to ear because he is just as happy as I am. Next, we creep up to the bedroom door where I turn the knob ever so softly.

I know Danielle is into some kinky shit, but she knew damn well not to even think about handcuffing me to a bed when we used to fuck around. But, I'm glad this simp ass nigga is into shit like this because he just made our job a whole lot easier.

"Hold up! What the fuck is this???" Roc yells in a panic.

Me and Larosa both run into the room in different directions, making sure it is secured. After sweeping the room, we stare down at Roc as he is handcuffed to the bed. His face spells terror and his aura breathes fear.

"Look, look, you can have everything," he stutters.

"This shit is deeper than money, nigga!" Larosa furiously says as he hits Roc with the butt of his gun, knocking him out.

"Where the keys to these cuffs?" I demand as I search

for them.

"On the dresser," Danielle replies as she wiggles her way into her tight skinny jeans.

"Uncuff him from the bed and cuff his hands," I yell to Danielle, making another urgent demand. "Let's go!"

The darkness makes our kidnapping easy as there are no witnesses to see us throwing Roc in the trunk.

I call Black and put him on speaker as we drive off.

"Hello…" he says.

"We got him," I confirm.

"Take him to the spot. DMG."

"DMG."

Click.

~ EMPRESS ~

"EARTH TO EMPRESS!" CHANTE CALLS AS SHE throws a pillow at me.

"Huh?" I say confused, totally wrapped up in my thoughts about Renardo.

"Whoever you're textin' must be talkin' good because you completely zoned out," Chante says in a teasing manner.

"It's probably that boy she met when she was at work," Olivia butts in.

Olivia thinks she knows everything. Well, in this case, she is right, but who asked her for her ten cents anyways?

"No, it wasn't," I lie, not wanting to satisfy Olivia's ego,

"If it wasn't him, then who was it?" She counters.

"Yeah, who was it?" Chante, Fallon and Alexis now want to know thanks to Olivia.

"Okay, okay, okay," I say. "It was him and he wants to take me out on Saturday."

"Yaaaaaaaay!!!!" We all scream.

This moment is identical to the lunch break scene in Grease with all the repeated "tell me more's" that the girls are demanding of me right now.

"So, is this an official date?" Fallon asks.

"Well, he didn't call it a date, but he did ask me if he could take me out… so I guess it is!" I say with a smile.

"Can we see a pic?" Alexis asks.

"He's supposed to be sending me one… I guess he got side tracked. But, when I tell you girls he is fine. He is F-I-N-E!"

We all laugh.

"If he is as fine as you say he is, then I need to take a trip to Rockdale and find me a man," Chante comments.

"Well, what color are his eyes?" Olivia asks.

"They're a deep dark brown, almost black. I swear I drown in them. They're the type of eyes that smother you and keep secrets. His eyes are mysterious. He's so dreamy," I say as I clutch a pillow to my chest.

"Is he tall?" Alexis asks.

"Well, I gotta look up –"

"But, you're only 5'2," Olivia interjects.

"Yeah, but it's not like he's 5'3," I retort, rolling my eyes. "I would say he's about 5'10 or 5'11."

I do not mind the girls asking questions about Renardo. I can talk about him all day. I can't wait to see him this weekend. I have already mapped out the outfit I will wear in my mind. I wonder what business does he has to take care of? Hopefully, I will hear from him soon.

"Enough of Empress' lover boy. We need to pick a movie," Chante says. "What about *Fifty Shades of Grey?*"

"Yeah," Olivia, Alexis, and Fallon say in agreement.

"Ugh, we've seen this movie about fifty times," I say,

combating the "yeah's."

"Well, let's count this as the fifty-first time," Chante says. "It's my house so I get the final say so."

"Whatever," I reply, opening my hands to express that I don't care. I am not trying to argue. Besides, it is just a movie."

"Now, Christian is the type of guy to go crazy over, Empress. He has money which he is generous with and he is into freaky, good, sexy sex. I would gladly sign whatever contract he wants," Chante adds.

"Don't you want more than sex or money?" I ask shaking my head. "Don't you want a meaningful romance like the one in *A Walk to Remember*?"

"This is a romance," Chante argues.

"How?" I ask. "The girl is just a horny virgin, and the guy is into bondage and all that 'call me daddy' shit."

"Empress makes a good point," Alexis chimes in.

"Yeah okay, to each her own. Let's just watch the movie," Chante says.

~ NARD ~

CONGO AND BLACK SNATCH ROC OUT OF the trunk once we pull up to the spot. Minutes later, by the time me and Larosa enter the house they have Roc tied and gagged to a chair.

"Larosa, it's show time for you!" I say, hyped up off adrenaline. "Let's get CJ back!"

I throw Roc's phone to Larosa and he wastes no time locating Jaz's info because he is Roc's emergency contact. Larosa presses the green call button anticipating on to talking to Jaz. The phone rings six times until it reaches voicemail. Larosa hits the red end call button and calls Jaz again. The phone rings another six times and there is still no answer.

"I swear to God, if your uncle has done anything to my cousin, I will kill you both, my nigga!" Larosa screams out to Roc in frustration.

"Don't lose it, Family," I tell Larosa. "Stay focused. He will pick up eventually."

"Eventually might be too late, my nigga," Larosa panics.

Getting up in Roc's face, Larosa says in a terrorizing tone, "If he doesn't pick up this damn phone, I will think the worst and I will do the worst to you! Believe that!"

With the gag removed, Roc tries to make an appeal, "Come on man, I don't even have nothin' to do with none of that shit! I don't beef, my nigga!"

"Well, I'm sorry to tell you, you just got caught up," Larosa heartlessly says.

Still attempting to reach Jaz, the phone continues to ring six times and go to voicemail.

"I believe you are going to leave your uncle a message," Larosa says with a vicious look on his face.

Suddenly, he swiftly pulls out a switchblade and cuts deep into Roc's skin, from the left corner of his mouth up to his left ear. This was not a cut, this was a full blown, forceful thrust into his face. An image zooms into Roc's mind. A whirling vortex of angles, shades of silver and white plunge through shades of red and brown, as if he is visually able to follow the blade of the knife shooting through his skin and muscles. It is a deep, ever so deep, pain with insatiable throbbing. The pain comes in waves of intensity, sometimes sharp twinges, sometimes dull pounding, all around and inside the area of the wound. Heavy, red blood drips on the concrete floor as Roc lets out a piercing, inaudible scream of agony and torture.

Good thing that there are not any neighbors nearby, or else, our cover would be blown. Me, Black, and Congo hurry and grab Larosa because he has lost focus.

"Why the fuck did y'all grab me?!?" An angry Larosa yells.

"Because he is useless to us dead, nigga! And we will never get CJ back that way," I say just as loudly, trying to talk some sense into his head.

"Brothers, there is no need to argue!" Black yells, as he notices Roc's phone on the floor and picks it up. "Jaz will hear about this incident because everything was being recorded on his voicemail."

CHAPTER TWELVE

"LOOK, I'M ABOUT TO GRAB SOMETHING TO eat. Call me and give me updates if something changes," Jaz tells KG.

"Aight bruh, I got you. Bring me some Krystal's. Chilli cheese pups with extra chili. Don't forget, man," KG says.

"Just handle business," Jaz says frustrated.

Pausing as he walks out of the door, Jaz thinks, *"We've had this nigga, CJ, for about 18 hours and still no word from this nigga Larosa... This nigga must not give a fuck about no one but himself... I will find this nigga and enjoy killing him... Betrayal is worse than death and that's what he's done..."*

Jaz walks out of the front door and hops in his red '86 Buick Regal with T-Tops on 24s. Immediately, he notices that he has notifications on his phone from missed calls and a voicemail. Talking to himself out loud, he says,

"What the hell does my nephew want?" Jaz says to himself as he dials into his voicemail. He only has to hear three seconds of the message to know what is going on. His head instantly drops in disbelief. For the first time in his life, Jaz is frightened. Wasting no time, he

calls Roc's phone. Larosa answers Roc's phone on the second ring.

"So, are you ready to negotiate or do we have to lose lives?" Larosa asks.

"On God, my nephew had better be okay!" Jaz yells as he hears Roc's horrific screams in the background.

"I don't believe you are in the situation to be making such demands," Larosa fires back. "For every action is a reaction, remember that."

"You are absolutely right, but you forget one thing: you robbed me and that's what started everything! I treated you good my nigga –"

"Hold up, I'm going to stop you right there. We are not about to talk about that robbery because I have no friends, so if you not Family then fuck you. Don't never show me too much."

"Nigga! I treated you like Family. So, what the fuck you talkin' about?!?" Jaz furiously screams into the phone, not understanding Larosa's disposition.

"But, you are not Family, fuck nigga. If you want me, you come get me. I ain't running!"

"Bet that up! But until we meet, how do you want to do this swap out? How do I know Roc is still alive?"

"You heard him on your voicemail, did you not? But, I haven't heard CJ yet. I'm just goin' by your word because I know you not that stupid."

"We not swappin' out until I hear his voice," Jaz declares.

"Either you take my word or we can hang up right now and once we hang up, I can't promise you he will be OK. Just the thought of me losing CJ will cause me to bring severe pain that will cause any man to take his last breath," Larosa threatens. "So, the ball is in your court. Hell, what will you tell your sister when she finds out her baby boy done came up missing because of you? Tragic."

"I will call you in an hour," Jaz says after a brief pause. "Have my nephew at a secure location and I will do the same with CJ."

"Say less."

Click.

Jaz hops out of his car and runs back into the house.

"Strip that nigga naked and drop that nigga off in the cut!" Jaz abruptly instructs KG.

"Say what?" KG asks, puzzled.

"They've got Roc!" Jaz frantically yells.

"How the fuck did they get Roc?" KG asks.

"I don't know! Just strip that nigga! We will deal with these niggas later, but for right now I've got to get my nephew back before my sister finds out he is missing."

"Aight, bruh." KG says.

~ NARD ~

"SO, IS HE READY TO SWAP?" I ASK LAROSA AFTER overhearing the phone call with Jaz.

"Yea, he's ready. We gotta drop this nigga off at a secure location. You got any ideas?" Larosa asks.

"Yeah, actually I do…" I slowly say as the wheels in my mind turn. "This will send a message."

"Where???" Larosa asks, mystified.

"In that nigga Jaz's front yard," I answer with a smirk.

"What!?!? Do you think we can pull that shit off?"

"Nigga, we can pull anything off," I say, fully confident in my quickly devised plan. "We gon drop that nigga off in a hot box. He will be in the trunk tied up."

"What will the message be?"

"We can touch whenever we want, so walk lightly,"

I say, looking Larosa dead in the eyes.

~ EMPRESS ~

THE MOVIE IS NOT HOLDING MY ATTENTION, because I have seen it so many times. Naturally, my mind wonders about the one and only Renardo. From our conversation, he seems so mature. What will he be like on our first date? I'm curious to know.

It is so hard practicing restraint. I want to call and text him sooooo bad, but I won't. I don't want to seem too eager. I would look sooooo lame. Besides, what would I say? "Hi, just checking up on you?" We have not even gone out on a date and I am not his woman, so why would I be so concerned? Ugh, I have to get this boy out of my mind or else he will drive me insane!

Chapter Thirteen

"HELLO?" JAZ SAYS AS LAROSA PICKS UP THE phone. "Your boy is standing in the cut."

The cut is a path that is the gateway to three different hoods, including Larosa's. It is also a jackboy's dream, due to all the traffic that comes thru on late nights. Larosa even used to sit in the cut on Friday and Saturday nights, waitin' to catch a drunk muthafucka slippin', but that was awhile back when he was a lil nigga. Now that's petty change to him. If he's going to take penitentiary chances, then it's going to be for sumthin worth it.

"This better not be a setup or your nephew is a dead man," Larosa fires back, knowin' how shit goes down in the cut.

"I always keep my end of the bargain," Jaz firmly states. "Just know this beef ain't over baby boy."

"My nigga, just know what you doin'. No one is bigger than the Mob. Remember that shit!" Larosa threatens through gritted teeth.

"This situation will get bloody so prepare yourself," Jaz says, laughing at Larosa's audacity.

"You are late," Larosa snickers back.

Jaz pauses and in a fit of rage screams, "Where the

fuck is my nephew and what have you done to him?!?!"

"Just chill," Larosa condescendingly says. "You're gettin' ahead of yourself. Once my people secure CJ, I will send you to go get your bitch ass nephew. Don't worry, Roc is close by."

After minutes of anxiously waiting, Larosa finally receives the million-dollar text confirming that the Family has secured CJ. He feels a great amount of relief while asking Jaz, "Are you at home?"

"No," Jaz lies.

"Why are you lying? I see your car from where I'm standin'," Larosa says.

Feeling the immediate pressure, Jaz grows dismayed and grabs his gun out of his safe.

"No need to panic. If I wanted to kill you, you would've already been dead," Larosa reminds Jaz. "Anyways, there is a black Chevy parked in your front yard and if you look in the trunk, you will find your lil nigga," Larosa says as he bursts into laughter and hangs up.

Jaz hears laughter and grabs his .44 Bulldog. Cautiously, he exits through his backdoor and creeps toward his perfectly manicured lawn. When he spots the black Chevy, his heartbeat quickens because he does not know where Larosa is hiding. His breathing becomes erratic as he unceasingly scans his front yard which is lit by the moonlight and the outdoor light on the side of his house. All the while Jaz is unaware that Larosa has vanished into the night.

"*On God, I'm going to dead this pussy ass nigga,*" Jaz says to himself.

Slowly creeping towards the black Chevy and poppin' the trunk, he quickly regrets it because what he sees makes his heart drop as tears well up in his eyes. Jaz wastes no time getting Roc medical attention.

"FAM, everything good on my end," Larosa says to Nard, barley givin him a chance to answer the phone. "I'll be at the spot in ten."

"That's a bet. Everyone is here. We're waitin'. Love."

"Never Enough."

Click.

~ EMPRESS ~

"EMPRESS, IF THIS WAS YOUR MOVIE IT WOULD be called *Fifty Shades of Church*," Olivia attempts to tease me as the ending credits roll.

Since the film has ended, this means a movie discussion is in order. It's normally a time when us girls have a deep, philosophical discussion about what we would have done if we were the female lead in whatever film we watched. Tonight, it seems I will be in the "hot seat" and asked what would I do if I were the main character in this movie. Oh, boy!

"Na, it would be called *Fifty Shades of…*" Alexis says as she struggles to complete her sentence while snapping her fingers. "What's the name of that guy Empress is totally crushing on?"

"Uh… uh Narco!" Chante says with a smirk, trying to be funny.

"Ha-ha, you mean Renardo," Fallon laughs as she chugs down her can soda. "She kuh-ra-zy about him."

"I am not," I say with a shy smile.

"You are too!" Fallon teases.

The house alarm goes off as Chante's mother enters their home to find us girls have invaded her den.

"Hi, Dr. Gamble!" We all say in unison.

"Hey, girls!" Dr. Gamble excitedly says as she makes room on the couch and places her Louis Vuitton briefcase on the carpeted floor. "I'm surprised you girls are up this late. It's nearly 1 a.m."

"How was the ride to the airport? Was it packed?" Chante asks her mother.

"When is Hartsfield-Jackson not busy?" Dr. Gamble replies. "Your father and I had dinner there while we waited on his flight. He is so excited to go to Kansas for the AMC Theater convention. He just loves meeting other movie theater owners."

"I know," Chante says. "He's been talking about meeting Wang Jianlin, the richest man in China, all month."

"Girl, isn't that the truth," Dr. Gamble says with a laugh. "So, what juicy girl talk did I just walk in on?" She asks as she reaches her hand into the popcorn bowl.

"We're just talking about Empress' love life, mom," Chante says.

"Or lack thereof," I interrupt.

"A beautiful girl like you?" Dr. Gamble ask. "Now that's totally unacceptable. Well, now, what are we going to do to fix this situation?"

"I need to meet a guy," I say with a smile and much declaration with Renardo on my mind.

"That's a start," Dr. Gamble says with playful sarcasm as the girls and I giggle.

Getting up from the couch, I walk across the room dramatically with my throw blanket wrapped around me.

"Not just any guy," I continue. "He has to look good."

"Of course," Fallon say with a giggle. "We don't do ugly boys."

"I know that's right," Dr. Gamble joins in.

"It's not all about his looks though," I add. "This guy will have to be charming and sweep me off my feet."

"Ah, a nice old-fashioned romance," Dr. Gamble comments.

"Hmmm…maybe. This guy will have to make me fall soooo hard for him through his love and loyalty for me. I'm talkin' about, some actions speak louder than words type of love," I say, caught up in my fantasy.

"He has to be handsome, intelligent, and most importantly, kind," Dr. Gamble adds, pumping up my dream guy.

"Exactly!" I innocently and doe-eyed say. "He has to be sweet and respectful. And does not attend Brook High."

The girls instantly roll their eyes, not liking my statement because they feel as though I am dissin' their hometown and our school.

"What, you think you too good for Brook High?" Olivia asks in the most defensive tone.

"No, no, it's nothing like that. I just want something different," I say, still partially under Renardo's invisible spell. "I want a guy who means exactly what he says. Someone who has real love for me and is selfless in his love."

CHAPTER FOURTEEN

~ NARD ~

"THIS SHIT HAS GOTTEN OUT OF HAND," BLACK says as he paces across the Somerset hardwood floors of his home. Pointing at CJ, he continues to be firm in his lecture, "Y'all have allowed this brother to come into harm's way because of the love you all have for money. Y'all niggas need to learn that it's not all about you and what you do not only affects you, but others as well, sometimes the ones you love. I cannot turn a blind eye to this incident because you've allowed this brother to come into harm's way. Not only was he harmed, but now we are at war. I love you both, but, my love comes with discipline. What do y'all have to say about this situation?"

"Well, I will never admit to nothin', but I will apologize to my brother for placing him in this situation," I say, looking straight ahead, avoiding eye contact with Black. "I pray that he finds it in his heart to forgive me for not being there when that pussy ass nigga was doin' this shit to him."

Every time I look at CJ, I become infuriated because my brother looks bad and it is all me and Larosa's fault.

"I promise you CJ, everything will be taken care of in due time," I add.

"FAM, you know it's all love and this could've happened to either one of us, but I was slippin'," CJ manages to reply with his busted lip and black eyes.

He may be young, but he has heart. That's one thing I respect about him.

"Nard," Black says, barely giving CJ a chance to finish his sentence. "That shit wouldn't have happened if y'all didn't do that fuck shit!"

I do not like how Black is coming at me and I dislike how he puts emphasis on the word 'y'all'. Damn, I know me and Larosa fucked up, but I do not need Black reinforcing the shit.

"I hear exactly what you are saying," I reply, not doing a good job of controlling my aggression. "But, Black, I've got rights as a brother. Please do a thorough investigation on this incident before you act off presumptions," I firmly add, looking Black directly in the eyes.

"All this shit is my fault and I take responsibility for my actions and of Nard's," Larosa jumps in, trying to stop the tension that is building.

Not believing my ears, I look at Larosa as though he has two heads.

"FAM is right, bruh," he says looking at me. "None of this shit would've never happened if it wasn't for my greed and temper. I had no self-control. You were only dragged into this shit because you knew I needed you to have my back."

The more Larosa talks, the more I shake my head. This nigga must think he is Usher, and this is his confessions. I don't know what the hell Larosa is thinkin' right now. He continues going on and on, diggin' us into a deeper hole. Enough is enough! I can't take any more of this shit.

"Well, guess what, FAM? I don't know what this nigga talkin' about. I ain't did shit," I interrupt, directing a menacing glare towards Larosa.

"Well, Nard, the first step to forgiveness is admitting and acknowledging your wrong," Black says, finally taking a seat on a bar stool.

He sits, I stand.

"No, that's called stupidity," I say with a smirk. "You wouldn't tell a judge, 'I want you to forgive me for killing these two niggas.' Why? Because that judge is going to give your dumbass two life sentences."

"I know that's right," Black says through his laughter. "But I'm no judge. I am your brother who wants to see you both do better. Better than what I did when I was younger."

Me, Larosa, and CJ sit quietly and listen as Black continues.

"Do you think I haven't done the things y'all doing? I have and probably more, but I've grown into a better person. It took losing my older brother, Forte, to the system for my eyes to open. That's one reason we began this truce with the YGC crew - to end this senseless beefing."

"I've heard of Forte," I say.

"That's big bruh to all of us, FAM," Black says remorsefully, not wanting to discuss Forte any longer. "I don't want y'all going through the same things I did in order to learn the lesson of life," he continues. "Life itself is the greatest teacher. Remember that."

"Now, that's real shit," CJ says as he applies pressure to his busted lip with an ice pack.

"That's DMG," Larosa agrees.

"I hear you, FAM," I add. "And I love you Eternally, but I'm goin' to hold the truth of this incident to myself and strive to do better. You are just going to have to do your investigation. I know I do wrong. I'm not perfect, but I will never tell on myself. I will never make the same mistake twice. And that's DMG."

"That's Love, Gentleman," I say as I shake everyone's hand.

"I swear that nigga stubborn," Larosa chuckles, as I try to exit.

"That nigga is a damn Aries," Black adds.

"Ha!!! No, I'm just Hard Nard," I say with a smile, correcting them.

"You right though, FAM, life itself is the greatest teacher," CJ says, disregarding our joke and bringing focus back to Black's original statement.

CJ points at me and adds, "That's what it's goin' to take for this brother to learn."

Chapter Fifteen

~ EMPRESS ~

IT IS SATURDAY NIGHT AROUND 7 P.M. BUT THE sun has set which makes it feel later than what it really is. Even though he has not rung the doorbell yet, the loud music blastin' from Renardo's car alerts me he is here to take me out on our first date.

Neither my mom nor Trapp is home which makes tonight perfect for a date. I don't need them grilling me about who I am with and how long I will be out.

I scramble to find my Chance by Chanel perfume as the doorbell rings. It smells so good. I know Renardo will love it. I try to collect myself as I head down the steps. I have to come across as saucy and not nervous.

His eyes light up at the sight of me as I stand in the doorway. It is no coincidence that I am wearing my gray form-fitting sweater dress that hugs my body in all the right places with my black Jeffrey Campbell thigh high boots. The heels give me the perfect height to match Renardo's tall stature.

"I like your outfit," he says, biting his bottom lip which is so sexy. I wish he would do it again.

"Thank you," I nonchalantly say, playing it cool even though I'm thrilled by his compliment.

"You look very stylish as well," I add, sincerely returning the compliment. He has on a tan tailored Ralph Lauren bomber jacket with a nice crisp white t-shirt underneath, white True Religion jeans, tan Louis Vuitton Hockenheim loafers with an LV Initiales belt to match.

"If I haven't told you already, I love your car," I remark as we make our way to the driveway. "It's sittin' pretty on those 24s." Tracing my fingers across the hood, I add, "The clean white paint job with the burgundy stripes is niiiiiiiice!. What year is it?"

"Thank you. It's an '84," Renardo proudly says, opening the passenger door for me.

Impressive! He is quite the gentleman, and he just scored even more points with me. Boys today are so rude and do not know how to treat women, but Renardo seems to be the opposite. Not to mention, he has his own ride, and it is DOPE!

"This is really nice," I remark once more enthralled with the peanut butter interior and leather seats.

"I'm glad you like it. I worked hard to save up to buy and to restore it," Renardo says, closing his door.

"I bet!" I reply, still admiring the fine automobile.

"Hmmm… you said this is an '84," I say, thinking out loud. "So, that makes this model part of the first four generations of the Monte Carlo. The fourth generation to be exact."

"Yeah, it is. How do you know that?" Renardo asks in amazement.

"I know a little bit about a lot of things," I respond with a giggle. "This car is sexy."

"And how do you determine sex appeal?"

"Well, power and performance," I say, looking seductively into Renardo's eyes. "I mean, the Monte Carlo SS is the crème de la crème of ol' skool cars. And then there's the physical characteristics."

"Yeah, that's right. Appearance counts," Renardo says with a cool smile.

"Oh yeah, definitely," I add, running my fingers across the peanut butter dashboard.

"I'm surprised a nice, sweet girl like you would like a car like this," Renardo says. Staring at me intently he adds, "You sure this isn't too hard and rough for you?"

"Not all," I say with a smirk. "This is a classic… everlasting. Definitely a turn on."

With a minute of total eye contact, Renardo and I seem to connect on another level. He grabs my left hand and ever so gently kisses it. I cannot help but blush. Then he starts the ignition and with one crank, we are off into the night. A pleasant look fills his face as it does mine.

———◆———

WITH HIS SWAG IN FULL EFFECT, RENARDO coolly hands his keys over to the parking valet like a BOSS. We confidently stride into Luca with me adorning on his strong chiseled arm. Luca is a swanky, five-star restaurant that celebrities, politicians, and anyone with major influence in Atlanta frequently visits. Grand is the only word to describe this place. The food and service is terrific. The ambiance is intimate. The furnishings are elegant. The lighting is warm, and the colors are harmonious. The staff's chic uniforms bounce well off the suave decor. Without a doubt, we are the youngest people in the restaurant. Even if things don't pan out between Renardo and me, just being here at this glamorous establishment is a memory for a lifetime. I feel like royalty tonight.

For about twenty minutes, Renardo and I fill each other in with little facts about ourselves. *You know, "getting' to know you" type of stuff like our favorite colors, hobbies, horoscope signs, etc. Being that he is an Aries and I am a Sagittarius, we are both fire signs. Hopefully, we can ignite each other's flames. According to astrology, we are very much compatible as his sign is "The Hero" and mine is "The Philosopher".*

I tell him of my aspirations to be an entrepreneur and pop star. Talking over the romantic background music playing, I explain to Renardo, who is lookin' soooo good, "Yeah, I think I'm a mix of impulse and fiction when it comes to writing songs. I want to own my own music publishing company. I've been researching the moves I need to make to bring my dream into fruition."

Renardo is truly an old soul. I love his southern city drawl and the way his eyes twinkle as I speak. I think I have found myself a true Georgia boy.

He offers his advice about the music industry, saying, "There is a bunch of crabs in the industry who are only out for self. Just make sure you choose wisely on who you want to be your producer, but first finish high school and go to college, so you can have something to fall back on."

"One thing I know is that I definitely don't want to work at Krystal's forever. Can you believe somebody tried to give me a $2 bill a couple of days ago?"

"I haven't seen a $2 bill in forever," he says reminiscing. "It is hard to get rid of them. I remember one time I made a jug for some money, well there was about $50 worth of $2 bills and I didn't want them. I tried to exchange them for $10 bills or any type of money because every store where I tried to spend the $2 bills, the people who worked there would look at the bills like they were fake. I even had an Arab dude at a gas station refuse to take the money."

"So, what ended up happening?" I curiously ask through the midst of both our laughter.

"Well, I was mad at the fact he wouldn't take the money, but eventually I ended up spending it all."

Renardo smiles as he takes a sip of Hennessy.

The waiter must have assumed, like I did when we first met, that he is older than his age because he did not get carded. He has such a maturity about him that I can understand how someone could think otherwise.

"I enjoy listening to you talk. I can't believe you are single. I guess this is my cue to step it up," Renardo says with a quick smirk.

Wow! If only he knew I am patiently waiting for him to do so. Though Renardo has an air of mystery about him, we seem to know each other well already. We click so naturally. We're so comfortable with each other that nothing is forced. Familiarity is seemingly a part of us.

"So…tell me more about yourself. I find you very intriguing," I say, stirring my drink with a thin black straw.

"There is not much to tell about me," Renardo replies in a serious tone.

Who does this guy think he's kiddin'? Have we not been talking for the last hour-and-a-half? I could see he had a story to tell when I first spotted him. He is very guarded, but hopefully the closer we become, he will eventually drop his guard. He's already let me in somewhat from our first phone conversation and when he told me his full government name which I love because as he said he rarely gives that information out.

"I don't believe that," I disagreeably say. "Who are

you Renardo Wade?"

"I'm just another nigga from Rockdale."

Renardo's answer leaves me intrigued because he has said nothing, yet hints at more to come.

"Sooooo, what position do you play on the field?" I harmlessly ask. I seem to be talking too much. I guess the fruity tropical drink with Vodka that Renardo ordered me has gone to my head or maybe it is pure adrenaline from being in his presence.

He takes off his jacket and his bulging biceps are just as distracting as his deep dark eyes. There are still sooooo many things about him I have not figured out yet.

"Let me guess, running back?" I answer my question with yet another question.

"And why do you think running back?" He asks as his eyes beam.

"Mmmm...I don't know...you look fast," I laugh.

"Well, I am fast," he says with a smile. "I've been fast all my life."

"Really? This is something else to add to our list of things we have in common. I was awarded a badge a few years back for being the fastest girl in DeKalb county!" I enthusiastically say.

Renardo looks me up and down as he takes another sip of Hennessy. "Empress, I'm not buying that," he says with a chuckle.

"Well, don't I look fit?" I say, taking a slight offense.

"Definitely. You are definitely fit and fine," he says looking me up and down again. "But, you just don't strike me as an outdoor, sweating in the sun type of girl."

I laugh at his comment because I don't like to sweat in the sun, but I am fast though – at least I think I still am.

"Let's race around the track one of these days to see

who is faster," I say loving a challenge.

I extend my hand and he extends his. "Bet," he says as we shake hands on my proposal.

"Back to your assumption though. Yes, you are correct. I can play running back plus other positions. Tight end, wide receiver, and cornerback."

"Wow, so you play both offense and defense?"

"Yeah. Those are just some of the positions I can play. I can pretty much play any position on the field," he proudly says. "How do you know so much about football?"

"My older brother, Trapp, played football growing up and my mom would drag me to all the practices. You will have to invite me to one of your games."

"About that…" Renardo's voice trails off. "Empress, I have to tell you that…"

Oh boy! I knew this date was too good to be true. What bad news is Renardo going to lay on me?

"I…" He drawls. "…I used to play football until I got kicked out of regular school. Now I attend Alpha Alternative School." Folding his hands together in a defensive way, he continues, "Please don't think of me as ignorant because I am not. I'm very intelligent."

"Alpha Alternative? What is that?"

"I keep forgettin' that you not from Rockdale. It's the alternative school for 7th -12th graders that the school system claims are too bad to attend regular public school," he informs me.

"Oh, okay. We have one of those in DeKalb called Off Campus on Memorial Drive. Who names these schools anyways?"

We both laugh while shaking our heads. "Right," he agrees. In a serious tone, he adds, "The school system is discouraging if you ask me. It's like they are saying if you don't make it here, then you are finished. But I won't allow myself to fall victim to all these fuck ass systems."

"How did you end up at Alpha Alternative?"

"Fighting," he remorsefully says as he gazes into the air. "I bet I would have a football scholarship right now, but this is my fifth high school in four years. So, now all my credits are fucked up. Alternative schools do not have athletic teams, so I guess that's one of my dreams that won't come true."

"It's never too late. You never know what the future may have in store for you," I cheerfully say.

"That's right. I love your upbeat energy," he says with a smile. "It's so refreshing, considering all the negativity that surrounds me." Rubbing his hands together he adds with a sigh, "I've had some struggles in this life, Empress."

"Renardo, if you don't want to talk about this we don't have to," I say, reaching my hand across the table, sensing he is becoming uncomfortable. I hope I am not offending or making him upset. I have soooo many questions. I just want to know everything about him. From the smallest of details to larger life altering things. I just hope I'm not being invasive.

"No, no, it's all good," he says. "I've been bounced around from group homes, to fosters homes, to juvenile detention centers, which I'm not proud of, but you know it is what it is."

"So, are you an orphan?"

"Not exactly…my parents are alive," he sorrowfully answers, sadness taking over his dark lively eyes. "I had to become independent at a young age. They gave me up. Right now, I am a ward of the state until I turn eighteen. They gave up on me because they were not ready to be parents, so they consider me a delinquent. But, really I just needed guidance from them."

"Oh, wow," I say, shaking my head in disbelief.

How could his parents abandon him? I just can't fathom how parents could willfully turn their backs on their children and sleep at night. From what he has told me so far, it seems that his parents think he is an inconvenience and don't want to be bothered. It hurts my heart to know that they have treated him so cruelly.

"I have come to the realization that no one is born a parent, so I cannot place any blame on them," he continues.

"Wow, I don't know if I would have that perspective if I were you," I comment while looking into his sweet weary eyes.

"Just like I'm a child who needs guidance, they were young adults who also needed guidance on how to be parents. Still, I have gone through so many struggles in this lifetime because of them. I have no one in authority that actually cares about me. That's why I'm so family-oriented because I don't want anyone to go through the things I've gone through during my childhood. I know the importance of having family support. Once I have my own children, I will never abandon them, no matter what the circumstances are."

"I agree," I say before taking a final bite of the delicious buttered bread roll.

"Most people can't understand something like this," he says.

"I understand," I say, our eyes connecting. "I will always be there for my children. I feel like abandoning a child is ultimately unforgivable."

"So… was it tough being a foster kid?" I hesitantly ask.

"Well, one thing is for certain, it forces you to grow up fast," he says with a snap of his finger. "No one cares, you know?" Totally empathizing with Renardo, I lightly place my hand on top of his. He continues, "No one makes sure you are doing your homework, or wakes you up in the morning for school, or make you lunch, or cook you dinner, and all that good stuff. It's just too much bullshit. That's why I ran away. I couldn't take it anymore. I'm tired of the lies. I wouldn't wish foster care on any child."

"I imagine your life is very chaotic and unpredict-able."

"It can be, but I maintain," he replies. "Look at me now. I'm having a romantic dinner with a beautiful woman. I would say things are much better now."

"I feel like I'm a reporter or something," I say, trying not to blush as we finish our meal.

"No, it's all good, Empress."

"Well, I don't know about you, but I've had enough of the past," I say before taking a sip of water.

"Exactly," he agrees. "I only want to focus on the future."

"I'm glad we had this conversation," he adds, motioning for the waiter to bring the check for our lovely meal. "Just know that we can talk about anything and I will not lie to you."

Once the waiter brings me the slice of Devil's Food cake I ordered to go we head out of the restaurant. Holding my hand and leading the way, Renardo turns to me and says with a smile, "I know for a fact we are forming a lifetime bond because you already know too much about me. I feel like I can trust you with a lot of things."

———•———

I DO NOT WANT THIS SPLENDID NIGHT TO END as we arrive outside my brick duplex. Judging from how Renardo parked his car adjacent to the driveway, I can tell he does not want the night to end either. With the hazy street light nearby, we stare at one another for what seems like an eternity in the dim light. We share an instance between a glance where the world seems to freeze; an intense moment, a perfect moment. Renardo pulls closer and goes for a kiss on my forehead like a true gentleman. So pure, so sweet, so tender. He pulls away showing restraint which is so sexy. His kiss on my forehead is unidirectional. It does not anticipate a reply nor does it need one. But, it gives me a silent indicator that he has good intentions. Most boys I have dealt with kiss me right away and try to come onto me too strong and too fast. Renardo is different. He's smooth, he's got game, and he's a gentleman at the same damn time. That's super-HOT!

"What are you doing tomorrow?" He asks.

"Work, but I'll try to wake up early, so I can work on my music."

"That's cool," he says with warm eyes.

"Who knows, I may just write a song about you," I say with a smirk as my hand slides across the glove compartment.

"I would like that very much," Renardo says with a pleasant look on his face as he nods. "How long have you been writing songs?"

"Since I learned how to read and write," I say with a smile.

"Do you remember what your first song was about?"

"Yep. A mop and a broom," I answer, causing us to

laugh. "My mother says I will run out of things to write about one day."

"Do you think that will happen?"

"No way," I reply. Looking out the window and up at the stars in the sky, I mumble, "The eye is not satisfied with seeing, nor the ear filled with hearing."

"Ecclesiastes," he remarks, bringing my attention back to him.

"I love Ecclesiastes," I say, our eyes permanently fixated on each other.

"It's definitely one of my favorite books in the Bible," he says.

"Whenever I get discourage, I read it. It brings me peace and puts my mind in perspective," I elaborate.

"Yeah," he says with a sigh. "I know what you mean. Have you ever – "

As Renardo is about to ask me a question, my hand slips and the glove compartment pops open where two guns idly rest.

"OMG! What the fuck?!?" I scream.

Even though I live in a crime ridden community, I am totally freakin' out!

"Damn, I thought I locked that shit!" Renardo angrily mutters to himself as he closes the glove compartment.

"Um...maybe I should leave now," I say, still shaken up. "I'm scared."

"You don't have nothin' to be afraid of," Renardo reassuringly says as he grabs my hand. "You were not supposed to see those. I hope this does not change the way you feel about me or give you a bad impression."

"No... it's just that... I did not expect to stumble upon these and I certainly did not expect for you to have them," I say, on edge and worried.

Talk about being held up at gunpoint! There are more twists and turns than I could imagine tonight. I have never seen nor touched a gun until now. This is my first time being exposed to not one, but two guns. Why would such a sweetheart like Renardo need guns? Maybe he is a big game hunter. After all, we do live in the south. Or maybe he's a Second Amendment purist who needs protection…but protection from who?

"Why do you have them?" I hesitantly ask, not sure if I really want to know the answer to my question.

"Empress, I'm really not tryin' to speak on this," he answers, trying his hardest not to sound defensive. "Just know you will never have to worry about nothin'."

Clearly, he is avoiding the question. But why? Does he have something to hide?

"Well, I hope you know what you're doing with these," I blurt, still trying to wrap my head around the situation. "I just read an article about a boy - around our age, who didn't know how to use a gun. The gun misfired, and he killed his best friend. These sorta things happen all the time."

As I speak, Renardo's dreads bounce as he shakes his head. He exhales, lets out a long sigh and says, "Empress, please do not worry because you have nothing to worry about. Please don't ever -"

Suddenly, he stops talkin' dead in his tracks.

Tap.

Tap.

Tap.

"What the -" Renardo jumps.

"Oh no, it's my mother!" I say.

"Empress! Empress! Is that you?!?" My mother screams through the window. "If you don't get your ass in this house right now!"

How embarrassing! I did not even see my mother pull into

*the driveway. I guess I was so into Renardo and this whole
gun situation that I was not paying attention to anything else.*

"Shit, it's my mom!" I say to Renardo, trying not
to feel embarrassed. Letting down the window, I say,
"Mom, I want you to meet Re- "

"What? I'm not trying to meet no nappy-headed
little boy! Get your ass in this house this very minute,"
she yells back.

"Ugh," I say for lack of better words, even more agi-
tated.

"It's all good, Empress," Renardo says, looking at me
in the most tender and affectionate way. "At least your
mother cares about you. I enjoyed our date tonight."

"I did too," I say with a bashful smile.

"You better get in the house," Renardo says, giving
me a sweet kiss on the lips. "Looks like your mother
drew a crowd out here."

*To my horror, he is right! It seems like all of the neighbors
are outside lurkin' to see how much further my mom can
embarrass me.*

"Call me when you can," Renardo says as I get out
of his car.

"Okay," I say, with a short, quick smile, still not over
the humiliation my mother has caused.

*I hate to leave Renardo and I am damn sure not ready to
face my mother in the house. Here is another time where I
wish I could be invisible again.*

Chapter Sixteen

~ EMPRESS ~

I DREAD WALKING INTO THE HOUSE. TEASES AND laughs from the neighbors fill my ears which do not make it any better. I hoped that my date would be over before my mom got home, but clearly, there was a mis-calculation of time on my part.

I try to close the front door without making a sound, but it makes no difference. My mom is standing front and center in the foyer. Before I can even turn around, she lets me have it.

"Do you know what time it is? It is 11:45 at night! What do you think you are doing being out this late? Whose car were you sitting in?" She questions like a drill sergeant as I hang my coat in the hall closet.

I can barely think straight from the guns and the embarrassment she has put me through. My coat falls off the hanger, but I do not bother to pick it up. I am not in the mood to play 21 questions with her.

"Mom, that's Renardo's car," I say in a slightly annoyed tone. "The guy I've been telling you about all week. I was just tryin' to introduce him to you, but you forced me to get out of his car."

"Damn, right I did. No daughter of mine is going to

be sittin' in some nappy- headed boy's car. Stuff happens to little fast ass girls that sit in boys' cars. I don't know what you think this is. I'm not raising a teenage hoe who is goin' to turn up pregnant. You done lost your damn mind!"

Wow, my mother has completely gone off the deep end. What "stuff" is she talkin' about, and why doesn't she trust me?

"Mom, what are you saying?" I respond, rolling my eyes. "I'm seventeen years old! I should be allowed to have some freedom. I get good grades while workin' two jobs. I don't get into any trouble. Besides, do you think I want to be a baby mama?!? I am going to be somebody. I will never play myself like that!"

Oh boy, why did I just do a slick turn up? Now I gotta wait for my mother to erupt like a volcano because now she really will blow.

"And just who do you think you're raising your voice at girl?!?"

"I'm sorry, mom," I apologetically say because I am totally over the conversation and need to neutralize the situation. "But, I just don't understand why you are so upset. I like this boy and I would like for you to be supportive and give him a chance."

"That's all good and fine," she says in a much calmer tone. "But, if he is from Rockdale he's probably runnin' around and gettin' into all types of trouble. These boys out here ain't nothin' but thugs!"

"He's different mom!" I say in his defense. "He's not like the boys Trapp hangs with. Please, mom, try to understand that I just might fall in love with him."

"Love?!?!" She laughs, yells, and screams all at the same damn time. "Yeah, probably in a puppy love sorta way."

"No, in a serious way," I retort.

"Empress, I don't want you to throw your life away on some stupid adolescent infatuation."

"It's not like I'm doing anything wrong!" I fire back. "We were just sittin' in the front of the house."

"You have one more time to raise your voice at me, Empress," My mom says giving me a stare down that rivals Claire Huxtable's. Too bad this isn't *The Cosby Show* and I can't cut to commercial break. Mom continues with her lecture, "You sitting in front of the house is not what this is about, Empress. If this was about you sitting in front of the house, we would not be having this conversation. This is about you breaking your curfew for some boy."

"Since when do I have a curfew?" I ask, callin' my mother out for some rule she just made up.

"You are really tryin' it, girl!"

"I'm just sayin' –"

"And I'm just saying it is not responsible to be out this time of hour with someone I don't know nothing about in this questionable area."

"Well, you could have gotten a chance to know something about Renardo, but you told me to come in the house. C'mon mom, why are you giving me such a hard time?"

"I've always been able to trust you Empress, and I want to keep it that way, okay?" My mom says as she looks me in the eyes in a caring and mothering way.

"And you still can mom," I say, giving her a hug.

"I know I can," she says. "It's him I don't trust."

~ NARD ~

TRAFFIC IS NON-EXISTENT AS I DRIVE BACK TO my spot after taking Empress home. I lean my seat back as I cruise the streets, recapping the night. I am very impressed and intrigued by this woman. She has one of those faces you will never forget. She is gorgeous. There are many dimensions to her beauty.

Her brown skin glowed all night and fit well with her hazel eyes and dark hair. Throughout the whole night, I was under the spell of her warm, inviting eyes that sparkled with joy. I can't stop thinkin' about how smooth her hands are and how amazing her smile is. Kissing Empress was a dream come true because her plump lips are naturally soft. Did I mention how fine she is? I love her tiny frame. Her flat stomach balances out her well-proportioned breast and ass. The gray dress she wore tonight showcased all her curves. She is simply mesmerizing.

Besides her physical attractiveness, her mind has me in awe because she has ambition, unlike a lot of these females out here. She actually sees beyond the average and wants more. Two great minds like ours will eventually be a force to be reckoned with. Not to mention, she has confidence that oozes out of her pores. She loves herself and others. And she is independent, too. She is a naturally good woman. Nothing about her is forced or fake. She genuinely listened and cared about what I had to say tonight. Now that I think about it, I have got to really like this woman because I exposed a lot of shit about myself tonight. I told her things that I have never expressed to another living soul. Not only was she understanding, but she was also encouraging.

Then I love that she isn't out there. No one knows her as being fast and givin' the pussy away to everyone. She knows how to carry herself in public due to the self-respect that she has for herself. I also love that she respects others. I find her empathy, curiosity, and open-mindedness so sexy. Then she is not hood, so I don't have to worry about her bringin' unnecessary drama.

I believe I have found my Queen. She possesses all the right qualities that help sustain a long-term relationship. I wonder how she really feels about me. I just hope I'm not moving too fast for her, but I need her as my woman standing by my side. She has to feel some way about me, or else she would not have asked all those personal questions. I'm afraid of this feeling, but I don't believe I can stop it. This feeling is inevitable -

My phone rings interrupting my thoughts. "Hey, pretty lady," I say, answering the phone with a smile because it is Empress.

She must have read my mind.

"Hi, Renardo… I was just, um, thinking about you and our date," she says in the cutest voice. I sense her blushing through the phone.

"I was actually just doing the same thing," I say, still smiling. "It kinda got me spooked though because you just called right now."

"Oh, did I call you at a wrong time?" She asks with a hint of concern in her voice.

"Naw, nothin' like that," I say. "I believe our spirits are in tune… you probably won't understand what I'm sayin'."

"No, I believe I do… soulmate," she interjects.

I was hoping she understood what I mean and she does. This woman is just right for me.

"Exactly!" I reply, not concealing my excitement. "I believe God brought you into my life for a reason. I want you to be my woman, Empress. I strongly believe if you are my woman, I will be complete. I already feel complete when I'm in your presence. If my feelings were not this strong, I would not have revealed so much about myself tonight."

"Renardo, it would be my pleasure to stand hand in hand with you. I was waiting for you to pop the question."

I wish I had asked her when we were in person, but God has answered my prayers because she said yes. In this moment, I will give anything to kiss her.

"I would have asked you earlier. But as you know, we were interrupted unexpectedly by your twin," I explain. We both laugh at my reference about how much she and her mother resemble each other.

"Yes, that was sooooo embarrassing!" She says through her giggles.

"It's all good because at least you know someone cares about you and loves you," I reassuringly say. "She just wants you to choose wisely when it comes to men."

"Well, without a doubt, I know I am choosing wisely."

"Most definitely," I say while smiling. "Now, I'm not perfect. But, know that I have your best interest at heart."

"I pray that is true… just promise me that you won't hurt me."

"It is true. I'm not the average - I promise. But allow my actions to speak louder than my words," I say with the utmost confidence.

"We shall see," Empress says.

Chapter Seventeen

~ EMPRESS ~

EVEN THOUGH RENARDO AND I HAVE BEEN dating each other for little over a month now, I find it way too hard to keep a smirk off my face as he texts me about how boring his class is.

Renardo: This science class is so boring.
Empress: I bet. The science class I am in right now is boring too.
Empress: What subjects do you hate the most?
Renardo: Science, Writing, and History.
Empress: I love history! Why don't you?
Renardo: Because it's boring lol. I'm making my own history as we text lol.
Renardo: I feel like my life is important enough to be in history books.
Renardo: So, if they don't want to put my life in the history books, I don't want to read about nobody else.
Empress: Valid point. But history repeats itself. It's good to know what people did in the past so we won't make the same mistakes in the future.
Renardo: I want to see you.

Empress: I want to see you, too.
Renardo: How about today?
Empress: We shall see :)

I laugh at myself for texting "we shall see" because I so badly want to see Renardo, but I have to play it cool. I cannot let him know that I am falling madly in love with him.

A couple of minutes go by and my phone lights up and vibrates on my desk, after Renardo Snapchats resting on his desk.

He looks both' miserable and adorable.

"Isn't he so cute?" I whisper to Olivia, making sure not to disturb the class while Mrs. Rozier is teaching.

Glancing at my screen she nods in approval while she takes notes. I pose for a quick selfie with a pouty expression and send it to Renardo. Two minutes pass before he texts me back saying, "You look sexy when you make that face :) "

"He is sooo dreamy!" I think to myself with an undeniable smile.

A couple of more minutes pass by and to my delight, Renardo sends me a picture that he forgot to send me yesterday of him with his baby blue puppy Pitbull.

"Psst," Olivia says, trying to get my attention.

"Yeah," I say, drawing hearts in my notebook with my pink ballpoint pen.

"Didn't you tell me he goes to an alternative school?" She whispers.

"Yeah, so?" I answer in a whispery tone.

"Girl, you are trippin'. He may be cute and all, but I would never pass up Church for a guy like him." Olivia says with slight disgust.

"You better check your tone and what do you mean a guy like him?"

"I mean, I'm just tryin' to figure out what possessed you to go out with a... hoodlum?"

"Hoodlum?" I ask, giving her the side eye. "Hahaha, you sound like my grandma, and if you are referring to my man, he's not hood."

"Puh-leze! Who are you foolin'? Why else would he be at that school for thugs? While you're wasting time with him, you could be planning a future with Church."

"Damn, can you fall off Church's dick?" I say in aggravation. "Since you soooo concerned about him, why don't you go out with him? Unlike Church, Renardo is sweet, mysterious, and quiet. I am without a doubt his type of woman. Notice I said woman, not girl."

Olivia giggles but starts talking her bullshit again. "It's one thing to be crushin' on that nigga, but you're getting serious. Church is safe and harmless - clean cut and you know he has a future. You don't know what this Renardo nigga is capable of.... he may be slick dangerous and he is from Rockdale. You know they are crazy out there!"

"Shut the fuck up! Don't be ignorant," I retort in a whisper as I roll my eyes and shake my head. "You're judging him based on superficial things and assumptions. Listen, if I want to date Renardo, I will and nobody can stop me."

"Empress, you're being stupid!" She semi-yells, getting loud.

Every action causes a reaction, so I, in return, get louder. "Bitch, who are you calling stupid?!? Don't you ever call me stupid! Stay out of my fuc – "

"Ladies, ladies what's going on back there???" Mrs. Rozier demands as she claps her hands together, interrupting me and Olivia.

"Girl fight!" A group of immature boys in the class yell.

"I got $5 on Empress!" Cameron shouts.

"Hell naw, I got $10 on Olivia! Empress don't got them hands, bruh," Dex yells.

"Boys!" Mrs. Rozier screams. "Now, you all know I don't tolerate profanity in my classroom. Girls, what is going on back there?"

"Everything is fine back here, Mrs. Rozier," Olivia says, lying through her teeth. "Sorry for interrupting class."

"Is that right, Empress?" Mrs. Rozier asks me as she wipes her eyeglasses on her shirt.

Taking a moment to think, I decide to keep the peace and I nod my head and answer, "Yeah, Mrs. Rozier, everything is fine."

"Good!" Mrs. Rozier says as she continues with today's lesson.

My eyes search high and low for the time. Disappointingly, twenty-five minutes are left before this class ends. Looking around the room, I can count on one hand how many students are paying attention. I am definitely not included in this count. Everyone is bored except Tommy who is the modern day teenage black version of Bill Nye the Science Guy. He's always reading some science book or quizzing a random person about a scientific fact. Currently, I have no idea what is going on, but I hear Mrs. Rozier say something about a magnetic field.

"*Magnetic field,*" I repeat to myself. It is as though a light bulb goes off in my mind as I instantly scribble in my notebook, crafting a song.

The lyrics flow:

You have a cosmic power

That brings me back to you
Magnetic field
I'm always attracted to you
And that's how I want it to be
It's simple philosophy
Some say it's in the stars
That's why I'm never going too far
I can't stay away

*The words perfectly express the connection I feel between
Renardo and me.*

~ NARD ~

*THE BELL RINGS AND IT IS FINALLY LUNCH
time. I don't know where Juke went, but I do know that I
am hungry as hell. That nigga prolly trying to put his macc
down on the new girl that started yesterday. Lunch is only
thirty minutes, so I'm going to walk up the street to Subway.
I'll catch him later.*

"Luv, Family," I answer the phone as I grab a bag of
Lays to go with my footlong Sweet Onion Chicken
Teriyaki Sub.

"Luv, FAM," Black replies. "Listen, Nard, I've let
this whole situation go too far, especially as an elder
brother. If possible, I'm going to have a meeting set up
for Jaz and me to talk. How much money was taken?"

"Bout $7,500. Why do you ask?" I answer with sus-
picion, sitting down a booth.

"I ask because that money you took is going to be
replaced if he agrees to peace. This beef began with
money so it should end with money," Black harshly
says.

"My nigga, with all due respect, I'm not giving

nothin' back and I'm quite sure Larosa feels the same way. That shit took," I say, trying to control my temper and ready to smash this delicious looking sub in front of me.

"I didn't call you to argue, Nard," Black says, growing annoyed. "If you want to keep the money, then prepare yourself to deal with the consequences for being insubordinate. One day you will understand the reason I'm doing what I'm doing."

"You always sayin' that shit, but I'll never understand. That is a low blow. You are forcing my hand," I fire back, equally annoyed with Black as he was with me.

"I'm forcing your hand to do the right thing," he replies.

"The right thing?" I sarcastically question. "Oh, now you want to do the right thing?"

"You've got to change your ways, bruh," Black says.

"You must forgot who I learned my ways from?" I shoot back.

"You are absolutely right. But, I'm trying to make things right before it's too late," Black says, growing short on patience with me.

"I hear you and I overstand. But, I have morals and principles on what I stand on and I'm not going against that to pay that money back," I firmly state.

Black lets out a long sigh. "Do you see how everything has occurred from that one incident?" He asks. "I was proud of you because I saw you finally striving in a direction better than what I taught you, but this one incident caused you to get knocked off your square and go back to the basics."

Honestly, he is absolutely right, but, I am too stubborn to ever admit this to him.

"Black, nothin' you say can change the way I feel," I

nonchalantly say.

"Nigga, you got defense like Richard Sherman!" Black says with a laugh. "You need to stop that shit." In a more serious tone, he says, "Let me ask you one last question."

"Shoot," I coolly say.

"How much money is in this world?" He questions.

"Shit, you can't count it," I answer confidently.

"How many of you in this world?" He questions.

"There is only one of me," I say confidently, yet growing tired of his interrogation.

"How many of me is in this world?" He questions.

"There is only one of you," I reply, lacking the confidence of my previous responses because I understand where Black is going with this.

"The reason I'm askin' you this is so you can see what I see," Black says, finally revealing his logic. "Materialistic things come and go, but once we are gone you can't bring us back. We're gone forever. That is why human life is the most valuable thing on this Earth, especially the people you love. You have to come to understand that it is not all about you, FAM. The decisions you make in life not only affect you, but the people around you who love you the most."

Damn, I'm speechless because that shit was deep.

"I want you to think about everything I'm tellin' you, lil bruh," Black adds.

"Love," we both say, ending the phone call.

~ EMPRESS ~

TRAPP DROPPED ME OFF AT KRYSTAL'S NEARLY fifteen minutes before my shift starts, so I walked across the street to the Shell gas station to buy some lottery scratch-offs.

Miss Mable has me hooked. I never played scratch-offs at all until I started working at Krystal and Miss Mable would send me to go get her some while I was on the clock. Sometimes, she would even let me keep some for myself. I later found out the money she was giving me was coming straight out the cash register. SMH. Did I mention earlier that Miss Mable thinks she is a slickster? She is one of those old people who think they know everything and can con everybody. Anyways, I have been on a winning streak lately, so I want to press my luck. Perhaps, Renardo entering my life is the reason I have had so much good luck. Even though I am underage, I am cool with all the employees at the gas station, so I am never asked for ID.

As I walk back to Krystal's, I see Willis sittin' down on the side of the building, smoking one of those disgusting Newport cigarettes.

Willis works on the grill, so he is always smelly and hot. He is in his late twenties but stays makin' passes at me. A couple of times, I had to curse him out for purposefully trippin' over something or coming so close to me just so he could rub against my ass. I cannot stand this onion smelling, perverted guy with his widow's peak, yellow teeth, and dirty, grease stained uniform. I swear he never washes it. I am relieved that I do not have to work with him because his shift ends when mine begins. Ugh, I do not want to even talk to this guy, but it is too late to turn around now, being that he has already seen me.

"Hey, Empress!" He yells as I walk closer to the building.

"Hi, Willis," I respond with way less enthusiasm.

"Miss Mable in there trippin' already," he says, tryin' to make conversation. "I'm so glad I'm leavin'. I can't stand that old bitch. She always gettin' shit started."

Now, Miss Mable does do and say some foul things, but I

am no fool. I will not agree or deny anything Willis is saying because he is just as messy as she is and he will go back and repeat what I said to anyone who will listen, all while adding false information.

I simply shake my head at his comment.

"You know we've been gettin' complaints from customers about you and your lil boyfriend when y'all be out here during your break, kissin' while he's feelin' on your booty," Willis says as though he feels some type of way.

"Huh?" I say becoming defensive. "Jake hasn't said anything to me about that."

"Well, we were talkin' about it and he doesn't like it," Willis says. "Especially when you come up in here with those hickeys on your neck."

Now my blood is boiling. I had done my best to cover the hickeys by applying aloe vera and cocoa butter and even make-up. Renardo warned me that the hickeys would be visible, but I am not goin' to refuse his love bites. They feel soooo good. My knees are getting weak just thinkin' about them. I just love when he sinks his teeth into my neck like a vampire. You would think we were characters from the Twilight book series. I guess we could be considered the real-life Bella and Edward in more ways than one. Anyways, that is beside the point. Back to the subject at hand, who does Willis think he is to be discussing anything about me with Jake?

"I don't care what Jake has to say and fuck the Krystal's policy," I respond, infuriated.

"Dang, Empress," he says, surprised at my reaction. "See, that nigga got you changin' already. I ain't never heard you talk like this before."

"What?" I say totally pissed off with him.

"Yeah, I've noticed a change in you over these last weeks. Why do you like him anyways? You normally like those clean-cut Carlton Banks lookin' dudes," he says.

"Willis," I state, being completely done and over the conversation. "You can take those so-called observations you've been making and go fuck yourself."

"I probably would like that," he says with a twisted laugh as he puts his cigarette out.

The guy is such a sick perv.

CHAPTER EIGHTEEN

~ NARD ~

I THOUGHT TAKING A NAP AFTER SCHOOL WOULD help ease my mind, but it is hard to sleep when I keep hearing Black's voice echoing in my head constantly saying, "Give the money back... give the money back." I still can't believe he is on that fuck shit.

I hit up Larosa because I wonder if Black has tried to convince him that this bullshit is the best thing to do.

"What's poppin'?" Larosa answers his phone.

"Have you heard from Black?"

"Naw, what's goin' on?"

"A lot is goin' on because he trippin' hard. He talkin' about giving that $7,500 back to that nigga Jaz."

"Say what?!" Larosa yells.

"You heard exactly what I said," I say as I let out a long sigh while shaking my head.

"Has that nigga lost his damn mind?!" Larosa exclaims.

"Shit, I'm wonderin' the same thing," slowly tumbles out my mouth due to the disbelief I still have over Black's remarks.

"FAM," I say after taking a sip from the glass of water

on my nightstand. "He talkin' 'bout exposing what we did if we don't."

The phone line goes silent. I do not even hear Larosa breathing.

"Hello????" I question, hoping he's still on the line.

"I'm still here, FAM," Larosa says after another minute of dead silence. "I'm just thinking."

While Larosa's brain digests what I just told him, I catch my puppy nipping at a pair of my sneakers in my open closet.

"Hey, get your ass out of there!" I shout to the Pitbull.

I usually love my puppy's raw and wild energy, but right now I am in not in the mood to play around.

"So, how is this supposed to go because I know this nigga and if we give the money back, it's not goin' to stop nothin'. The beef will continue until he's dead or we are. This shit is way deeper than money right now," Larosa states.

"Well, try tellin' that to Black," I snap back. "He feels as if he can persuade Jaz to end this."

"Well, I would love to be present at this meeting, so, when is it?"

"We're having a group call tonight at 6," I inform him. "I will call you then."

"Do that. Love."

"Already."

~ EMPRESS ~

AS THE NIGHT WINDS DOWN, FEWER CARS FILL the drive-thru, which pleases me. Maybe I can take a quick break. Standing on my feet for eight hours straight can be gruesome. Drive-thru responsibilities are like entering the

Wild West. As a cashier, I never know what I may face. An angry customer, a flirty customer, a broke customer that hopes I give them free food, a scam artist that acts like I shorted them on change, or a con artist that gives me counterfeit money.

Two years ago, when I first started working at Krystal's, there were a few times when I unknowingly accepted counterfeit money. Blame it on naivety and letting compliments go to my head! What can I say? I was very green back then. Miss Mable would always help me straighten my drawer out so that I would not be short at the end of the night. If my drawer came up short and Jake found out about it, as the General Manager, he could either fire me or take it out of my check. I appreciated Miss Mable lookin' out for me early on because I really needed the job to help take care of my family. Who am I kiddin'? She probably was responsible for my drawer coming up short. You know - sneakin' and takin' when she was sending me to the Shell to buy her scratch-offs. She probably was doing it for gas money since she always complains about how far her ride from Decatur is from Rockdale.

"Empress, come sit down," Miss Mable says as she motions for me to come to the table she's sitting at in dining area.

"What's goin' on grandma?" I say with a smile as I sit down.

"Oh, nothin'," she responds as she takes a bite out of her square Krystal burger. "I've been watchin' you and that young man you're dating. You like him, don't you?"

"Yes, I do," I proudly confirm as my eyes beam. "He's sooooo sweet and soooo different from any boy that I have ever dated."

"I know what you mean," she says as she sips her sweet tea from an extra-large Styrofoam cup.

"Really?" I surprisingly say.

"Yeah, your little boyfriend reminds me of some-one I used to know many, many years ago when I was a young girl, about your age," she replies, wiping the corners of her mouth with a napkin. "I didn't always look like this. I was foxxy, as we used to say back in my day."

Miss Mable knew someone like Renardo? Ha! I can't even begin to imagine Miss Mable as a teenager. That had to be ages ago. My interest is peaked.

"Tell me more," I say.

"Well," she says with a pause. "He was very good lookin'. They used to call him Satin because he was so smooth just like satin sheets. Have you ever seen that old blaxploitation movie *Willie Dynamite?*"

"Yeah, I have."

"Well, Satin had a huge, bright purple Cadillac with gold trimmings and animal print seat covers - just like the one Willie Dynamite drove in the movie. Every-body used to go crazy over that car. Men, girls, and chil'ren. This was before car alarms, so Satin used to pay either a homeless man or some lil kid to watch the car every time he parked," she chuckles.

Still recalling her past, Miss Mable continues, "Chile, when I tell you he was a good dresser, a fast talker, and a mean walker, you better believe it. When I say good dresser, I mean from head to toe. He was sharp! He wore nothin' but the best custom suits, fur coats, and flashy hats. Like J.J. used to say on *Good Times,* he was "DY-NO-MITE."

We both laugh at her J.J. impersonation.

"So, I know he kept you lookin' fly."

"Chile, you know right," she replies with a grin. "I had nothin' but the best when I was with him. He even had some ghetto artist paint a portrait of me."

"Really?" I ask as my eyes widen.

"Yes, it's hangin' right in my living room."

"Take a picture. I gotta see it," I say with a giggle. "That was really sweet of him. He must have really loved you."

"Satin made quite the name for himself," she continues. "He had power within the city and he was involved in some terrible things on the streets. He had niggas workin' for him. Back in my day, they used to call 'em street runners. People warned me to be careful with him."

"Well, were you?" I inquire, wanting to hear more of the story.

"I fell head over heels in love with him," she says with a wide smile. "He made a lucrative livin' and life was good then."

"Alrite, grandma!" I playfully approve.

"But," she continues as the wide smile suddenly leaves her face. "They were right. He was dangerous."

"Really?" I disappointingly ask.

"Yep, really. Lookin' back, I made a big mistake. People told me to be careful and I should have listened to them. I loved Satin, but he was so selfish and greedy. Where there is greed and the quest to be second to none, one is always confronted with jealousy and envy from their fellow peers. Let's just say the heat started comin' down hard on him. For as smart and ambitious as he was, Satin was an arrogant dumb nigga. He didn't want to deal with reality. He wanted things to continue the way they had been when he was on top. I guess he thought he was gonna be king forever. All that ambition, but he had no vision. He never thought about tomorrow, he only thought about the present moment. I would always try to convince him to start a business to go legit, but he steady blew money and had legal fees. What was I thinking? Just because a nigga can sell dope doesn't mean he knows anything about running a business. Eventually, everything fell apart and I've been working here ever since."

For an ephemeral moment, I do not know where Miss Mable mind goes, but an aura of sadness begins to fill the air. Snapping back to reality, she looks at me and warns, "And you... you should listen to what people are tellin' you. You're too smart and you have a bright future ahead of you. You've come too far to get caught up in some foolishness like I did."

"Aw, c'mon Miss Mable. I'm not tryin' to hear a lecture."

"Chile, this ain't no lecture. I'm thankful to God that I got out when I did. He nearly destroyed me," she says. "I may pick on you from time to time, but I like you, Empress. You are focused and these other girls are not. Just remember, men are like a box of chocolate."

"Huh? How so?" I ask. "Please, don't tell me you're about to quote *Forrest Gump*?"

"No, chile," she says through her laughter. "Would you just listen? I'm tryin' to drop you a jewel before a customer comes."

"Okay, okay, I'm listening."

"Just like a box of chocolate, one man can be filled with many temptations. I think our job as women is to pick the 'best box of chocolate' for ourselves, if you know what I mean. All candy boxes are filled with temptations, so you should pick the box filled with the temptations that you feel are worthy of your time and consequence. Remember, it's all about moderation. Now with chocolate, you can moderate your indulgence with a minimum amount of consequences.

For example, makin' sure you don't get cavities or maintaining your weight by not eatin' more than you should."

"How about moderation with men?" I ask with a Cheshire grin.

"Now men, well, the moderation is hard because there are some men who are irresistible, to say the least."

"Yeah, I know what you mean."

"But," she continues. "Usually, they come with major consequences. The very least being heartbreak."

"Heartbreak?" I dismally repeat.

"Yep, heartbreak," she confirms. "You see, when it comes to men, moderation does not exist. Either you are all in or it's nothin'."

Getting up from the table, Miss Mable begins walking off. "So, I want you to think about what this wise old lady just said to you," she pauses and says. "Your little boyfriend seems like an old-fashioned disaster in the makin'. I know, from words I speak. Pay attention!"

Ugh, Miss Mable too? Why can't anyone just be happy for me? It is only out of the respect that I have for the elderly that I will not say anything combative to Miss Mable.

"I hear you," I dryly respond, rolling my eyes.

CHAPTER NINETEEN

~ EMPRESS ~

EVEN THOUGH GEORGIA IS A SOUTHERN STATE, contrary to popular belief, we can have pretty brutal winters here. When it finally gets cold, it gets cold. The sky is clear blue. The air is fresh. The birds are chirping. The trees are bare, but they add to the beauty known as winter. I love to take a moment and enjoy God's coloring book that we call Earth. The freshness of winter and the limitless sky have a way of elevating my spirit. I know anything is possible.

I do not know what has possessed my little sisters, Gabi and Cinnamon, to want to ride their brand-new bikes and tricycles outside in the dead of winter on this beautiful Sunday morning. Today is my only off day this week, so I plan to relax and worry about nothing. There is not a sacrifice that I will not make for my family. I saved up for months to buy them these Christmas gifts, so I do not mind watchin' them ride the bikes; despite the cold weather. I am just glad to see that they are enjoying my gifts.

Renardo is so sweet. He bought Gabi a Nintendo DS and gave her a $25 gift card so she can buy all the Wing Nook and American Deli that she wants. He also bought Cinnamon the American Girl Doll of the Year, Lea Clark. I was not surprised in the least that he spent a $150 on a doll because he has given so generously throughout our relationship. I have to say that this was pretty extravagant, but he knows how much my sisters and their happiness means to me.

Gabi is a nine-year-old fourth grader who used to be the baby of our family until Cinnamon came along three years ago. I gave Cinnamon, whose real name is Lea, the nickname because when she was born, her face was covered with brown freckles that I thought looked like sprinkles of cinnamon. As you can see, the silly nickname stuck.

It is freezing cold out here! My nose is red and my hands are nearly frozen. The black knitted gloves my mom gave me for Christmas do not come close to keeping my hands warm as chilliness seeps through, numbing my fingers. If it was not for the nightfall colored Meilani Ugg Boots Renardo bought me for Christmas, my feet probably would be frozen. The black scarf I have wrapped around my lower face and neck keeps falling each time I yell at Gabi and Cinnamon for going too far up the street.

Even though our duplex loft is in a quiet, neutralized area in the neighborhood, this is still Field Stone and it is nothin' for some shit between rival gangs to pop off or an altercation between neighbors to occur. Just three months ago, a bullet had ricocheted and killed an elderly old lady on the west end of this humongous neighborhood.

To those on the outside of the nonexistent gates, Field Stone seems like a terrible place to live due to violence, drug dealing, and break-ins. But to my family, this is the best place we have lived since I was Gabi's age. Even though we struggle, we have a beautifully decorated, three-bedroom duplex loft. My mom managed to decorate on a budget and she did an exceptional job. Anytime someone visits us, they always make a remark on how nice our home is. The woman who we rent the duplex from prides herself on the fact that our unit is one of a kind and does not share floor plans with any of the other duplexes in the neighborhood.

When we first moved in, Trapp became cool with nearly everyone in the neighborhood. He is one of those types of people who always fits in wherever they go. His connections and the fact that we live on the mellow street in the neighborhood play a large part as to why we never experience break-ins. Even though I rarely go outside to socialize and chill, everyone knows me because of Trapp. The 'lil sis pass' seems to work everywhere. My mother always says Trapp attracts what she calls the 'strays' of the world. Every other day, someone is sittin' at our kitchen table, calling my mom, 'mama,' as though she has birthed them. My mom does not mind. She says people are naturally attracted to good hearted people and even though we have little, she is always willing to share. Field Stone seems to offer my family and me stability even in the middle of all its chaos.

"Gabi! Don't pedal so fast! You're leaving Cinnamon behind!" I yell loud enough from the mailbox so that Gabi can hear me up the street. Poor Cinnamon can barely keep up on her red Radio Flyer tricycle.

"Ssssh! Ay, girl you gonna wake up the whole hood," Stacks says as he walks thru the cut with four other guys.

I instantly roll my eyes at him.

I'm not sure how he got his nickname. I can only assume it is because he is always flashing his money every opportunity he gets. Stacks is a little taller than me, probably 5'5 and is in his early twenties. I think he suffers from the Napoleon complex or what Trapp calls 'the little man syndrome' because he always wants to be seen and heard. The only plus about him is that he is stylish. He is fresh today with his black Polo cap, white polo sweater, and black polo boots.

"Where yo brotha at?" He says as his custom 18

karat yellow gold, 6 bottom grill and diamond earrings gleam in the sun.

"I don't know," I answer while keeping an eye on Gabi and Cinnamon.

Looking me up and down, Stacks turns around to his clique of four and says, "Ay, man… y'all gon 'head to the spot. I'll catch y'all in a minute."

All the boys seem to say something different to let him know that they are cool with leaving as they dap him up before walking away. Stepping closer to me, Stacks pulls out a wad of cash from his saggy True Religion jeans and begins to act like he is counting it.

"Babygirl, you lookin' like a movie star out here," he says as he pretends to focus on counting his stack of money.

Not impressed with his corny line, I roll my eyes.

"Whew," he says with a smirk. "It's cold out here, but you don't have to be, baby."

"Shouldn't you be catching up with your homies?"

"In a minute, in a minute," he responds. "So, who was that nigga you were sittin' with in that Monte Carlo? Hahaha, I heard Mom Dukes made you go in the house." He laughs referencing the embarrassing situation that happened nearly three months ago.

"That wasn't funny!" I quip, totally over him and this conversation.

"Mom Dukes did right tho," he says. "So, who was this nigga?"

"My boyfriend, Renardo. And don't ask me nothin' about him because it's none of your business," I reply with an attitude, seeing my breath form with each word I speak due to the coldness.

"Ain't nobody concerned about that young nigga. Especially not Stacks," he says with an obnoxious laugh.

I hate it when people talk in third person, so I roll my eyes at him once again.

Noticing I am unimpressed by his blatant display of cash, Stacks places the ducats back in his pockets once and for all.

One thing that I adore about Renardo is he is not a show-off. He has never tried to buy me or pressure me about sex. Renardo is truly a breath of fresh air from all the polluted boys that fill the world.

Stacks follows me as I walk up the street to tell Gabi and Cinnamon to come back to the house.

"You know I've been tryin' to get at you since y'all moved over here, but that nigga Trapp say you don't talk to none of his partnas," he says.

"That's right," I coldly respond.

"It's cool, shawty," he says, his eyes scanning my body. "You know Stacks stay playa anyways. I'ma holla at you later."

I am so glad he is finally leaving. The way guys harass girls can be so embarrassing and aggravating. I wonder how some of them build up the courage to act a fool the way that they do.

All of sudden, Stacks stops dead in his tracks and does a 360 in the middle of the street. He heads back in my direction as though he forgot something.

Dang, what else does he want?

"You said that nigga name is Renardo???" He asks as his diamond earrings gleam extra bright from the sunlight.

"Yeah?" I wearily say as I try to figure out why this name strikes a chord with him.

I mean, I know Renardo has lived out here most of his life and he knows a lot of people, but I hope Stacks isn't one of his so-called partnas. I hope my baby has better taste in friends than this fuck boy.

"Renardo? Renardo? Renardo?" Stacks repeats while snapping his fingers as he stares into space. After a few seconds pass by, he pauses in mid-finger snap as he finally recalls the name. "Aw man, don't tell me you talkin' to that nigga Nard with the dreads," he says.

"Yeah, that's my man," I confidently reply.

"Damn, lil mama, at least I don't rob. You talkin' to a thievin' ass DMG nigga," he declares, shaking his head.

"*Theivin' ass DMG nigga???*" I repeat back with a hint of confusion in my voice.

"No... no... you must be thinkin' about someone else," I say confidently to Stacks.

"Really? Come on now. How many niggas you know name Nard? That young nigga was beefin' with my YGC homies right here in the hood a while back," Stacks says.

What is Stacks telling me? I did stumble upon Renardo's two guns, but is he using them to commit robberies and hurt people??? He did tell me that he is familiar with Field Stone, but is it because of a gang beef??? No, of course not. What am I thinking? He is too busy with school.

"Ha! That young nigga don't know what to do with a girl like you," Stacks add. "You need a real nigga like Stacks, who gonna show you the finer things in life. That nigga ain't got no class. None of them DMG niggas do. See, Stacks makes real money, baby. Not rob people for they shit."

What the hell is Stacks saying about my sweetheart and why is he talkin' in the third person again? Oh no, Stacks can't be talking about my sweet baby! A robber? DMG? No way.

"Bye, Stacks," I say, pulling my black woolen hat over my frozen ears. "You just hatin' right now. I'm not about to listen to this bullshit you talkin'. You just makin' stuff up."

"Stacks, hatin'? Never. All I'm sayin' is don't get stuck on him, lil mama. He ain't gonna do nothin' but bring heat your way. If he cares 'bout you, he would leave you alone. You a schoolgirl. You don't need that kinda street nigga in your life."

His phone vibrates and he looks down to see who it is. He answers the phone and tells the person to hold on. Looking at me, he says, "Look shawty, I'm 'bout to bounce this time forreal forreal. You know my mixtape comin' out in the summer. If you act right, I'll feature you on it. I've been seeing your stuff on YouTube and listenin' to you on Soundcloud. You soundin' good."

Totally tuning him out at this point, I give a weak, "Thanks."

My thoughts are so clouded right now that I can't think straight. I know Renardo can be very quiet and serious at times, but does that mean he is harboring secrets? I need answers. Is Renardo playing me for a fool? He promised that he would always be honest and that he would never hurt me. I have to talk to Renardo immediately!

CHAPTER TWENTY

~ EMPRESS ~

IT IS A SCHOOL NIGHT AND RENARDO HAS picked me up from CVS, my other job, so we can talk about the Stacks situation, which has been weighing heavily on my mind for the past couple of days.

He has a bright idea to stop at Yogurt Paradise, a frozen yogurt shop on Dogwood Drive. It is a cute, brightly decorated shop with neon colors. All the employees wear the cutest ol' school 1950s lookin' uniforms with white paper hats on their heads. To some extent, it is the frozen yogurt version of the world's famous Varsity drive-in restaurant.

"This yogurt fye, baby," Renardo says as we stand in line looking at the menu.

I am somewhat annoyed with him because he has not called me in two days. I am also feeling conflicted due to every thought and opinion I have heard about him. Yet, I can't help but stare at him in a loving way. I can look at Renardo all day. With his strong jawline and beautiful profile, he is a work of art - devastatingly handsome. He should seriously think about modeling or acting.

"We close in ten minutes!" A cashier shouts to alert everyone.

"I guess we will have to take ours to go, baby," Renardo says with a smile. "I know the perfect place."

"Where?" I ask.

"So, the lady speaks?" He sarcastically remarks with a slick smile. "This is the first thing you've said all night," he says, rubbing his thumb underneath my chin.

With my lips in a pout, I fix my eyes back on the colorful menu trying not to entertain Renardo.

"I just love it when you look like that. Give me a kiss, my sexy baby," he says, leaning down to plant a sweet kiss on my lips.

Loving the sensation of his lips on mine I cannot hide my smile.

"Now that's what I like to see," he says, looking at me as though I was the only girl in the world. "Go ahead and decide on what type of yogurt you want, baby."

With so many flavors to choose from, I do not know where to start.

"They have the best soy-based yogurt here," Renardo raves.

So, he likes to eat healthy, huh? I wasn't expecting that, but I love it. I love a man that cares about what he puts in and on his body.

"I'll take the black sesame frozen yogurt," he tells the cashier.

"And what about you ma'am?" She asks.

"Black sesame sounds different. Is it good?" I ask Renardo, Unsure of what flavor to choose.

"Yeah, but it is different. I think you have to acquire the taste, baby," Renardo says with a laugh.

"Okay, that means no," I say, causing him and the cashier to laugh.

"I will stick with what I know. I'll take the pineapple

mango frozen yogurt," I tell the cashier.

After paying for the yogurt, Renardo drives to Johnson Park. We walk silently pass the swings while eating our frozen yogurt. Finally, after 10 minutes of walking on the bike trail, we sit on the brown wooden park benches.

The park is different at night, but I guess everything is different at night. Even though it is cold, we are warm in each other's company, underneath the starry sky. I hate the conflict and turmoil I have been suffering through lately. I can barely focus at school or at work. Today at CVS, an elderly lady became upset with me because I told her that the Depends were on the wrong aisle. The conversation I had with Stacks has caused me to become unfocused. I need to clear this up now!

"Baby, there are so many people saying so many different things about you. Everyone has an opinion or a judgment about you. None of it is unbiased, you know? And I'm just thinking and I can't stop thinking. What's goin' on with you? With us? People are telling me I should be afraid of you… that you will only hurt me… that… that… you rob and hurt people. Have you been completely honest with me? Where is our relationship going? And I feel like…"

Looking into Renardo's dark eyes and sweet face trips me up. "And I feel like I'm rambling on and on right now… like an idiot, so you can just stop me anytime you want," I say with a smile.

"Baby," Renardo replies with a quick, tensed smile. "I know some people say bad things about me… but they don't know me. I don't care what people think. I just want you to continue to draw your own conclusions about me based on how I treat you, what you see, and what you know."

"That sounds fair," I say with a smile. "I should have never entertained anything Stacks was saying."

For a split second, Renardo looks away. But within an instant, he refocuses on me and our conversation again.

"There's just one last thing he mentioned..." I say as my voice becomes a little shaky.

"What is it, baby?"

"Well... um... he said that you are a..."

"C'mon, baby," he patiently says. "It's okay to say whatever it is that you heard."

"Um... is it true that you are a Dirty Money Gangsta?" I hesitantly ask, not sure if I want to know the answer.

"Be honest with me, baby," he says as he places his cold, rough hand on top of mine. "Have I ever treated you badly or disrespected you? Have I ever embarrassed you in any way?"

"No, not at all, baby," I say sincerely say as I caress his face. "You've been a complete gentleman."

"That's good to know because I was taught to be a gentleman and to keep my word, which you have, Empress," he states as he stares at me intently with his dark eyes. "My word is all I have," he continues. "I debated with myself about when I should tell you, but I didn't want to scare you off, baby. Yes, I am apart of DMG, but we don't go around terrorizing neighborhoods and killing people like the media portrays. There are so many things I want to share with you and I will in due time. I grew up rough and have gone through a struggle that most can't even fathom. Just know and understand that I have morals and principles that I stand on firmly. I hope this does not change the way you feel about me. I don't give a damn about what people think of me, but I care about your opinion, Empress. I have ambition beyond the streets."

"Baby," I say with a long sigh as I try to process everything. "I can't believe you didn't tell me. What does this all mean?" I search his eyes hoping to find the answer.

"It means what you want it to mean, baby," he responds as his eyes hold mine. "I am the same man I was an hour ago before we started talking about this."

"I know that, baby. I just don't want a similar situation to happen again," I say as we hold each other's gaze. "I don't ever want someone to shock me, catch me off guard, or tell me things about you that I do not know. It makes me look like a stupid, naïve little girl and it makes me question you."

"There is nothin' stupid or naïve about you," Renardo says, letting out a sigh. "Listen, baby. The less you know about certain things the better. I will never allow anyone to hurt or disrespect you. And you will never look stupid. Baby, you do not have to worry about no bullshit poppin' off because I'm goin' to keep all that away from you." His eyes widen and soften as he loses his train of thought. "There you go again with those eyes," he says with a smile.

Out of nowhere, Renardo wildly kisses me. He likes to kiss me so much that I think he is addicted to my smooth-as-honey kisses. As a little girl, my grandma would always say 'kisses don't lie' which leads me to believe Renardo is telling the truth. I recently read an article on a blog that detailed how kissing is far more intimate than sex. Crave and intensity charges Renardo's kisses, so I will have to agree with the article. Kissing is a great metaphor for intimacy. With each kiss we allow the core of ourselves to land on one another's tongue. We breathe each other in, the good and the bad. Whew! Did

I mention that Renardo is a fantastic kisser? I could kiss him all day and night.

"So, are we good? Can we move forward?" Renardo asks, breaking our steamy lip lock.

"Yes, baby. We are definitely good," I reply, dropping any doubts.

CHAPTER TWENTY-ONE

~ NARD ~

"SO, WAT'S UP WIT YOU AND THAT GIRL, Empress?" Juke asks as we are ridin' through the city.

"Things couldn't be better, my nigga," I reply, cutting on the heat because its freezing.

"I can't believe you actually settlin' down, my nigga. Ever since you've met her, you haven't been hangin' out with the crew," Juke truthfully points out.

"My nigga, there comes a time when a man has to grow up. I want a wife and children one day. Hangin' out with the crew every day is not going to help me find that. I love y'all niggas more than I love myself, but I must move forward and plan my future," I explain. "Anyways, you know I'm always here to support and help y'all in anything that y'all need me to, so just don't think I'm gone because it's nothin' like that."

"I hope so, FAM. Because I would hate to see you fall for this girl and she turns out to be different than what you believe her to be. You know these hoes ain't loyal," Juke says with a laugh.

"No need to worry about that, FAM," I respond. "This woman is far from the average woman. Trust me."

"Speakin' of women, you know Danielle is mad with you, right? She told me not to even bring up your name. What did you do to her?" Juke questions.

"I didn't do shit to her. She will be aight, watever, it is."

"You might wanna call her cause she actin' like you offended her in some way," Juke shoots back.

"I'll do that later. But ain't that that nigga, Stacks?" I ask as I point out the window.

"Yea, that's that nigga. So, wat?"

"Nothin'. Just chill. I gotta holla at this nigga real quick," I say as I whip my car into the Taco Bell parking lot where Stacks and a couple members of his crew are posted trying to pull some women.

"Wat's good, lil nigga?" I tell Stacks as me and Juke hop out of my MC to pull up on him.

A look of surprise is written all over his face as he angrily asks, "Who the fuck you callin' a lil nigga?"

His response causes me to laugh because he is such a short ass nigga.

"Nigga, don't get hard in front of your audience," I shoot back. "I need you to be very careful on how you choose your words. You are a hustler, Stacks. So, stay in your profession."

The women who he and his crew just met whisper and mumble about the ongoing scene as they try to figure out what is going on.

"Nigga, I'm a man of many professions," he states, refusing to get embarrassed by me.

Again, I burst out into laughter. "Let me guess, one of them is havin' my name in your mouth while talkin' to my woman?" I fire back.

"Wat the hell you talkin' 'bout?" Stacks asks.

I bet he's probably cursing himself for ever mentioning anything about me to Empress.

"See, I didn't pull up on you to go back and forth with you, but to warn you. Find yourself something safe to do. Keep my name out your mouth, nigga," I say firmly while walking back to my car, but locking eyes with each and every person standin' around Stacks to make sure that my statement is felt.

Stacks reluctantly nods as he watches me and Juke drive off.

———————

"NOW WAT THE HELL WAS ALL THAT ABOUT?" Trapp asks Stacks as he puts his Newport out in the cement.

"Watever it is, we not tryin' to be involved in none of this bullshit," one woman interrupts as the rest of the women walk off. "We gone."

"Hell, ask your sister. That's her nigga!" Stacks fires back as he takes his fitted cap off.

"So, you tellin' me my sister talks to Nard? Hell naw! Wat the fuck is she thinkin'? Does she know what this nigga do for a livin'?" Trapp wonders, shocked by the revelation.

"Nigga, I tried to warn her but you see wat came about that situation," Stacks responds.

"Imma have to talk to her and see wat's goin' on with her and this hot ass nigga," Trapp says while scratching his head.

"Shit, I guess," Stacks says as he looks around the parking lot. "That nigga done ran off the hoes. Fuck him. Tell your sister that young nigga better watch his back."

~ NARD ~

AFTER DROPPIN' JUKE OFF AT his crib, I take his advice and call Danielle to see what's wrong with her.

"Wat do you want, nigga?" Danielle answers the phone with an attitude.

"Damn, my nigga. Wat the fuck I did to you?" I ask.

"Nothin'," Danielle dryly replies.

"Shit," I say, not understanding why this girl is so angry. "I can't tell because you clearly got an attitude with me. So, wat's the problem?"

"Nigga, stop actin' dumb!" She yells into the phone. "You know wat the fuck wrong with me. I seen you in traffic with your new girl this weekend."

"So, and?" I reply, aggravated that she wants to be all in her feelings. "You and me ain't together. We been stop fuckin' and there is absolutely nothin' goin' on between us other than us being Family. So again, I ask, what is the damn problem?"

Hurt by my words, Danielle instantly pours out her feelings on the line. "The only reason why we're not together is your choice because you stated that you wasn't ready for a relationship," she says in a mocking tone. "I always thought you would come around and choose me to be your woman. I thought maybe if I was loyal enough, I could win your heart. But, now I see you played me."

"No, I didn't play you, Danielle. We never had a con -nection. You don't know how to be by yourself. You are weak-minded and I need a strong-minded woman

by my side and you're just not it."
   "Nigga, FUCK YOU!"

Chapter Twenty-two

~ EMPRESS ~

*IT HAS BEEN A LONG FEW DAYS, BUT I AM GLAD
the matter with Renardo has been squared away. It was
weighing on my spirit, and I'm too young for all that. Right
now, I am soaking in a nice bubble bath in the small tub /
shower combo. I always find that bubble baths are a nice way
to bring peace and balance to my mind. Hopefully, no one
disturbs me.*

*Is Renardo a robber, or isn't he? The question plagues my
mind as the warm water covers my body, causing me to close
my eyes and dream.*

*The setting is in the 1940s, just like the old film noir and
gangster flicks I watch on TCM. Romantic candles illumi-
nate the huge bathroom. The bathtub is also huge. In fact,
it is a Whirlpool that has eight multi-directional jets. Did I
mention that I am draped in shiny diamonds? Diamond earrings, diamond necklace, and diamond bracelets on both wrists.
Marilyn Monroe sang it best when she said, "Diamonds are
a girl's best friend." Indeed, they are! Loving every minute, I
hum the old song, 'Don't Worry, Be Happy' as I luxuriate in
the calming, yet invigorating bath.*

Ooh-ooh-hoo-hoo-ooh hoo-hoo-ooh-ooh-ooh-ooh-ooh

Don't worry

Woo-ooh-woo-ooh-woo-ooh-ooh

Be happy

As I hum, I am startled as a shadowy figure emerges from the bathroom door. It is a man wearing a nice black trench coat, a black fedora, and black leather gloves. Oh, did I forget to mention he's toting a machine gun and aiming it at me?!?!

The mystery man is none other than Renardo Wade.

"Hey, what are you doing in my dream?" I ask.

"I don't know, sexy lady," he responds still pointing the gun at me.

Our dialogue mirrors the film noir genre – fast paced and poetic.

"Are you gonna flirt or shoot?" I ask in a seductive manner, still treading in the warm bath water.

"Whichever you desire, baby doll," he quickly replies with the gun still pointed at me.

Even though he poses a threat, I remain cool and sexy. "No better way to die than in a beautiful tub completely naked, wouldn't you agree?" I ask with a smirk.

Still aiming the gun at me, he walks over slowly to the bathtub and demandingly says, "Yeah. Give me the diamonds!"

"Diamonds? What are you talking about?" I ask, playing clueless.

"The ones around your neck and wrist," he coolly says. "They are worth a grip and I want 'em."

"Oh, these old shiny things?" I ask, still playing clueless. "Do you always get what you want?"

"All the time," he responds, never breaking eye contact with me.

"You know, when you first walked in, I couldn't tell if a gun was pointed at me or if you were just excited to see me," I say with a smile.

"It's hard to conceal big things," he replies with a smirk.

"Do you really think the most valuable thing in this tub is these cold, rough, inanimate baubles?" I ask, placing both of my arms on the tub's molded-in armrest.

"That's what I came here for, baby doll. So… give 'em to me," he says, stuttering as he admires my body which is no longer covered by the now fizzled bubbles.

"Well, if this what you really want," I say, unhooking the clasp.

In the process of handing him the necklace, it 'accidentally' slips through my fingers.

"Ooops," I say as the necklace floats to the bottom of the bathtub.

"Damn," he says with a smile.

"Oh, dang it!" I respond with a giggle.

"Gimme that," he casually demands.

"If you want it, you better come and get it," I retort, matching his casualness.

"You like to tease, huh?" He says as he finally puts the gun down on the marble floor.

I smile as he takes off his gloves and rolls up his sleeves to bend down and put his hand in the tub to search for the necklace. After ten seconds pass, he takes his hat off with his free hand and says, "Damn that!"

He kisses me as I pull him into the Whirlpool tub creating a big splash.

Boom!

Boom!

Boom!

Someone is knocking on the door, but it isn't in my dream.

"Empress! You've been in there for 'bout an hour.

Quit hoggin' the bathroom!" Trapp screams through the door.

Damn it! He would interrupt my dream just when it was about to become X-Rated. Ugh, playtime is over, back to reality. No more diamonds and this definitely is not a Whirlpool tub.

"Alrite, alrite!" I say loud enough so Trapp hears me. "I'll be out in a sec."

———◆———

AS I WALK TO MY BEDROOM, TRAPP WALKS FAST behind me.

He is so close I can feel his toenails on the back of my heels. I pay him no mind. I figure that he is being his normal, annoying self. He catches the door as I attempt to close it.

"Hey, what are you doing?" I suspiciously ask.

"I just wanna talk to my lil' sis," he says.

"Trapp, c'mon stop playin'," I say as I pull back my covers. "I have some homework to finish up before I go to bed. I don't have time to play with you."

"Well, wat I wanna to talk to you about is serious," he responds.

"OMG! You rush me out of the bathroom just to say you wanna talk. Can you just spit it out?" I say, becoming past the point of annoyed.

"Wat the fuck is goin' thru your head?!?" He yells.

"Whoa, whoa! Where is this coming from?" I ask. "And why are you yellin'?"

"Stacks told me you've been runnin' around with that hot ass nigga Nard!" He yells.

"Sssssh! Can you shut up?! Are you trying to wake

up mom?"

I do not want to hear Trapp's mouth, but I know I have to set him straight.

"Yeah, I am dating Renardo. So, what?"

"So, you call this nigga by his government?!?! Just how well do you know him?!?! This has gone too far!" Trapp continues to scream.

"Trapp, really? Why are you trippin'? He's a good guy," I defend.

"Good guy, huh? That nigga is dangerous. When we first moved out here, niggas used to say that he was too big for Rockdale. Wat the hell are you doin' with him, Empress?!?" Trapp asks as he shakes his head in disapproval.

"Renardo is not the guy you, Stacks, or anybody else is making him out to be. I'm sooooo sick and tired of people misjudging him," I retort, becoming more defensive.

"Misjudging him?" Trapp questions back. "I don't misjudge him. I've heard all kinds wild shit about him. That nigga is crazy. Empress, this ain't a game. You not seeing that nigga no more."

"Ha! Just who do you think you are, Trapp?!? Get out of my room!" I scream.

"Girl, you're in over your head! I'm tryin' to make sure you don't get hurt. No bullshitin'," he says.

"Out!" I scream as I point at the door.

I slam the door and lock it once he walks out.

I understand Trapp's concern because I am his little sister. But, I do not need him bad mouthing Renardo or asking me a billion questions. I am so tired of everyone trying to ruin my relationship by spewing hateful things with their pessimistic views.

Chapter twenty-three

BY DAY, JAZ AND HIS CREW CHILL AT HIS BANDO.
By night, they can be spotted at Club Libra - the only
decent club in East Atlanta. Rappers always come thru
and perform, which brings out the baddest girls on
this side of town. Jaz and his crew are always hoping
to get shown crew love. Since its Two Dollar Tuesday,
YGC will be in the club deep, lit as fuck and spending
money tonight.

As Jaz steps, up the sidewalk to enter the trap setup
at his apartment, his phone rings. Seeing an unfamiliar
number, Jaz makes a U-Turn back to his car for privacy and to avoid the loud sounds from the apartment.

"Talk to me," he arrogantly answers the phone outside.

"Jaz, what's goin' on? This is Black. I've been hearing
so much about you, but we've never met," Black says.

"Well, there is so much goin' on as you can see,
which has me puzzled as to why you are callin' me,"
Jaz aggressively says.

"I'm comin' to you with a sensible approach, trying
to resolve this issue and end this violence. We don't
need this in the community," Black says through gritted teeth, trying to remain calm.

"Oh, so now you want to come with a sensible approach - after Larosa and Nard robbed me?" Jaz sarcastically remarks. "Not only that, but harm was brought to my nephew."

"I apologize for that but what did you expect to come from you kidnappin' our brother?" Black shoots back. Realizing that his remark may have hit a nerve, Black quickly moves on to his reason for calling. "Look... listen," he explains. "This situation started with money, therefore it should end with just that. They were wrong for what they did, but the past cannot be changed so we shouldn't discuss it. Let's move forward."

Black's suggestion causes Jaz's face to tighten and his eyes to narrow. "So, you believe money is goin' to make everything right???" He questions without delay. "This shit is beyond money and I believe you know that, Mr. Black."

"So, you tellin' me you want to continue this nonsense?" Black asks as his frustration grows.

"I've said all I need to say," Jaz boldly states.

"Just know what comes with this, Jaz," Black sternly provides Jaz with a fair warning.

"Trust me, I already know."

Click.

"Turn that shit off!" Jaz yells as his marches in the apartment to find his YGC crew watching music videos and smoking weed. "If those niggas think this shit is over, then they will be reminded soon!" Jaz continues to yell. I want every nigga affiliated with that nigga, Larosa, dead on sight for what they did to my nephew - startin' with that nigga Nard first. I want Larosa to feel the pain of losing someone close!"

"Bruh, you are really talkin' crazy right now. Have

you gotten the greenlight from the elders about this shit? DMG is not to be taken lightly. Blood will be shed on both ends," KG reminds Jaz.

"I don't give a FUCK who or what they are, nigga!!!" Jaz screams as he throws an empty Cîroc bottle against the wall. "And everyone has been notified about this situation!"

The shattering glass and Jaz's loud voice causes all the boys and men to pause. They silently look at each other to figure out the root of Jaz's actions.

"Those niggas gave my nephew a Buck 50!" Jaz continues to scream. "A BUCK FIFTY!!! That shit is there for life and if anyone doesn't want to stand by me to avenge my nephew, then here is your opportunity to get the fuck on!!!" Jaz yells as he points to the front door.

Silence now fills the once lively apartment. Everyone seems to be frozen in their spots.

"I ain't with all that beefin' shit. I'm tryin' to get into some money," says an outspoken YGC member, breaking the long-standing silence in the room.

As he turns to walk away and head for the front door, a loud blast goes off. Before anyone can react, the outspoken YGC member's brain matter splatters around the room on everyone and the furniture.

"What the FUUUUUUUCK Jaz!!!" KG screams, astonished that Jaz just killed one of his own.

"I ain't got no sense when it comes to the people I love, NIGGA!!" Jaz angrily states, pointing his gun at KG. "So, is there anyone else who feels the need to express their opinion about who I choose to beef with?!?" Jaz questions the entire crew while aiming the gun at each and every one of them - one person after the other.

Eyeing everyone in the apartment, Jaz's menacing scowl leaves all their faces expressionless as corpses. The smell of burnt flesh fills the room. Everyone knows it is best to not utter a word.

"Clean this shit up," Jaz says before walking out of the front door.

CHAPTER TWENTY-FOUR

~ NARD ~

EMPRESS GETS TO WORK ON TIME, BUT SHE damn sure doesn't leave on time. Every time I pick her up from Krystal's, she always has to wait for the person who is working the third shift to appear. I'll be glad when she doesn't have to work this bullshit ass job anymore. She's too good for this kind of work.

A nigga she works with is parked next to me and I notice him lookin' at me crazy. He gotta be one of the niggas that Empress was tellin' me likes her. He better fix his face before I check his ass. Niggas only see the physical when they look at Empress. They don't see her true beauty as I do.

Finally, after about ten more minutes pass, my dream in motion is, at last, walking out those doors to be with me. A fast food uniform and a red visor never looked so beautiful on a woman as it does on Empress. Her eyes scan the dimly lit parking lot with determination to find me. She sees my car in no time and when our eyes meet her gorgeous smile melts my heart.

As soon as she sits down, she turns with her ample, full, soft lips and lays the sweetest kiss on me.

"Sorry for takin' so long baby," she says as she puts

on her seatbelt.

"It's all good, baby," I say as I turn onto the road. "Do you mind if we stop by my place before I take you home?" I hesitantly ask, unsure of how Empress will react.

"Okay," she responds without thought. "How was your day?"

I smile to myself because Empress is like no other woman I've ever known. She is not self-centered, and she cares about my well-being. When I'm with her, I feel like a little kid gettin' the gift I waited all year for on Christmas day. With Empress, I'm free to live in the moment with no baggage from my past. For the first time in my life, I see the beauty in this world. I just hope and pray to God that she is ready for tonight.

Chapter Twenty-Five

~ NARD ~

"MAKE YOURSELF COMFORTABLE," I SAY TO Empress as I walk into my bedroom, leaving her in the living room.

I'm so nervous. I pray everything goes right. I hope she does not hate me afterward, but I've got to get this over with.

A minute or two passes before I return to the living room.

"Did you find what you were looking for?" She asks so innocently.

"Um, yeah," I say as I sit down on the couch next to her.

For a minute, I awkwardly fidget with my hands, waiting for the perfect time to come. Empress starts tellin' me about her day at school and about an idea she has for a song.

"Empress, there is something I've been wantin' to tell you but I don't know how you will take it or feel," I blurt out because the perfect time never seems to come around.

"Baby, you can tell me anything," Empress says looking at me worried.

"I…" I nervously say. "I believe I'm falling in love with you. I've never felt this way for no woman. You might think it is too soon but what I'm tryin' to tell you is… that I… love you… and I love how you make me feel when I'm around you. For so long, I cared for no one other than my DMG brothers and sisters. You don't even have to say it back because whatever you tell me won't change how I feel for you. You've given me a reason to love again. I lost the feeling of love when my parents walked out my life, but you've given me a reason to live."

My hands sweat as time passes and Empress remains silent.

Fuck!!! She hasn't said a word, and to make matters worse, she is looking at me like I'm an alien. Damn, I knew I shouldn't have said nothin'. I've probably just blown the best thing I had going.

"Empress???" I timidly call her name, unsure of how she will react.

"Yes, baby???" She answers, looking as though she is hypnotized.

"Um, are you alrite???" I ask. "Did I offend you in some way??? If I did, I apologize."

"No, no, it's nothing like that," she says, still a little spacey.

A minute or two passes before she adds, "I love you too! I was so afraid to express my feelings… I just don't want to get hurt by giving you access to my heart."

"Baby, I will never intentionally hurt you… I will always take your feelings into consideration about everything I do," I reply.

I am thrilled that she loves me too. But, I hate that she's doubtful about me. I've got to get these negative illusions out of her mind.

"Have I ever showed you that I am a bad person?" Without giving her a chance to elaborate, I state my case, "Now I'm far from perfect, but I'm a survivor, Empress, and I do what I need to do to survive. Now everyone who knows me, knows that I am loyal to the people I proclaim to love and care for. Fuck anyone who is not in my circle. And it is what it is. My love comes with loyalty and my loyalty comes with love. I cannot have one without the other, or else it will be a conflict of interest. So, get me hurting you out of your head. Trust me. I'll give you my heart, and you give me yours, and let's live and build with one another."

One thing I know is that people do not want to see other people happy. Empress' head is being filled by some hatin' ass muthafuckas. I need this girl in my life. I need this girl to be with me. I need her to know that I will never ever harm her. I wish she would say something. My heart can't stand the suspense.

It seems like an eternity passes by before Empress parts her lips and effortlessly says, "Okay, baby. I trust you."

Excited and relieved by her answer, I take her hands into mine and lean forward to plant a kiss on her forehead. Even though both our eyes are closed, this kiss reveals how strongly connected our souls are. All of our worries seem to subside. I pull back and plant another kiss on her lips. Soft and slow, comforting her in ways that my words never can.

This is the love I have waited and prayed for. I thank God, every day for blessing this woman to enter my life. A love like this is to be cherished. Finally, I have my woman.

"I love you, Empress, for eternity. And hopefully, one day I'm given the opportunity to show you how much I really love and adore you," I say as we embrace.

"I love you too, Renardo," Empress says with a smile. "And I believe I love you more. I'm all in."

"No, we're both all in," I correct her with a smile, leaning in to kiss her once again.

~ EMPRESS ~

"WTF JUST HAPPENED?!?! DID HE JUST SAY WHAT I THINK HE DID?!?!" I ask myself as my mind races at 100 mph.

I just love it when Renardo kisses me like that. Wow! Oh wow! I just can't believe it! Renardo LOVES me! This explains why he has been acting so weird tonight. He doesn't know how happy I really am to hear those three words coming from him. Even though I was taken slightly off guard, I was thrilled the entire time and maybe in a state of shock. I loved every minute of looking into his eyes and saying those magical words, "I love you, too!"

All I can think about is him. When I try to think about important things like school and work, it is only temporary. Renardo defeats all my thoughts. I knew there was something special about him the day I laid eyes on him. I just didn't know what.

Everyone keeps tellin' me how dangerous Renardo is, but how can that possibly be true when I feel so safe with him? With him, I feel safe enough to express my dreams, fears, and opinions. I know Renardo feels safe with me too. He knows I will never repeat anything to a living soul. Since meeting him, I've wondered how I ever lived without him.

It's a scary thing to be this open and vulnerable, but I trust Renardo 100%. I can't waste my time listening to people who do not want to see us together. Without a doubt, no other guy can love me like Renardo does. He is everything that I want and more. I have fallen and I can only fall deeper. To quote Drake and Future, "WHAT A TIME TO BE ALIVE!"

CHAPTER TWENTY-SIX

"THESE NIGGAS A TRIP, KG," JAZ SAYS WITH frustration. "I pay these niggas to do one thing and they seem like they have a hard time doin' it."

Kicking a black folding chair over, Jaz continues, "Hell, my murder game better than these niggas and that's not even my profession. KG, I'm feelin' like I'm wasting my money because I'm not gettin' no results. Wat's the damn hold up!?!?"

"Listen, bruh. We are searchin' for these niggas, but we can't just go blastin' in those niggas hood," KG explains. "That would be a death trap. DMGs roamin' all over that muthafucka."

The thought of the permanent unsightly scar across Roc's face and the one hundred and fifty stitches it took to patch up the wound makes Jaz burn with anger. The scar serves as a constant reminder to Jaz that Larosa harmed someone he loves. He wonders what kind of effect walking around with a Buck 50 for the rest of his life have on Roc. The cause was not a simple "wrong place at the wrong time" incident. The cause was the beef Jaz had with Larosa which fuels his need to settle the score.

"Listen, KG. I love you like my brother and I trust

you with all my major affairs, but if you can't handle this simple ass assignment, then we are going to have a problem. I don't have time to keep explainin' to my sister why her baby boy's face is lookin' the way it is."

"I understand, bruh. Say less," KG says with a sigh.

~ EMPRESS ~

RENARDO PICKED ME UP FROM WORK, SO WE can chill at his spot for a few hours. To keep my mom from blowing up my phone or worrying about where I might be, I told her I had to work until 2 a.m. because the third shift worker was running late. This happens all the time on Thursday nights, so she won't suspect anything. I hate lying to her, but she will never let me see Renardo or any boy at this time of night. Not to mention, I do not know what Trapp has been telling mom about him.

"Gee, baby, you really need to decorate this place," I say, looking around his drab, less than fab apartment.

"Hahaha, I know. I needed a woman's touch and now that I have my woman, feel free to decorate," he says while grabbing a bottled water out of the fridge.

"Baby, can you bring me some apple juice?" I ask as I step out of my shoes to make myself comfortable on the black leather couch in the living room.

Shutting the fridge and walking over to the couch, Renardo kisses my neck from behind.

"This is not what I asked for," I say as he continues to work his magic on my neck.

One more love bite and my mind will completely go blank. It feels so good. His caresses leave me weak for desire. Just feeling his breath on my neck is enough to give my body goosebumps all over. He lifts my hair up gently as he brings his mouth closer to my neck.

"Bite me!" I command in a sexy whisper.

Just like a vampire, Renardo sinks his teeth into my neck while simultaneously using his warm tongue to brush over my skin. While kissing, he gently slides his fingers down into my bra, over my hardened nipples, moving his fingers in an almost rhythmic fashion. I get so deeply aroused by this, that I can barely hold still. *I crave him more than anything.* He bites his bottom lip as he slightly pulls on my hair, giving me that 'I want you sooo bad' expression.

In science class, we learned that many male mammals express their desire to mate by gripping the female's mammal neck with their teeth. Renardo is definitely expressing his desire to mate in this moment.

I can feel his erection emerging, which quite frankly turns me on. I can also feel his muscular body behind me, protecting and caressing me at the same time. My body seems to go into overdrive when he uses his tongue and teeth to bite my neck. *I have a deep curiosity and urge to see all of him. I want to feel him his gorgeous body pressed against mines. Skin on skin. I want him soooo bad, but this is not the right time.*

"Baby…. Baby… stop," I moan. "This is not what I asked for."

"But, it's what you need," he responds with a smirk, kissing me for the final time.

"Yeah… yeah," I say in a playful tone as I adjust my bra and open my laptop to start on my homework.

"Baby, you gonna watch *SportsCenter* with me?" Renardo asks as he turns on the television. "You know it's football season and I've got to catch the highlights," he says as he reclines in his La-Z-Boy.

"Oh please," I say while stepping out of my shoes. "The Falcons are some iron this year, so you already know how their game ended," I say, teasing him.

"Aw, baby, you can't do the home team like that. Even though I did lose $75 with those muthafuckas last week."

We both laugh.

"Let me do my homework first and then I will join you. You know what they say, 'business before pleasure,'" I say with a smile, stretching out on the couch.

My phone lights up notifying me that Alexis has sent me a text.

> **Alexis:** Don't forget about the Lady of Brook gathering in 3 weeks. Be sure to request time off from your jobs.
> **Empress:** I won't. Thanks for the reminder!

I had totally forgotten about the Lady of Brook gathering. I know this isn't the crowd Renardo normally runs with, but I know he will go to make me happy. Finally, my two worlds will join. Now, it's just a matter of convincing him that it will be fun.

"Baby…" I say in my sweetest voice.

"Yes, baby," Renardo answers, completely focused on *SportsCenter.*

"Remember that time I told you I was a part of a social clique at my high school called Lady of Brook?"

"Yes, baby. I remember. What about it?" He asks before screaming at the T.V. because some player made what he considers a stupid play.

"Well," I nervously start with a smile. "We're having a social gathering three weeks from now and we have to bring dates… so I… was… wondering… if you would like to accompany me?"

"Now baby," Renardo says as he mutes the T.V. "You know you don't even have to ask. Of course, I would love to take you."

"Great!" I excitedly say as I jump up and give him a great big kiss.

"There's just one thing," I add.

"What is it?"

"I love your style, but you have to be more… preppy for the event."

"So, what does that mean?"

"We're going shopping!" I say with a smile.

"Shittin me!" Renardo exclaims in fun, shaking his head. "There's no telling what you will pick out for me."

"Trust me, baby," I say, hitting him lightly across the chest.

"And that's why I'm afraid," he says with a chuckle.

"Watever," I playfully say as I crawl back to my laptop.

"Now that's one thing I hate doing - writing long ass essays because I think they are pointless," Renardo says, as he watches me type.

"I think it depends on the topic," I say while multi-tasking.

"As long as you get your point across and have five paragraphs with at least eight sentences, then everything should be straight," he continues.

"Maybe in middle school that was straight. But in high school and definitely college, that will not fly," I add.

"I know," he says, as his eyes focus on the T.V with the hope that his team will score a touchdown. "That's one thing I am going to dread when I decide to go to college within a few years."

"Why the delay?"

"Well, I just need a break. I'm tired of school right now."

"I understand that," I reply. "But, you definitely have to finish your education. You've come too far to throw it all away. There's a Malcolm X quote that I was taught in elementary school. My teacher Mrs. Wayfield really drilled it in our brains. 'Education is the passport to the future, for tomorrow belongs to those who prepare for it today.' Intellectual achievement lasts forever, baby."

"I know that," he says. "I promise baby, I'm going to strive to get my GED."

A couple of moments pass and Renardo is once again interested in the game on television. He feels me staring at him and asks, "What's on your mind, baby?"

"Well… if I tell you, you would probably think it's silly."

"C'mon, you can tell me anything. You know that," Renardo says making his way to the couch.

"Yeah, I know baby, but it's silly. You'll probably laugh."

"Make me laugh then," he says with a smile.

"Well, if you have to know," I say, running my fingers through his hair. "I've been trying to imagine what you'd look like without your dreads."

Looking at each other, we burst into laughter.

"So, you don't like my dreads?" He asks through his laughter.

"No, no," I say, still giggling. "Now, I have to tell you a secret."

"What is it?" He playfully asks.

"You're the first guy with dreads that I have ever liked. I don't like them on anyone else."

"So, you don't like my hair?"

"Yeah, I do," I say through my giggles. "It's just that I'm curious to see how you would look without them. Without a doubt you'll still be handsome."

"So, you asking me to cut my hair?"

"Well…" I say with a broad smile.

"I ain't, I won't, and I ain't," he says as we both laugh. "Just like Samson in the Bible, if my hair is cut I could lose my strength."

"Oh, please," I say, playfully rolling my eyes.

Time passes and Renardo turns to an action flick, which he loves so much. I love cuddling with him on the couch and the safe feeling of being held in his strong arms. Glancing at the clock, I notice it is now pushing 2 a.m.

"Baby, we've got to get ready to go. My mom will go Donkey Kong if I get in at 3 a.m.," I say, giving Renardo a kiss.

"You know we wouldn't have to worry about that if you moved in, right?"

"I know. But there is no way my mom is going to go for that while I am still in high school."

"I feel like that will strengthen our relationship because it will bring us closer together and we will trust each other more because we are goin' to be in this together," he explains, staring at me with those dark eyes.

"Honestly," he continues. "I believe we are ready to stay together. Now, you and this loud music in the morning, I don't know about. We are goin' to have to compromise. As long as you don't have music blastin' in my ears and I don't wake, everything will be good," he says with a laugh.

"I gotta have my music when I wake up," I say with

a giggle. "I'm a natural joyful person."

"And I'm not?" He asks with a chuckle.

"No, you're Mr. Grumpy," I teasingly say.

"I may be grumpy to those niggas out there, but I'm never grumpy to you," he says, giving me a peck on the cheek. "And I don't mind the T.V. being on either."

Wow! He hates sleeping with the television on, so this shows me the effort he will make to keep me happy.

"I truly love you," Renardo says, still holding my hands.

"I love you, too," I reply, my heart skipping a beat.

"I can't wait until you're all mine and all this 'seeing me when you're free from work' is over," he says. "I've told you before that I see a future with you in it and I'm serious. There is no doubt about it. You will soon see."

CHAPTER TWENTY-SEVEN

~ EMPRESS ~

I GUESS IT'S NEIGHBORHOOD DIFFERENCES because all the boys at Brook dress preppy. Maybe if Renardo attended Brook, his swag would be different...Nah, he is such an individual no matter where he goes, he will always be different. He's his own man, which I love, but it is also making this process difficult. We have been at the mall since 11 o'clock this morning.

"Ooh, how about this one baby?" I say, picking up a wool-blend navy cardigan sweater with brown elbow patches off the rack.

"No," Renardo says instantly.

"But, baby, it's soooo cute," I say, placing the sweater in front of me, pretending to wear it.

"Woman, I'm not wearing that Mr. Rogers lookin' bullshit," Renardo says with a chuckle.

"Baby, I know this isn't your style, but you have to look like a preppy schoolboy for the soiree. If you don't, they will turn us away at the door," I whine as I hang up the sweater.

"Baby, I don't like none of the sweaters we've been lookin' at for the past hour," Renardo says as he shakes his head making a confused face.

I love it when he makes that face. He looks sooo adorable, but he is not an easy man to please when it comes to fashion.

"These clothes, uh uh, they ain't my type," he continues.

Looking as if he has a bright idea, Renardo's eyes light up and he says, "I'll tell you what, let's compromise. I'll wear this bullshit if you let me pick out and buy an entire outfit for you.

"Okay," I say giving him a sexy kiss on the lips. I love how his hands always makes it to my ass each time we kiss.

"Get a room!" Someone passing by yells into the store, causing us to laugh.

"Come on, baby," Renardo says, grabbing my hand so we can exit the store.

The first place we stop, to my surprise, is Victoria Secret.

Now, I know Renardo is not trying to be funny. He said outfit, not lingerie.

I notice a sales girl eyeing him as we walk through.

She had better not stare too long.

"Hi, may I help you all with something?" She eagerly asks.

"Yeah, where are your sweat pants?" Renardo asks.

The sales girl walks us over to the PINK section and tells us about some sale the store is having.

"Is there anything else I can help you all with?"

"No, thanks," Renardo answers.

Has Renardo not been paying attention to my fashion sense? Well, giving him the benefit of the doubt, I am usually in a work uniform 50% of the time.

"Baby, sweats, really?" I ask.

"Don't be like that, baby," he says teasingly. "We

compromised, remember?"

"Yes, baby," I say with a bittersweet smile.

He is right. He is going to wear the outfit I picked out for him, so I can't be too mad.

"This is it, baby!" He excitedly says, picking up a raspberry jam PINK skinny jogger and matching jacket. "When I saw this, I said to myself, I'd like this outfit for my girl to wear. Try it on, baby. I know it will look good on you."

I'm not excited about trying on the joggers, yet I march to the dressing room enjoying Renardo's excitement. It takes me about five minutes to get out of my clothes and into the PINK outfit.

"How do I look?" I ask, modeling the outfit for him.

The way he's looking at me, you would think I have on a wedding dress.

"Perfect baby, just perfect. I knew it would look good on you. It makes your ass look good. Perfect," he says getting up from the waiting chair to kiss me.

Even though we have been dating for nearly six months now, I still love a compliment from Renardo.

"Thank you, baby. Let me change so we can go," I say with a smile.

"Naw, baby. Keep that on. You look too good to take it off."

"But, I have on heels. I'm goin' to look ridiculous with heels and a jogging suit on."

"Listen, I'm going to pay for this and then Footlocker here we come," he says with a slick grin.

OMG! What did I get myself into? I haven't worn sneakers since middle school.

At Footlocker, we ended up getting matching pairs of retro Jordans or as the sales guy, who kept correcting me said, Nike Air Jordan 4 OG '89 "White Cement" sneakers.

As we shopped today, I could see our future laid out in my mind. I love doing normal everyday things with Renardo. It is so cool, how we can be in public, but still retain our private world. Each time we kiss it is as though we are being exposed to voyeurism. Eyes observing us as we glance and smile at each other for no reason.

"Wow, baby. Do you realize that you bought me my first pair of J's? I say as I bite into the soft pretzel we bought at the food court.

"You've gotta be kiddin," he laughs. "Well, I'm glad to be your first."

As we put our bags into the trunk of his car, he pauses and says, "I enjoyed myself today, baby."

"So, did I," I say before kissing him. "Now going to work this afternoon won't be so bad all."

If kissing were a crime, we would surely be locked up because every opportunity we get, we show our affection through kisses.

"This was just what I needed," he says as he closes the trunk. "You're just what I needed. I am so glad you've come into my life."

CHAPTER TWENTY-EIGHT

"THIS NIGGA GOT ME FUCKED UP IF HE THINK he is just goin' to use me," Danielle rants to herself as she snorts a line of coke in the comfort of her bedroom.

Continuing to rant aloud to herself, Danielle says, "How could this nigga choose this bitch over me??? After all the shit I've done for him? I gave this nigga my all, and this is the shit he does?!"

With tears forming in her eyes, she gets off her bed and walks over to her dark wooden vanity mirror. As hard as she tries to hold the tears in, the hot streams of water creep down her face, ruining the thick black eyeliner she had on all day.

After starring in the mirror for five minutes, she screams, "Fuck him!!! I can't believe I got played!!!" Danielle, you slippin'. FUCK LOVE! FUCK HIM! I don't even know why I'm even stressin' over this nigga. He ain't shit anyway and most likely he will be dead or in jail soon. Damn, but I love him… Shit! Let me get the fuck out this house," Danielle says to herself as she dials her best friend, Erica's, number.

Finally, picking up the phone after five rings, Erica answers, "Hey, bitch."

"Bitch, I need you to help me get over this nigga," Danielle says.

"What nigga? I know you ain't talkin' 'bout Nard?" Erica asks.

"Bitch, you know it's only one nigga that stresses me," Danielle replies with a Newport dangling from her lips.

"Well, you need to get over that nigga cause that nigga all caked up with his new bitch," Erica says.

The more Danielle listens to Erica, the more her heart breaks.

"I know. That's where you come in at," Danielle says as she tries to keep her composure. "Take me out and let's have some fun."

"I got you, girl. We'll go to Club Libra. You know it be too lit. Just be ready when I get there," Erica replies with a lot of noisy distractions in the background.

"Shut up," Danielle replies in a friendly tone. "I'll be ready in an hour."

With Renardo still on her mind, Danielle hesitantly utters, "Say... where did you say you saw Nard and that bitch at?"

"Girl, at the mall today. They was all boo'd up. Look like he had took her shoppin'. I saw Victoria Secret and Foot Locker bags," Erica instigates.

Danielle did not think that her heart could drop even lower than what it just did. "Are you serious?!?" She screams.

"Yes, girl. They were all hugged up and shit," Erica says, making Danielle's heartache worse.

"That nigga never bought me shit! I FUCKIN' HATE HIM. I swear I'ma —"

Before Danielle can finish her statement, Erica interrupts, "Damn, girl. Calm down! You already know

Nard ain't shit. None of these niggas are. You need a drink. I got you on shots."

A turbulent rage of bitterness builds up inside of Danielle. She hears Erica, but she is mute to what she is sayin'.

"Dani? Dani? Are you still there?" Erica asks after holding the line with dead silence for a minute.

"Yeah, girl let's get turnt tonite," Danielle superficially says, snapping back to the present moment.

"You ain't said nothin' but a word! Give me an hour and a half," Erica says, smiling through the phone.

"OK, bye bitch."

"Bitch bye."

~ EMPRESS ~

"HAVE A GOOD NIGHT," I SAY TO THE customer as I pull the drive-thru window shut.

Oddly enough, Jake had phoned in around 4 p.m. and advised Egypt to keep most of the first shift crew on the clock because he expected a big rush since it is Saturday. We are heavily staffed, but it is greatly needed. Within an hour, we probably have served at least 100 customers.

"I'm goin' on break," Willis and April both say in unison.

"Dang, I thought this rush would never end," I think aloud as I walk to the soda fountain to fill my cup.

"I know!" Enrique says as he cleans the grill. "Me, Lewis, and Willis went thru at least 300 beef patties and 5 cases of hot dogs. It's 8 p.m. now… time for me to leave this bullshit."

"Hold up. Where you think you goin'? You here with me until eleven," Egypt chimes in.

"Huh? The fuck I'm not!" Enrique charges back.

"You better stroll your Mexican ass to the back and check the damn schedule," Egypt says as she restocks bags and cups.

"Aye, I done told y'all I'm not no fuckin' Mexican," Enrique shoots back in a slightly serious tone.

Enrique has a temper, and it is always hard to tell if he will take a comment as a joke or if he will escalate the matter into a full-fledged argument. Since I have to be here for a couple more hours, I hope this does not blow up. Reason being that I do not feel like being the mediator for Enrique's temper and Egypt's slick mouth.

"My parents are from Nicaragua. I was born in Nicaragua and I'm gonna be buried in Nicaragua. I'm 100% Nicaraguan, baby," Enrique says with a smile as Lewis laughs at his rant.

Lewis is in high school and has an after-school job because his stepfather will not let him live at home if he is not contributing towards the mortgage. He's a tall, skinny, quiet boy that can be easily influenced. With that said, he is easy to work with most times unless Enrique is working.

Coming over to stand by me, Enrique mumbles in Spanish, "Está loca... Does the schedule really say that, Empress?"

"Ay yi yi, I'm afraid so," I say with a giggle.

"Daaaamn, that's fucked up," Enrique says with a sigh.

"Naw, wat's gonna be fucked up is if y'all don't fully restock and these folks roll up in here," Egypt says as Enrique and I both roll our eyes.

"So, Empress, what's this I hear about you being all up in the mall on shoppin' sprees with your little boo?"

Egypt asks.

"Shopping spree?" I giggle and instantly cheese because Renardo is being mentioned. "Well, it's only natural that my sweetheart buys me things. He bought me my first pair of Jordans. Can you believe it? And some things from Victoria Secret."

"Victoria Secret, eh?" Enrique questions as he tugs his goatee and flicks his tongue out at me.

"Yeah man, that's what she said," Lewis says, giggling.

Knowing exactly what is on their minds, I interrupt them before they can say another word, "I'm a taken woman, so get those nasty thoughts out of y'all heads."

They both laugh.

"Can't we dream, Empress?" Enrique says, still giggling with Lewis.

"Egypt, who told you they saw me and my baby at the mall?" I ask.

"A little birdie," Egypt says.

Beep.

Beep.

Our headsets go off, alerting us that a customer has pulled up to the speaker box to place an order.

"Let's get back to work, y'all," Egypt says as I respond to the beep. "We have a long night ahead of us."

CHAPTER TWENTY-NINE

ERICA PULLS UP TO DANIELLE'S DUPLEX AN hour after their conversation in her 2008 silver Impala. As Danielle hops in the car, Erica says with a smile, "Hey, girl. I got a nigga I want you to meet."

"Erica, I'm really not tryin' to be bothered with a nigga," Danielle utters.

"Listen, I've been knowin' this nigga for a while and he cool and sexy. The only reason why I don't talk to the nigga is cause I've been dealin' with his home-boy and you know I don't get down like that," Erica explains.

Danielle snickers as she puts on her lip gloss. "Bitch, what's stopped you in the past?" She bluntly asks.

"I've changed, bitch. Before I was young and wild. Now I'm a grown ass woman," Erica replies, stunned by Danielle's bluntness.

"Yeah, yeah. But I'm still not tryin' to meet this nigga," Danielle responds.

"Didn't you tell me to help you get your mind off this nigga, Nard? What better way to do that than talkin' to another nigga?"

"OK, OK," Danielle agrees after a deep sigh. "Where are we supposed to be meetin' these niggas?"

"That's my bitch!" Erica says with an instant smile as they high-five.

"We meetin' them at the club," Erica tells Danielle as she backs out of the driveway.

"Free drinks until 12, right?" Danielle asks.

"You know it, girl," Erica replies as she makes her way out of Danielle's neighborhood. "You got your fake ID, right?"

"You just tried my Gangsta," Danielle replies while side eyeing Erica. "You know I'm 18 and it isn't like them niggas check IDs anyways."

Erica laughs. "I'm just sayin', it's 21 and up. Plus, it's hard to keep up with y'all bitches since I graduated three years ago. We're gonna have such a good time tonight."

"I hope so," Danielle replies as she looks out the window, mindlessly watching cars pass by. "I need to get my mind off that lame ass nigga Nard."

———◆———

A THICK CLOUD OF HAZY SMOKE LOOMS OVER Club Libra, hiding the decorated gold, black, bronze, and browns that cover the walls. The DJ has the club going wild with the latest and hottest music going on the turntables. The dance floor is crowded with people anticipating Gucci Mane's performance later tonight. Danielle vibes to the music in the VIP section. While throwing back a shot, Erica walks over with two guys.

"Dani, this is Smoke, and my baby, Heard," Erica points to each of the guys as she makes introductions. "Smoke, Heard, this is my main bitch, Danielle."

"Hey," Danielle says in a slightly tipsy and seductive manner, feeling her high.

"Wat's up, lil mama," Smoke replies, ready to put his macc down.

Smoke and Heard are both tall in stature and look like aging rappers with their dark Gucci shades, VVS shiny diamond chains around their necks, and diamond rollys around their wrists. They both look like BOSSES and Danielle can see why Erica rocks wit Heard. She is feeling Smoke's low fade and thick, groomed beard. She has never saw so much Gucci in her life. Smoke is Gucci'ed out with his Gucci dad cap, black Gucci tee, black Gucci shorts, Gucci socks and Gucci sneakers. He looks like money. The bottle of Ace of Spades he has in his hand indicates to Danielle that Smoke isn't scared to run up a check. The thought of revenge against Nard just got even better.

"Check this out, me and my mans here really ain't feelin' the club scene," Smoke says moving closer to Danielle, his clothes smelling funky from the loud he was previously smoking. "We was wonderin' if y'all wanted to go get a bite to eat and maybe have some entertainment at the crib."

"Awww, I was hopin' I could get my dance on and see Gucci, but if y'all ain't feelin' that then I guess we can do that," Erica says.

"Well, I'm not hungry. But, I'll ride," Danielle adds, after a loss of appetite from the drugs in her system.

"Looks like we 'bout to have us a night of fun," Heard says with a smile.

"Is that so?" Erica responds.

"Maybe," Danielle says, staring at Smoke seductively.

"Yes, we will. But in the meantime, follow us to the Waffle House," Heard says. "Matter of fact, Erica let

Smoke see your keys and hop in the car with me."

Without hesitation, Erica throws Smoke her car keys as they exit the club. Once they make it outside to the parking lot, Erica hops into Heard's black Audi A5 with matte black rims.

"Well, I guess it's me and you baby," Smoke tells Danielle as he watches her ass jiggle in the tight jump-suit she purchased from Fashion Nova.

"I guess so," Danielle says with a slick smile, opening the passenger door of Erica's Impala.

Chapter Thirty

~ NARD ~

"BAAAABY!" EMPRESS SCREAMS WITH A SMILE as she runs around the front counter of Krystal's, excited to have a surprise visit from none other than me.

"Hey, baby doll," I reply with a smile. "I was just thinkin' about you and I wanted to see you, so I thought I would stop thru and check up on my sexy lady."

I want to see Empress, but really, I want to show my face to all the hatin' ass niggas that are tryin' to throw salt on my name. I mean like damn, do niggas have anything better to do than to hate on another nigga? That's what separates me from the rest, they are small-minded and I'm great- minded.

As I scan the kitchen, I can tell exactly who the niggas are by the looks on their faces. To make things worse, I don't know none of these niggas.

I continue my surprise visit with a long kiss for my baby doll and a smack on that soft, phat ass that I love so much.

"Baby, how has your day been going?" I ask.

"The usual busy and boring," Empress tells me in her cute little voice.

"Well, I know it's almost closin' time for the dining area, but I was wonderin' if you could you take a break?"

"Of course, my baby love," she says with a smirk. "I don't wear this yellow shirt for nothin'", she adds, referencing that she is the second-in-command supervisor. "Let me clock out right quick," she says.

At this moment, the bell on the door chimes, alerting the Krystal employees that someone has entered the building.

"Hold on, Renardo. Let me take her order," Empress says loud enough so that I can hear her as she motions at the customer.

"OK, baby," I reply.

As I take a seat at the table, I glance at the woman who entered the restaurant. I try hard not to stare, but I am in disbelief.

I can't believe she is here! The way she is squinting her eyes, she recognizes me too.

"Hell naw," I tell myself. *That's not possible... I'm trippin'. But, she is staring... shit!* She must have recognized my voice.

"Welcome to Krystal's. May I take your order?" Empress says with irritation after repeating herself three times before she catches the attention of the woman eyeing me.

"My bad. I apologize. Can I get a number three with a strawberry Fanta to go?" The woman asks.

"Yes, that will be $5.78," Empress informs the woman.

After they make the transaction, Empress yells to the back, to tell her co-workers that she is taking her break.

She clocks out on the front register as the woman

waits for her order. Sliding in the seat next to me, she catches me turnin' my head from eyeing the woman whose order she just took. Shootin' the lady a sharp glance and then narrowing her eyes at me, Empress aggressively questions, "Wat is going on? Wat's up with that bitch, Renardo?"

"Whoa, baby. Wat's up with all that?" I shoot back.

"You tell me," Empress says without delay. "You've been eyein' that bitch, and she's been eyein' you since she walked in here. So now I'm asking you, wat's up with you and her?"

"Empress, can we talk about this later?" I plead.

"You're right," she condescendingly says, somewhat loudly in the sweetest, fakest voice I have ever heard. "I get off in an hour and I need you to wait so you can take me home, baby." With a demanding change in her tone she adds, "Then we can discuss the issue at hand further."

I clench my teeth tryin' to refrain from gettin' angry with Empress.

I have never seen her turnt up like this before. I hope she will drop the issue by the time she gets off.

"OK, baby, I will wait," I say.

Empress nods and gives me the eyes of an ice princess as she gets up to go back to work. Out of my peripheral vision, I can still see the mystery woman on the phone staring at us.

FUCK!

~ EMPRESS ~

I CANNOT BELIEVE RENARDO SET ME UP TO LOOK like a fool!!! I swear for a second, I could no longer decipher sounds. I felt like my head was submerged under water with a

loud party going on around me. My whole world just fuckin'
stopped. I can't wait to get off work! I want to know what the
hell is going on??? He has some fuckin' explaining to do! If
Renardo is cheating on me, I'm going to really let him have
it. Does he think I'm stupid? Does he think I'm blind? How
could he be so disrespectful? Did he think I wouldn't pick up
on the eye contact? Watching them make eye contact made
me feel like I was intruding or even worse... I had offended
him. It seemed like their eyes were holding a secret that only
they knew about.

Renardo was just soooo incredible when I first laid eyes
on him... now I just don't know. Stupid me. I thought he
was sweet - my sweetheart. He told me he would never lie
to me. After I had finally learned to trust, he goes and does
some shit like this. Even after I have been loyal to him. Ha!
Loyalty. I guess loyalty isn't everything. It has a price. I have
gone against the world for this guy and this is the thanks I
get. Everyone told me I was making a mistake, but I truly
believed what we have is true love. That bitch just better be
glad I am on the clock. She's not even that cute and she could
stand to lose a few pounds... But, who am I kidding? She
is gorgeous!

I will not tolerate disrespect. Who the fuck does Renardo
think I am?!?! I thought our connection was beyond the
norm. I thought our bond was strong. Silly, wasn't I?

I am so confused. I do not know if Renardo set this all up
to make me jealous or if he is a L.A.N.C.E - you know,
lying ass nigga cheating every day. I don't know what to do.
This is so complicated. My head is telling me to tell Renardo
to lose my number and forget he ever met me, but my heart is
telling me that he loves me and would never hurt me or disrespect me intentionally. I don't know which one to listen to.

Chapter Thirty-One

AFTER GETTING HER ORDER OF KRYSTAL'S, Bianca strategically sits on the opposite side of the dining lobby, making sure to keep an eye on the guy who has caught her attention. She lost her appetite while she was standing in line and is no longer hungry. The only thing on Bianca's mind at this very moment is calling her husband, Heard.

The phone rings until the voicemail prompt comes on and asks her to leave a message. She presses the end call button and dials again.

Annoyed that she still has not gotten an answer, Bianca gently places her phone on the table. "Why is this nigga not pickin' up the phone???" Bianca wonders.

As she continues to observe the guy out of the corner of her eye, Bianca draws a blank where there should be a memory. She stares into space, hoping she can drum up memories from the past. Thoughts run chaotically through her mind. Recollections take their own time. A light bulb finally goes off! The same eye contact she was making with the guy earlier was the same they had made months ago when he knocked on the Harvest Grove apartment door she had opened.

Sorting out the confusion silently, Bianca thinks, *"I just know that's the nigga who held me at gunpoint... his voice is sumthin I would never forget... and he has the same stature... I was about to brush this whole thing off, until his girl said his name... Renardo. Heard has been talkin' about deadin' some nigga named Nard for months now. There is no coincidence. Nard... Renardo. All I know is Heard said the niggas' names are Larosa and Nard and he will take care of things."*

Fear throbs through her heart as each moment of the past armed robbery seems to play on forever in her mind. She remembers the feeling of the cold, hard, deadly weapon pointed at her gut. Renardo grabbing her by the throat, demanding that she put everything in a bag. The harsh language that Larosa used. Loud footsteps echo in her memory. Her breath shortens as her heart races. Anxiety kicks in the more Bianca thinks about the terrifying experience. She can hear her pulse as she recalls the jeopardizing feeling of her personal safety. The uncertainty of her life being spared or ending during that moment still plagues her dreams every night.

She calls Heard again and there is Still no answer from Heard.

Bianca continues to think, *"Here is this muthafucka, Nard, and Heard won't even answer his damn phone. Another giveaway is that this nigga keeps glancin' at me tryin' to watch my every move. I'm gonna stay here until they close because I know he won't try nothin' in public or in front of his woman... at least I hope he won't."*

Chapter Thirty-two

"LOOK, BABY, I'VE GOT TO TAKE THIS CALL," Heard explains to Erica as he pulls into a Waffle House parking space.

"OK baby, take your time," Erica says hopping out the car to give him privacy.

Heard waits until Erica closes the door before he presses the dial button on his phone to call his wife, Bianca.

"Hello... baby? Baby, can you hear me?" Bianca answers in a whispered, panicked voice.

Immediately, Heard notices Bianca is in agony. Put on guard, he sits straight up and asks, "Baby, are you OK?!?!"

"No! That nigga who held me at gunpoint is here at Krystal's and he saw me," she frantically says in a whisper.

Heard instantly becomes enraged. Savage. Spiteful. He has wanted revenge since he spoke to Larosa on that early morning months ago. He is unforgiving and callous - taking no disdain for his woman lightly.

After pounding his fist on the dashboard, Heard regains his composure so that he will not unnerve his wife.

"Don't leave the building. I'm on the way," he slowly says in a calm tone.

"OK," Bianca faintly replies.

She is relieved, yet still frightened.

The call disconnects.

~ NARD ~

I WONDER WHY THE FUCK THIS BITCH KEEPS lookin' this way. Now she is on the damn phone. I know she callin' that nigga, Heard.

Damn!!!

I definitely don't need this drama right now, especially with Empress right here.

Fuck!!!!

I need to call Larosa.

"Say, FAM. I need you to pull up at Krystal's ASAP!" I blurt without giving Larosa a chance to say hello.

"Wat the hell is goin' on, FAM?!?" Larosa asks, alarmed by the frustration in my voice.

"Man, I just ran into Heard's bitch and she was ordering her food to go, but now she sittin' down babysittin' the damn food. She just got off the phone."

"Say less. I'm on the way. You strapped?" Larosa asks.

"Always," I effortlessly reply.

"Well, I'm 'bout to call Black and inform him on wat's goin' on."

"Bet. Just bring your ass."

Chapter Thirty-Three

"WE GOTTA CUT THIS NIGHT SHORT, LADIES," Heard explains to everyone.

"Aw, boo. I'm not ready for you to go," Erica says to Heard as she hugs him.

"I know, baby girl. But I got some business to handle," Heard informs her.

"Well, can I at least get $100?" Erica asks.

Heard reaches in his pockets, removes a rubber band from his money roll and hands Erica $500.

"Oooo, I wasn't expecting all this," Erica says with a smile as she folds and stuffs the hundreds in her bra.

"I'd rather give it to you than the hoes at Strokers," Heard says, as he hugs Danielle and squeezes her ass.

"We'll link up tomorrow night," he adds, before walking off.

"Ay, man, let me holla at you," Heard says, motioning for Smoke to walk in his direction.

"I got sumthin for you," Smoke says with a wink to Danielle as he lets her loose from his grip. "Let me see what my partna talkin' 'bout."

"Wat's good wit you, bruh?" Smoke asks Heard as he fires up a blunt. "I'm tryin' to smash shawty over there tonite," he says with a smile as he passes the blunt to

Heard.

"Nigga, not tonight," Heard says taking a hit.

"Fuck you talkin' 'bout?" Smoke asks with a cough.

"Smoke, we've finally caught up with them niggas... well, at least, just one."

"Who?"

"Nard," Heard states firmly looking Smoke dead in the eyes.

Danielle's heart sinks as she eavesdrops and hears her unrequited love's name mentioned. Even though she talks a bunch of shit about Nard, she can't bear to see any harm come his way.

"Does Nard know they comin'?" Danielle wonders to herself as Heard and Smoke hop in his Audi R5 and pull off in a hurry.

"Guuuuuurl, did you just hear that shit?!?" Erica asks Danielle. Not waiting for a response from Danielle, Erica continues, "It sounds like your boy is in trouble!" Still quiet, Erica mushes Danielle in the face to get her attention. "Bitch, you alrite?"

"Yeah, bitch. I'm good," Danielle responds, annoyed and not in the moment.

Taking a few steps back, Erica analyzes Danielle. She knows exactly what Danielle is thinking and goes off, "I don't know why the fuck you even give a fuck about that nigga. Especially after he has treated you like shit. Bitch, you dumb as fuck!"

"First off, I need you to mind your own mutha-fuckin' business before I go off in your shit," Danielle threatens Erica.

Seeing that Danielle is dead serious, Erica takes heed and shuts up.

"You don't know shit but what I tell you. After all me and that nigga done been through," Danielle says with an attitude. "I don't care what he did, but I don't wish death on him. I have to –"

"But Heard is my nigga. Ain't no way in fuck you about to warn that nigga," Erica cuts in.

"Who the fuck is goin' to stop me?" Danielle shoots back.

"Bitch, I've always been there for you every time you came cryin' to me about that nigga," Erica pleads.

"It's DMA or nothin'. Remember that. Don't never question my loyalty," Danielle threatens.

Hearing these words, Erica grows angry and builds up the courage to plunge herself at Danielle, knocking her against the car.

"Bitch, you done fucked up!" Danielle taunts Erica, knowing she cannot fight.

Furious, Danielle grabs and throws Erica to the ground. Terror consumes Erica as Danielle climbs on top of her. Erica knows Danielle has the upper hand. Beads of sweat pile on her forehead as she wiggles and squirms on the concrete. After minutes of defeat pass, Erica desperately grabs a handful of Danielle's box braids.

"Bitch, let my shit go," Danielle yells as she punches Erica in the mouth, drawing blood.

The harder Danielle punches, the more pressure Erica applies pulling Danielle's weave out. Embarrassed and even more enraged seeing her weave on the ground, Danielle pulls a razor blade out of her mouth. Seeing the move, Erica knocks Danielle off balance and flips her on the stomach. The commotion causes Danielle to swing the sharp razor blade, cutting Erica deep on her exposed back. Danielle takes all the fight out of Erica causing her to scream as she crawls to the sidewalk, crying and pleading with Danielle to stop. This brings even more attention to the customers inside the Waffle House and bystanders.

"Damn, wat those hoes got goin' on over there?" One man says to his girlfriend.

"Maaaan! I should've been recordin' so I could've sent this shit to Worldstar," another observer of the fight shouts.

A spirit of remorse comes over Danielle as she stands up and stares at Erica through glossy eyes. She tries hard not to cry because Erica is her girl and after tonight, she knows their bond will never be the same.

"Bitch, you are a fool," Danielle says with a slight chuckle.

With tears streaming down her face, Erica looks up at Danielle, bewildered by her statement.

"Bitch, what's so funny?" Erica asks as blood runs down her back.

"Do you even know why Heard beefin' with Nard?" Danielle asks, trying to give insight to the situation. Smacking her hands together, she continues, "Because I believe if you knew, we wouldn't even be fightin'. You fuckin' with a thirty sumthin-year-old married man, bitch! At least I had enough dignity to get the fuck on and not share a man."

The words cut Erica like a knife because she hears the truth out loud for the first time, but she reverts to denial. "I don't care!!!" She childishly yells as she looks up at Danielle in disgust. "At least I got a man, hoe. I love that man and eventually he will come around. I'll play my position for right now, but my time will come. Believe that!"

"I'm afraid that time may never come," Danielle mumbles as she turns her back on Erica to dial Nard's number.

———•———

"SO, WE GOIN' TO DEAD THIS NIGGA AT Krystal's?" Smoke asks.

"Fuckin' right," Heard replies without delay while speeding on I-20.

Seeing the puzzled look on Smoke's face, Heard continues to explain, "This Krystal's don't have any cameras, so that's one less problem we have to worry 'bout. The only thing we have to worry about is people seeing us, which is why we gonna put on ski masks. In and out. A smooth take out."

"Don't you think you need to tell Bianca to get the hell on???" Smoke questions.

"Once we are in the parking lot, we will call her to walk out," Heard informs Smoke. "Everything is gonna be smooth, man."

Chapter Thirty-Four

AFTER ENDING HIS CALL WITH NARD, LAROSA grabs his keys and hops in his '06 cocaine white Charger. Simultaneously, he calls Black. "Say, FAM," Larosa says.

"What's poppin', FAM?" Black answers.

"Nard in trouble," Larosa replies, shaking his head.

Trying to not wake his sleeping wife, Black excuses himself from their bedroom. He closes the door lightly and goes to their guest bedroom.

"Wat's goin' on?" He asks.

Larosa goes on to explain the situation to Black.

Despite knowing his wife will be furious with him because he promised to lay down his guns, Black agrees to be at Krystal's.

———◆———

FRIGHTENED NEARLY TO DEATH, BIANCA fumbles with her fingers as she tries to avoid eye contact with Nard.

"Is everything going okay, ma'am?" Egypt asks. It is a part of Egypt's job duties, as an assistant manager, to ask this question. She is supposed to always be focused on the customer experience, ensuring everyone is enjoying their meal.

"Um, I'm fine. Thanks," Bianca nervously says, trying not be seen by Nard.

"Okay," Egypt says as she moves on to make rounds with other customers.

"Where is this nigga at?" Bianca asks herself. "Just being in the same room with this nigga got me nervous. I wonder if he knows I called Heard. He keeps lookin' at me and it's spookin' me. My husband needs to hurry up."

~ NARD ~

GOD, I KNOW YOU AND I AREN'T ON GOOD terms but I pray that you can give me the strength to protect Empress. I don't know how tonight is about to play out, but please don't let my past come back to haunt her. If something were to happen to her, Lord I would lose it. God, grant me my request and I will hang my guns up for good after all this is over with Jaz. Amen.

My phone rings.

It's Danielle.

CHAPTER THIRTY-FIVE

~ NARD ~

NOT WANTING TO TALK TO DANIELLE, I DEBATE whether or not I should decline the call.

I decide to answer.

"Hello, Danielle. This isn't the time for drama."

"I know, I know," she anxiously says. "I was just callin' to let you know that Heard and Smoke know you are at Krystal's and they are comin' for you."

Grittin' my teeth, I wonder how the hell she knows this information.

———◆———

"BIANCA, YOU CAN COME OUT NOW," HEARD informs Bianca through a phone call. "Get in your car and drive straight home."

"OK," Bianca replies with a smile of relief as she hangs up the phone.

"It's about damn time this nigga came," Bianca says to herself as she throws her food away while taking one last quick glance at Nard who is staring at her with cold, dark eyes that could kill.

Glinting stars fill the vast, empty sky. Goosebumps cover Bianca's body as she steps outside in the cool night air. Scanning the parking lot, she looks for her husband's black Audi. She spots it in no time; breathing a sigh of relief because she knows her protector is here.

Longing for her husband's touch, she thinks, "I just want him to come home. Fuck this nigga. After all, he didn't harm me."

Something in Bianca's spirit nudges her to tell Heard to go home. The urge causes her to divert from walking to her silver Mercedes-Benz C300 and instead take tentative steps across the Krystal's parking lot to Heard's Audi A5. As she gets closer, she notices two dark figures creeping behind Heard's car. Feeling that something is not right, she naturally opens her mouth to scream.

Bianca's attempt to warn her husband of the imminent danger fails in a result of any audible sound she was about to make being silenced by a bullet piercing through her chest.

Instantly, Bianca becomes weak as the ejected gunpowder burns her shirt and skin. The psychological shock from being shot makes her lose all coordination. She becomes dizzy and collapses to the ground. Within an instant, everything she sees turns black. The sound of a blaring car horn resonates as she lays unconscious on the ground.

~ NARD ~

BEFORE I CAN ASK DANIELLE WHAT SHE knows, a hail of gunfire interrupts my thoughts. Adrenaline surges through my veins as I hang the phone up and draw my .40. Making my way towards my baby, Empress, I drop into a crouch unaware of where the shots are coming from.

Everyone is screaming as the sound of a semi-automatic rifle fills their ears.

Boom!

Boom!

Boom!

Gunshots fire quickly, magnifying the customers and employee's vulnerabilities as they hope and pray a stray bullet does not find them.

After a second of searching, I find Empress crying and shaking at the back of the restaurant in a corner. Horror fills her eyes. The scream she lets out makes my blood run cold.

"Baaaaaaby!!!!" She screams through her tears because she is glad to see me.

Instinctively, I grab her. "Ssssh!!!" I tell Empress so she does not give us away.

With my .40 still in my hand, I lead the way as we creep our way out of the emergency exit. Once we make it outside, the gunshots cease.

Now, a loud car horn is nearly bursting our eardrums as it blares repeatedly. The roaring sound reverberates in our ears and rings out across the parking lot. Hearing the car horn sound nonstop is a clear sign that someone is dead or unconscious. No time to worry about that now. Empress's safety is my only concern.

I lead the way, maneuvering us to my Monte Carlo SS. Quickly, I unlock the driver's door allowing Empress to climb in. I hop in after her and scan the parking lot quickly. While cranking the ignition, I notice Heard's black Audi A5 filled with bullet holes. I have no time to investigate further. I have to get Empress to safety.

CHAPTER THIRTY-SIX

~ NARD ~

THE WHOLE RIDE TO HER HOUSE, EMPRESS has not said a word and neither have I. How can I explain to her what just went down?

"Baby, are you OK????" I ask.

Not getting a response, I look at her and notice she is staring out the window.

"Baby???? I need you to say something," I plead.

"Baby...I...I freaked," Empress sobs as she snaps out of her daze. "I just witnessed people getting severely injured or possibly murdered and you ask me if I'm Ok?"

She stares into space again.

"Well, to answer your question, no I'm not OK, Renardo," Empress states matter- of-factly. "I don't understand why a FUCK-ING shoot out would happen in the parking lot of my job. Out of all places, there? Really?!?!" Empress yells out the question while shaking her head. She continues, "I hope and pray all of my co-workers are okay. What if we were hit, baby??? I mean, we were just innocent bystanders."

I quietly drive with no answers because I know I am

the cause of this shootout.

If Empress only knew the shooting took place to protect her. Tonight, is the first time I have ever felt fear, and it is because I want to keep the love of my life safe from any danger. I can never tell her I am behind all this, especially if people have lost their lives. I do not believe she would forgive me. See, Empress values the lives of strangers. Me? Well, I hold no value of life. If I don't love you, then I can give two fucks whether you live or die.

Snapping out of my train of thoughts, I realize Empress is crying and my heart sinks because I can't feel her pain nor can I take it away.

I grip her hand and kiss it. "Baby, don't cry. Everything will be ok," I reassuringly say.

"I'm sorry for screaming at you, baby. But I just can't stop thinking. What if we would have been killed? What if I would have lost you?" She weeps.

"That's not gonna happen, baby," I say as I pull her face in for a kiss.

For a minute, everything seems to be ideal as we tightly hold one another's hand as I cruise down the street headed to her house. Our eyes focus on the non-busy street as we tune out the outside noise. Together, we feel safe and comfortable. No worries. No fears. If only for a little while.

Out of nowhere, Empress let's go of my hand and says, "But, I can feel it in my spirit that someone died, baby. Doesn't that bother you???"

I grow quiet before answering.

"Baby, I've grown to only worry about myself and the people I love. I can't show any emotions to people whom I don't know," I explain.

With my left hand gripping the steering wheel, I wipe the tears from her eyes with my right thumb as I continue, "You might say it's cold, but I look at it like this, if I were to die today, who would actually care enough to go to my funeral? I believe you can answer that due to how many people have slandered my name, even though they have never even held a two-minute conversation with me."

As we pull into her driveway, Empress looks emotionally distressed and exhausted.

"Baby, I hate that you feel that way. But, it would shock you how many people would mourn your death because I would die myself if I were to lose you," she sorrowfully responds. "You are a good man and everything people say about you does not ring true because I have never seen you do any of the things they say you do. I don't listen to what people say and I never will."

"I love you, Empress. Just know I will always protect, comfort, and give you my all until my last breath and even in the afterlife. Thank you."

"I love you too, baby. But, why are you telling me thank you?"

"Thank you for being you," I say, ending the night kissing her soft lips.

As I watch Empress walk inside her duplex and close the door behind her, I dial Larosa's phone.

He picks up after the first ring. "What's good, FAM?" He asks.

"Everything is good," I respond.

"That's the business," Larosa says, pleased to hear my response.

"I will head in your direction tomorrow because I'm headed home to rest," I inform him.

"I'll be here," he tells me.

"Love, Family."

"Never Enough."

Click.

Chapter Thirty-Seven

~ EMPRESS ~

ACROSS THE STREET, A CAR MISFIRES AND IT causes me to flinch as I peek out of my bedroom window to see exactly where the noise is. I skipped school today because I did not feel like dealing with questions and stares. More than that though, I do not feel safe. I feel so helpless. I know the shooting was not anything I could anticipate or prevent. Still, I feel defenseless.

I could barely sleep last night and when I finally began to dream, it quickly turned into a nightmare. I woke up in a cold sweat feeling like my dream of masked invaders entering Krystal's and taking all my co-workers hostage was real, but the most frightening thing is… some aspects were true.

"Empress!!!" Alexis and Chante say in unison as they burst through my bedroom door, never more relieved to see me.

"Heeey! What are you girls doing out here???" I say as I run to give them a hug.

"Krystal's was trending last night on Twitter," Chante says worried.

"Yeah and we were callin' your phone last night, but no answer. Of course, we are worried," Alexis explains.

"Everybody at school is," Chante adds. "We had to come and see how our girl is lookin'."

"Not too hot," I half-jokingly say as I tighten my comfortable pink robe which I have had on for most of the day.

"There's a rumor goin' around school that you got shot," Chante says as they take a seat on my bed.

"What?" I question, becoming upset.

"Yeah, girl. People are sayin' all types of wild things," Chante rambles.

"Chante!" Alexis interjects, seeing I am in no mood to talk about dumb hearsay. "How are you, Empress?"

My emotions get the best of me as I flashback to the previous night, causing my eyes to fill up with tears.

"It was so... so... unbelievable," I say, grasping for words.

I take a moment to gather my thoughts and blow my nose. I cry as though I have a never-ending flow of tears. Emotional agony flows out of every pore of my body. Being in my presence causes Chante and Alexis to cry a little too.

"The shots were soooooo loud," I explain.

"How did you keep yourself from not getting hit?" Chante asks.

Barely able to get the words out, I stutter, "I - I - I threw myself onto the floor....in a corner. I am truly blessed."

I place my hands over my eyes because the memories of the crime scene are just too much for my mind. The girls begin to rub my back to try to soothe and console me.

"I'm so thankful Renardo was there and he brought me to safety," I say as my tears dry up.

"Hold up, did you say Renardo?" Alexis asks. "What

was he doing there? OMG! This little crush you had has gone too far. Are you two always together?"

"What?" I ask, puzzled by Alexis's comment.

"Yeah, Empress," Chante chimes in without giving Alexis a chance to answer. "We think you are spending too much time with him. Like you don't even spend time with us anymore. Are you seriously thinkin' of bringing him to the Lady of Brook soiree?"

"Ugh!! I scream. "Don't start this shit. I get so tired of you bitches tryin' to down my man. You have never even met him, so what is the reason for all the hate? Yes, he is my date for the Lady of Brook soiree. Who the fuck is yours?"

"Empress! We just sayin' –" Chante explains.

"Naw," I angrily cut her off. "I'm not going to let you all continue to bash a person that I happen to love dearly. From jump, y'a'll have been jealous haters sayin' slick shit. Just because he comes from Rockdale does not make him a bad person or less than the fuck boys at Brook. He has treated me with more respect and has loved me better than any nigga in fucking boujee ass Brook."

"Look, Empress, we didn't come here to raise your blood pressure," Alexis says. "We came to make sure that you are okay."

"No, y'all came here to talk shit about my man," I say as I show them to the door. "I am not a victim. I'm strong and I don't need y'all sympathy. Do yourselves a favor and get the fuck out my house."

"Empress, why you gotta act like that?" Alexis asks.

"I'm not actin' no way. Just leave," I instruct them.

"Shit, you don't have to tell me twice," Chante says as she walks out the front door with an attitude.

I gladly shut the door behind them.

~ NARD ~

ENTERING BLACK'S FINISHED BASEMENT, which his wife calls his rustic man cave, he is the first person I see sitting at the large mini-bar. Congo and Larosa are in the game area playing Madden on the PS4. An indescribable feeling of gratitude comes over me because I feel as though I owe these brothers greatly. I will always be there for them by any means. When I had no one, they were there for me. That is why the bond we share is unbreakable. I smile as I step toward the bar to shake hands and embrace Black. Larosa and Congo pause the game and join us at the bar where I shake their hands and embrace them too.

"I want to thank y'all brothers for the support last night. I'm forever grateful," I genuinely say to them.

After they did their thing last night, Black and Larosa split up and hopped in two separate cars where they met later at the designated spot. Congo was a getaway driver.

"What's understood don't have to be explained. You know it's nothing but love, FAM," Black replies.

"My nigga, I know you would've done the same thing for us. That's why we didn't hesitate," Larosa adds.

"Fuckin' right," I respond with all seriousness.

"No one is bigger than the Mob. These niggas need to instill that shit in their mind," Congo affirms.

"Soon they will see. Once we wipeout Jaz and his crew from the city," Larosa proclaims.

"Alrite, let's move forward. What happened last night stays there. Understood?" Black insists.

"Understood," we all answer in unison.

"Now, we have a small problem other than the Jaz incident," Black continues. "I've inquired some information concerning that shootin' last night, and it seems like we had a survivor... Heard's woman. But she's in a coma and labeled critical condition, so if she ever comes out of that coma, we all know what needs to be done."

Me and Larosa both nod to confirm that we understand what Black means.

The more I think about the situation, I feel that it is only right for me to get my hands dirty.

"FAM, if she is ever released from the hospital, I will deal with her myself," I vow.

"Handle that business. No slip-ups because she can be our downfall," Black sternly says as he looks directly into my eyes.

"Trust me, FAM, I don't miss," I confidently tell Black.

"Wat about Jaz and his crew???" Congo asks Black.

"We've got brothers lookin' for them. It seems like they've gone into hidin' because we've had no luck in finding them," Black replies. "But they will be found. Y'all just stay on point."

"Already," I reply.

At this moment, my phone rings. When I look at the screen, it is none other than my baby, Empress.

"Pardon me, Family. Let me take this call."

"Handle your business," Larosa says as everybody nods as I step outside onto Black's deck.

"Hey, baby doll. I hope you are feeling better today," I say with warmth and care.

"Um...better...I guess...I just wish you were here," she says, still sounding a little somber.

"After I finish handlin' this business, I can stop by and get you out the house to help soothe your mind from what happened last night. Would you like that?" I ask, wanting to uplift her spirit.

"I would love that baby," she says in a joyous tone. "Where are you planning to take me?"

"It's a surprise, baby. But, I believe I know just the place."

"Baaaaaby, now you know I hate surprises."

"I do too, baby But, guess what?" I ask with a smile.

"What?" She eagerly responds.

"I'm not telling you," I say with a laugh. "So just go ahead and get sexy for me, which will take no effort because you stay stunnin' and beautiful even on your worst days, which I don't think you ever have."

I can tell Empress is blushing through the phone, as she says, "Awwwwww baaaaby, OK. Only for you. I love you."

"I love you more, baby," I reply.

"No, you don't," she playfully teases.

"If you only knew, baby. I will see you in an hour," I say before I blow her a kiss through the phone.

"OK, baby," she replies as she blows a kiss back.

As I step back inside the house, my mind wanders back to last night, to an issue that needs to be addressed.

"Say, y'all, I've got sumthin to tell y'all that's been botherin' me all night," I announce to the brothers.

"What is it, bruh?" Larosa asks with concern.

"Right before the shootin,' Danielle called me to let me know that Heard was comin' after me at Krystal's and I'm wonderin' how the hell did she know that shit. As soon as she told me, less than a minute later guns were fired. I know I never called her and even if one of y'all called her, none of us knew for sure that Heard's woman called him. So, how was Danielle so sure that he was comin'?" I ask everyone.

"Say what?!?!?!" Larosa explodes. "Call her ass right

now and tell her she needs to get here now!!!"

"Calm down, Larosa," Black calmly states as mumbles of speculation fill the room. "Give the sister an opportunity to give us all a reasonable explanation before we start jumpin' to conclusions."

"Black's right. So, call her Nard and tell her to meet us here, but don't tell her why," Congo suggests.

Hearing Black and Congo's advice, I agree it is only fair because that is her right as a sister. *I just pray she has a reasonable explanation.*

Danielle finally answers on the sixth ring. "Thank God you are OK!" She wails into the phone.

She seems to walk away from all the loud noise that surrounds her to a much quieter space.

"Where the hell have you been?" She asks. "You had me worried. I called your phone all last night."

"I was at home, but I had my phone off because I needed some rest," I dryly respond.

"Wat happened last night? Are you OK? All I heard was shootin' and then the call disconnected," Danielle asks as I become even more skeptical.

"We will discuss that later. I need you to get to Black's spot as soon as possible."

"OK, I will be there in 30 minutes."

"We will see you then."

CHAPTER THIRTY-EIGHT

~ EMPRESS ~

I LOOK OUT MY BEDROOM WINDOW WITH MY eyes focused on a street I have no interest in. Cars pass by, but there is only one car that I care about and it hasn't appeared yet. Who was that woman Renardo was making eye contact with last night? The thought of Renardo with another girl makes me want to vomit.

Where is he anyways? He is an hour late, and he hasn't been answering my calls. He is really pushing me to the breaking point of my patience. I'm so torn right now because I want to believe the best, but his actions are showing me otherwise.

He drew me in with his genuine sweetness. I miss him all the time, especially when we are apart... especially right now. But right now, he has turned my mind into its own prison with thoughts of the worst in full bloom. My mind keeps replaying our last moments together before the shooting took place. What I saw...his reaction...what he said.

I re-read sweet texts that he sent me in the past to try to convince myself that Renardo couldn't possibly be interested in another girl. The stroll down memory lane is not working. I just keep thinking about the way he was looking at her and the way she was looking at him. They definitely know each other and I want answers.

~ NARD ~

AS DANIELLE STEPS INTO BLACK'S BASEMENT, she is shocked to see so many people. Other brothers and sisters were called in to hear Danielle's explanation of last night

"Danielle, come in and take a seat," I instruct her as I take the floor.

The surprised look on her face says it all. She is probably wonderin' wat the fuck is this all about and why didn't I tell her all these brothers and sisters would be present.

"Danielle, me and a few other brothers have a question for you about last night," I state.

At once, she frowns with confusion but remains silent.

"How did you know Heard was comin' for me at Krystal's? Now, please give us all a reasonable explanation of how that was possible."

"Really, Nard???? Really??? Are you really trying to question my loyalty or better yet slander my integrity?" She questions.

Within an instant, Danielle is about to snap but she catches herself due to everyone being present. With her voice cracking, she continues, "Never in my life would I betray you or anyone else who stands on the same principles and teachings I do. For you out of all people to question me, hurts deep. But, if an explanation is what you want then that's what you'll get."

Danielle explains the previous night's events which make me feel like shit. She is right. I am wrong to ever question her

loyalty after everything we have been through.

As she tells her story, she looks directly at me as though she wants me to feel her pain. *If this is her intentions, the plan is workin' because I feel awful. I cannot bear to look at her as she concludes her story. I want to step out the room, but I can't. I called this meeting, so I have to be present.*

Suddenly, Danielle takes a seat in a tan armchair.

I would have never known she was finished because I tuned everything out. I knew she was tellin' the truth. Black brought me back to the present moment when he stood to speak.

"Well, it seems as though this sister's story sounds valid. What do you think, Nard? Black asks.

"I agree and I also apologize for ever questioning you, Danielle. Sincerely, please forgive me," I say, trying to connect eyes with Danielle even though her eyes evade mines.

Disregarding my apology, she stands up to give one last look at everyone in the room, saving me for last. "I would never have thought in million years I would be questioned after all I've done and given to you all," she says slowly with a sense of defeat.

No one stops her as she walks towards the door because every member in the room feels guilty.

Chapter Thirty-Nine

~ NARD ~

"DAMN, I KNOW MY BABY IS GOIN' TO BE MAD at me," I say to myself as I am driving to Empress' house.

One hour has turned into two and a half, and I have 6 missed calls and 3 text messages from her. I'm preppin' in my mind what I will say to her because knowin' her the way that I do, I just know the first words out of her mouth will be, 'Renardo, where the hell have you been?' I just hope she is fully dressed and ready to go once I get there.

Knock.

Knock.

Knock.

When the door opens, it takes a minute for me to look down because no one is in my line of vision. Two, tiny adorable girls stare up at me. They are Empress' little sister's, Gabi and Cinnamon.

"Hey, Nard!" They try to say in unison, but Cinnamon trails behind.

"Hey, girls! Why did y'all open the door without asking who is it?" I ask, concerned about their safety.

"Empress told me to get it," Gabi answers.

"Oh, okay. But since y'all are both tiny and cute, y'all

better use the peephole next time," I suggest.

"Okay," Gabi says as I step into the duplex. "Thanks again for the gift card!" She adds with enthusiasm.

"If you keep makin' good grades, then I'll buy you some more gift cards," I say as I take a seat at the circular family table in the kitchen.

"Yay!" Gabi responds happily.

"Do you want a hot wing?" She asks.

"No, I'm good. But thank you," I respond.

I have never seen a skinny little kid who loves hot wings as much as Gabi.

"Can you girls tell Empress that I am waitin' for her?"

"Okay!" They say as they race each other up the stairs to Empress' room.

Cinnamon drops her American Girl Doll and ends up losing the race.

"That doll too expensive to be droppin', Cinnamon," I playfully yell.

I have never seen a doll that was $150. I thought the doll at least talked, but Empress told me it doesn't. It's just a very exclusive doll.

A few minutes pass before Empress comes down the steps lookin' gorgeous as ever. Even when she dresses casual, she still looks sexy as fuck. Today she has on distressed jeans, a Beyoncé tour t-shirt, which clings to her body, and a flannel shirt wrapped around her waist with laced up black Doc Martens.

Standing on the last step with her hands on her hips and with so much attitude she says, "So, you've been waiting on me, huh?"

Ignoring Empress' attitude, I jump out of my seat and hug her. "Baby, you look so good," I say stepping back and admiring her.

"Renardo, you're three hours late and you have

answered none of my -"

"Let's not get into this now, baby," I say grabbing her face and drawing her into a kiss.

I hope this will prevent any potential argument, but I notice she is not into the kiss. Her eyes are open, her head is straight, and she's not standing on her tippy toes like she normally does.

Still holding her face, I step back and look directly into her eyes.

"My baby doesn't want to give me a kiss?" I ask.

Empress looks at me with a cold expression and rolls her eyes as she walks out the house to go to my car.

I put my hands over my eyes as I exhale.

I know I have got to tell her what is going on. I just don't know how.

~ EMPRESS ~

I   AM SO PISSED WITH RENARDO THAT I CAN'T even think straight. Does he seriously think a kiss will make everything better? The more he talks, the angrier I become. He shows up late to our date, and he has not been answering my calls and he thinks I'm just supposed to go along with the flow? SMH.

"Renardo, where the hell are you taking me, anyway?" I ask, annoyed by him.

"Whoa, chill baby," he says, taken by surprise with my tone. "It's a surprise. Plus, you know I don't like it when you say my name like that. I'm, Baby."

Lightly rubbing his right hand on my thigh, he insists that I call him "baby".

His masculine touch sends an instant shock of electricity through my spine. The hot moisture between my legs is distracting. It is as though his fingers have short- circuited my mind. I'm under his spell and I think I am in love again.

I just know he isn't cheating on me. Yet, the thought of him and that woman at Krystal's hovers over me like a halo. To prevent problems, as Renardo always says, I'm just going to suppress the thought and stop being defensive. I will apologize for acting mean and let this go.

As I open my mouth to offer a sincere apology, Renardo's phone begins to vibrate. Taking his eyes off the road to see who it is, he ignores the calls.

Oh, hell no! I wonder who is calling or texting him. Is it that woman from Krystal's? Ugh, I don't know. I am going to try to put it out of mind because I do not want to ruin our date. But, I have to let Renardo know he is not slick and I see what is going on. Fuck it! I'm going to let him have it.

"So, you're ignoring her calls now?" I condescendingly ask, assuming it is the woman from Krystal's.

"Huh?" Renardo says, sounding clueless.

"You heard what I said. What the hell is going on?"

"Nothin's goin' on, baby," he calmly replies.

"It does not seem like nothin'," I retort.

"It's nothing baby," he says with a hint of frustration.

"It's nothing baby," I mock him in a high-pitched voice. Pounding my hand on the dashboard, I say, "I'll be the judge of that."

"Calm down, baby. Got Damn!" He says as he swerves into a shopping center parking lot.

"No! I'm not going to calm down. First, you were starin' the bitch down at Krystal's. Now she's calling your phone?!?!""You must think I'm a fuckin' idiot!?!?" I say as I open the passenger door. "All I've ever asked for is total honesty. If you want to get sumthin goin' with that bitch just let me know -"

"I don't even know that girl!" He says, cutting me off.

"Could've fooled me!" I yell, enraged. "I saw how you were lookin' at her! You don't know her, huh? So, what...you wanna fuck her?!?!?"

"I'm not tryin' to go thru this shit!" He yells as I slam the door.

Looking straight ahead at him as the bright lights from the car blind my eyes, I scream loud enough so he can hear me from outside, "You're free to do what the FUCK you want! I'm gone!"

"Baby! Baaaaaaby!!! Bring yo muthafuckin' ass back here!" Renardo yells as he rolls down his window and I walk off.

"Baby! Please come back," Renardo yells as one last plea.

"For what?!?!" I yell stopping dead in my tracks.

Taking a few steps forward, Renardo looks down as he runs his fingers through his dreads and says in the smallest voice, "I need you, baby. Please come back. Please."

With tears in my eyes, my heart cannot help but warm to him. I've seen him vulnerable before, but not in this way. This is different. Instead of seeing my enemy, I see the fragile soul that I fell in love with.

I walk back towards his loving arms that are waiting for me.

~ NARD ~

"FIRST OFF, BABY, I PROMISE YOU THAT I HAVE been faithful to you and you're the only woman I'm interested in," I say while kissing her forehead and hugging her warm, slim body which is comforting to the touch. "It's some things I've been keepin' from you."

As a slight, cool spring wind moves between us, I clear my throat. I prepare myself for what may be one of the most difficult moments of my life. For tonight could determine if I lose the love of my life. *I know I have to tell Empress some details, but I am struggling because I don't know how much I should reveal. Knowing Empress, she will have questions, concerns, and worries. I'm afraid of what her reaction will be, which is why I have been dreading this day since the night of the incident. Yet, I can no longer avoid the issue just like I cannot ignore the sped up beating of my heart as it pounds heavily.*

"Baby," I say as I let out a slow, controlled breath. "I know and understand that you have been having doubts about our relationship due to what you saw at Krystal's the other night."

Empress gives me one of those "you damn right" looks, yet she gives me enough respect to remain quiet and allow me to speak. Looking into her eyes, I hope to rekindle the warmness that those beautiful eyes normally generate towards me, but right now nothing can break her icy glare.

"Empress," I continue. "This is God's honest truth. I don't know that woman personally and I don't have nothin' goin' on with her."

"Then why the hell was y'all eyeing each other down???" Empress questions with a spark of anger.

Instinctively, I know Empress is goin' to fire so many questions at me about this woman. To prevent further problems and to prevent Empress from sayin' something she may regret, I hold one hand up with the gesture for her to slow down and just listen. Once I get her full attention, I continue, "That woman was the wife of someone I had bad dealings with and she knows her husband is lookin' for me. That is why we were starin' at each other."

Empress stares directly into my eyes, trying to find any sign of a lie. Through her icy glare, I hope she sees this is the truth. After a moment of her eyes interrogating mine, she nods slowly and says, "OK baby, I believe you. But, I have one more question and I want you to be honest."

"What is it, baby?" I ask, relieved that she believes me. "You can ask me anything. But, know it's certain things I don't want you to ever get exposed to."

"What do you mean by that, Renardo?" Empress questions with irritation.

"I mean…there are some things I believe should be left unsaid to save the face of the person you love or care for."

"Baby, you have lost me. Can you elaborate?" She responds, looking confused.

Knowing her next question, I cannot allow her to ask it because I will have to lie in order to save my integrity and dignity on what I stand on. But, maybe she will understand what I'm about to tell her.

"Baby, sometimes knowing the truth about things can change the outlook on how you see the man you love. Like I've told you before, I've done some bad shit in my lifetime and I'm not proud of a lot of things. Therefore, to save face with you, I'd rather not go into details of my past or things I may be involved in. Dealin' with me, you must love the good and bad about me, but I promise I will always keep you happy."

Looking as if she is in deep thought, Empress sits quietly on the hood of my Monte Carlo SS. God, I hope she doesn't ask this damn question because it will hurt like hell to lie to her.

"It's funny you say that I need to love the good and bad about you," Empress says with a slight grin, breaking her silence.

"Why do you say that?" I ask, curious to know the reason for her statement.

"Because that is something my mom taught me. She said when I fall in love I would have to love the good and bad about the man because no one is perfect."

"Oh, yeah?" I say, pleased and surprised by her answer. "Well, your mother is a very smart woman," I say with a chuckle, trying to ease the tension in the air.

"I want you to make one promise," Empress says.

"What is that baby?"

"One day can you enlighten me on everything that you are into?"

"Baby, that will take time. I just can't make that promise," I reply with an exaggerated sigh.

"Renardo, I'm for you, not against you. Remember that. But, I can't stay in the blind forever," she says with her eyes wandering around everything except me.

I hate for Empress to feel as though I am hiding things from her or being dishonest. I wish I could tell her, but I just can't right now. But, I need her trust and I need to know that she loves me.

"That's Understandable, baby. Just know I can't promise you no time soon," I state pulling her into my arms.

"OK, that's all I ask. I love you."

"I love you, too," I say before kissing her sweet, soft lips I fell in love with.

CHAPTER FORTY

~ EMPRESS ~

AS WE PULL UP TO THE HIGH MUSEUM OF ART, Renardo notices the shock register on my face before I can hide it. A sly grin comes across his face.

"Aw, baby," I respond with my eyes saying so much more. "I love you."

"I love you and I love putting a smile on your face. Now let's hurry. I think the show has already started," he says, planting a sweet kiss on my face.

I was totally not expecting our date to be here. Renardo is full of surprises and that is one thing I love about him. Not to mention, he knows nothing about art and he thinks it is boring. But for me, he's willingly here because he knows this makes me happy.

"Baby, take a picture of me in front of the recreation of Warhol's *Big Electric Chair*," I eagerly say since tonight's exhibition centers on famous artworks re-created by local artist.

I take at least five pictures with different poses because I am always unhappy with the first few shots. After settling on a good shot, we make our way through the museum holding hands. Our fingers intertwine as though they intend to stay this way permanently as we walk around the museum. I'm not really sure where Renardo's head is, but he does a good job of amusing me as I admire the artworks. There is a buzz of excited talk throughout the museum. Everyone here is enjoying the experience, including me.

"Oh wow, baby. This is a great imitation of Van Gogh's *The Starry Night*. He was a post-impressionist painter," I enthusiastically say. "Don't you just love how the painting is brimming with whirling clouds, shining stars, and a bright crescent moon?"

"You can see all of that from this?" Renardo confusingly says with a chuckle as he points to the painting.

"Yeah, don't you?" I innocently ask.

"Hell naw," he says with a chuckle. "I just see a bunch of colors in a swirl."

"Baby, you've got to learn to appreciate art," I say as he wraps his arms around my waist.

"Well, I appreciate one fine art piece."

"Oh, yeah? And just what is the name of that art piece?" I say stunned.

"It's a real fine masterpiece and only God Himself could have created it."

"Hmmm…an ancient art piece…I wonder what art piece you are referencing."

"It's not ancient," he says with his arms still wrapped around my waist. "In fact, it's a modern piece that is right here in this museum."

"What's the name of the piece?" I ask, curious to see this great artwork Renardo is alluding to.

"Empress Cunningham," he says with a huge grin on his face as he gives me a kiss on the cheek.

"That was sooo corny, but sweet," I say, nearly blushing. "Thank you, baby, for taking my mind off what happened last night."

"You deserve it, baby," he says. "I don't ever want to see you crying like you were last night. Anything I can do to make you happy, I will. These things are just paint on canvases. You're the one who makes tonight special."

"I'm sorry baby for assuming the worst," I say as we gaze into each other eyes.

"No need to apologize, baby," he says. "It's my fault we're going through this. I shouldn't have hidden that from you."

"No more secrets?" I ask with a smile.

"No more secrets," he agrees with a smile.

Chapter Forty-One

~ EMPRESS ~

"BABY, ARE YOU SURE YOUR MOTHER WILL not trip if you stay over tonight?" Renardo yells from his couch as I dry off from taking a shower.

"Of course not!" I yell back continuing to dry myself off.

"So, you're telling me that your mother knows you're here with me?" He asks, muting the TV while flipping through the channels.

"Of course, not!" I reply as I wrap the towel around my body. "I told her I was spending the night at Chante's."

We both laugh as I make my way to the couch.

"I love you, Booskie," he says, looking into my eyes.

"I love you, Booskie Wooskie," I say with a smile, giving him a pleasurable kiss on the lips like he knew I would. With my lips, I feel his mouth stretching wider than it should, battling between a broad grin and kiss. I've never kissed a better kisser than Renardo. Each day, our kisses seem to get better and better and grow more passionate. He's the only man on Earth for me. The only one who can take my breath away.

"Alrite, you can't call me that in public," Renardo says with a chuckle.

Over the past couple of months, Renardo and I have adopted calling each other these pet names. Where did Renardo get the name Booskie? I have no idea. But there was something organic and sweet about it the first time he called me 'Booskie'. We were talkin' outside, on a sunny afternoon and he looked me directly in the eyes and blurted it out. It was as though my name alone was not enough to express what he felt. As they say, serendipity is the essence of love. For the sake of cutesy and rhyme, I added 'Wooskie' to the term of endearment.

"Let's pick a movie to watch, baby," Renardo says hitting the Netflix button on the remote. "After going to the museum and seeing all that soft shit, I need to see some action."

"Yeah, yeah, yeah," I say cuddling up next to him.

Ha! Action. I'm ready to see some action too, but just a different kind. I have only had sex one time before, so my nerves are through the roof. I know before meeting me, Renardo fucked his share of girls, but he has been patiently waiting for me.

What if I'm awkward? What if I don't know what I'm doing? What if my anxiety gets the best of me, and I freak out? What if I make a complete fool of myself? Will Renardo still love me tomorrow? Did I seriously just ask myself that question? Of course, he will always love me. I can't psyche myself out. After six months, Renardo loves me, and most importantly, he fully respects me. There is no man more deserving of my body than him.

There was so much pressure for my first time to be special, but it was really uncomfortable to say the least. I was scared as hell. I felt like having sex was something that I had to do, mainly because I was listenin' to my friends. Being the only girl in the squad carrying a v-card was not cool. I couldn't graduate high school as a virgin.

As a freshman, I had made the choice to wait until I met the right boy, but over time, it felt like that would never happen. I was embarrassed because I was a seventeen-year-old virgin. I did not really care for the guy who was my boyfriend, but I felt pressured. It hurt like hell even though it only lasted a few minutes. There was no love involved. It was terrible, and I'm not even sure if he popped my cherry. My moral principles had waived, which was a bad choice on my end. Virginity is sacred. Even if all my friends had lost theirs, I should have waited for the right person. I don't want my body used as a vessel or receptacle for someone to relieve their hormones and stress. YUCK! I want to know the man before deciding if I want to know his manhood.

Finally, in Renardo, I have found someone I love and care about. I only want to share my body with him because I know when we make love it will be another expression of how deep our love for one another goes. I know Renardo will be tender and gentle. Just thinking about the feel of his rough hands against my soft skin gets me good and moist.

"You know, I love being here with you," I say to Renardo as he reads a movie description on the Netflix menu. "I feel so good and safe with you. I can't even describe it."

"I feel the same way too, baby," he says in the most romantic voice ever as his eyes instantly meet mine. "I promise you that you will always be safe with me."

"I love you sooo much, baby," I say gazing into his mysterious dark eyes.

"I love you more," he says lost in my gaze.

"Never in a million years did I think I would meet someone like you," I say with tears of joy filling my eyes. "I never imagined that I would get swept off my feet and fall in love in this way. It's like everything is happening organically, yet instantly. The first time I saw you, I knew you were something special. It was just so natural and easy."

"I didn't think you liked me at first," he says with a smile. "I couldn't figure you out."

"You didn't think I liked you?" I repeat with a smile. "Here I am in love with you and you don't even know the half of it. Baby, I've been crazy about you since the first time I spotted you at Burger King."

"Na, I don't believe it," he says with a chuckle.

"If you only knew," I say shaking my head. "I had the biggest crush on you. After seeing you for the first time I ran back to Krystal's and told anyone that would listen that I had seen the finest man in life and I had to get to know him."

"You're jokin'," Renardo say with a smirk, flattered by my revelation.

"I promise you, I'm not," I say blushing with a giggle. "I absolutely embarrassed myself going on and on about you - the boy from Burger King. I think it was your dark eyes and smile that did it for me."

"Well, you know I only smile when I'm with you," Renardo says as I run my fingers through his dreads.

"You have no idea what you do to me."

"It only balances the power that you hold over me," he says with the cutest smile. "I need you so much."

"I need you, too," I say, my lips meeting his. "Your eyes are…so dark…so mysterious…so sexy," I add while stroking his gorgeous face.

"You are so beautiful," Renardo says as he delicately kisses my forehead.

"Wouldn't you like to take a closer look?"

Renardo nearly does a double take, as he questions, "Are you sure, baby?" His eyes mixed with skepticism and arousal.

With lust in my eyes and love in my heart, I nod to indicate yes. My towel is no hindrance once Renardo undoes the knot. His eyes flicker up and down as he observes me. There's something about him that lights me up from the inside. There's something about me that melts his tough, hard body exterior. I have never wanted anyone more in my life. His dark eyes devour my body making my skin tingle. I love kissing him deeply as my tongue explodes into his mouth. He lets out a soft, gruff noise as his hands roam my body, cupping my breast and caressing my ass.

With my hand between our bodies, I cannot help but touch his dick. I thrust my right hand down his Nike basketball shorts and down into his Ralph Lauren boxer briefs.

Drawing in a deep breath, his head falls back.

"Damn, baby," he slowly says.

Gently, I touch the side of his face with my left hand, kissing him ever so lightly.

Our eyes never lose focus of each other as my right-hand trails across his back and around his hip. I can feel that his erection has raised quite a tent in his Ralph Lauren boxer briefs. I stare in admiration of the length and width of his dick as he comes out of them. Feeling his dick get hard through his clothes differs greatly from seeing his manhood full on. It's amazing how his dick is bobbing and growing before my eyes. It will be a lot to handle, but I am wet, ripe, and ready.

"You're so sexy, baby," I say licking my lips.

"This is your dick, baby," he says with eyes of desire as he holds his dick in his hand.

As he takes me in, everything changes. I feel his bare chest against my plump breast. My pussy is as warm and as wet as it has ever been. My tongue loves the feel of his six pack as I slowly tickle his toned torso. Renardo exhales as I stimulate his dick by jerking my hand slowly, up and down. His dick continues to grow and expand in my hand by the second.

"Mmmmm…baby that feels so good!" I whisper as his tongue teases my hardened nipples.

Seeing how much I like this and feeling the juices of my pussy flow, Renardo sucks on each nipple like a hungry baby while nipping at them with his teeth.

"Damn!" I moan as my body bucks.

Grabbing my face, he kisses me as though he will suffocate without me. Quite simply, we are each other's air supply. My tongue gently caresses his lips as I kiss him sweetly. He wastes no time slipping in his tongue. Our tongues wrestle as the passion between us brews. We pause every so often to intake air.

With a naughty grin, I carefully make a circle with my thumb and forefinger, sliding it down his shaft with a feather like touch. My other hand gently clutches his balls.

"You like that, baby?" I ask as a large drop of clear liquid materializes on the tip of his dick.

Renardo replies with a series of slow and steady nods. I smear the leaking fluid around his dick as if it is a finger painting. My hand shuffling up and down his dick seems to hypnotize him. No doubt he is turned on.

Lightly, he rubs his hand across my pussy lips and feels the dampness that the conditioned response my body has for his generates. His fingers glisten with my moisture.

"Play with your pussy with your other hand and spread it around, baby," he says ever so sexy.

I do just that as I continue to stroke his dick with my hand. I can feel the pressure building and a need to release. Looking directly into my eyes, Renardo lets out some sort of primal sound and shoots a long, warm, unbroken ribbon of cum across the room. I can't believe how much cum he shoots out. Some even gets on my hand. Nothing can describe the feeling of knowing that I can cause his body to react this way. It is exquisite. I can't believe he is still hard!

"Wow!" I say with a huge grin.

I follow his lead to the bedroom, with my fingers laced between his. This moment is finally happening. I can't believe it! I have been in his bedroom countless times, but never for this reason. I never knew my fingers could be so delicate. It feels like I am holding the finest threads of gold.

Laying me on my back, Renardo slowly climbs down next to me, approaching me like a predator stalking its prey. His gorgeous face stares at me intensely, making my body feel as though I'm on fire. My pussy is as wetter than it was the very first day I saw his gorgeous face.

Pinning my hands over my head, he bites my neck which causes a height of undiscovered pleasure. The sensation is different than what I'm used to. I like it ALOT.

Wanting to give him full access, I spread my legs wider, my pussy throbbing for more of Renardo. He rubs my bald, wet pussy with his three fingers. He's making me all juicy and dizzy with arousal.

"I want to taste you," he says with his eyes full of want and passion as he stares at my glistening pussy.

"I'll be gentle," he whispers so softly, looking me square in the eyes. His face travels up to my mouth to plant one long French kiss. After our tongues unbind, his tongue makes a trail from my lips to my flat stomach before he circles my belly button in a teasingly fashion. I quiver out of nervousness.

"It's okay, baby," he stops and says. "Let it all out."

I hadn't realized that I was holding my breath, censoring myself. He repeats circling my belly button with his tongue four more times, making me moan, "Oooooo…baby." Each time my pitch rises higher than the last, as I fully enjoy the man I love exploration of my body.

My pussy drips as he makes his way back to my neck and sinks his fangs in, sending me into orbit.

"Bite me again, baby. Bite me!" I scream in delight.

He bites me alrite, but not in the place that I want. Instead, he clamps down on my stiff brown nipple. "Baaaaaby," I cry out as both pain and pleasure move throughout every nerve of my body. Releasing the clamp, his tongue soothes the scorching pain. Gently sucking each nipple, he reaches down and feels the heat stemming from my pussy.

Kissing my inner thighs ever so lightly, he moves closer to the warmth he has waited an eternity to taste. Slowly, gently, he kisses and licks around my pussy. I love the way he takes his time to explore…never rushing and savoring all my juices along the way. My pussy lips yield to his touch, moistening, opening.

Uncontrollable moans escape my mouth, increasing his passion as his tongue flicks across my clit in circles. My hips sway which causes Renardo to grin devilishly. The thrilling sensation surprises me as it spreads from my head to the tip of my toes.

Putting his hands around my thighs and onto my stomach, he slides his tongue from the start of my ass crack all the way up to my clit. Even more love juice flows from my pussy. His tongue teases my tight hole until my legs shake. Crave fills his eyes as he licks up every bit of my sweetness.

"Mmmmmm…Fuck! Don't stop, baby," I moan out along with other obscenities, completely engulfed in his pleasure.

My body squirms and my breathing increases as he gently sucks on my clit. The feel of Renardo's wet, stiff tongue inside of me is possibly the best thing I have ever felt. Louder and louder my moans become as his tongue picks up momentum.

My mind races with thoughts of gratification while my heart pounds as he buries his head deep in my pussy. His saliva covered tongue cuddles my wet, juicy pussy as though it is a paint brush and my pussy is a canvas.

He places his hands on my hips to hold me still and to keep me from moving away. I can't help tossing and turning as the mounting pressure builds up inside me. It feels as though I am going to explode from erotic euphoria. Yet, it feels so foreign – too good to be true, so I wiggle to free myself from the ecstasy. Everything seems too much for me to handle. But, damn, it feels so fuckin' good. Deep down I want more. He has created a need in me that only he can satisfy. I can't resist. I want all that he has to give me.

Lightly I push Renardo's head inward as a signal for more direct pressure on my clit.

"Don't stop, baby…Don't stop, baby," I whisper as he comes up for air.

"I gotta breathe, baby," he says with a chuckle.

He inserts two of his fingers in my dripping wet pussy while his other hand plays with my breast, causing my nipples to become rock hard. I can hear the moist sound of his fingers quickly coming in and out of my pussy as my breath heightens.

The more he sucks on my clit while fingering my pussy, the more my body craves to cum. Fallon told me that you're not supposed to hold your breath when having an orgasm - which I think I am having for the first time, so I breathe out. His fingers churn my insides into butter and his tongue dances across my sensitive clit. I lock my knees together and squeeze his face between my thighs. The speed of me having an intense orgasm is an inevitable.

"I...I-" I try to speak to tell him how good it feels and that I am about to cum, but my voice tears away in breathless moans. I grab his dreds between my fingers, trying to relieve this pent-up energy inside of me.

His tongue hits my G-spot while his fingers rub my clit aggressively. I squeal in delight. Unknowingly, this turns Renardo on and he brings his lips back to my left ear.

"Is this my pussy?" He whispers.

"Yes," I answer breathlessly.

"Tell me this my pussy," he orders with a grin.

"This is your pussy, baby," I moan as he parts my pussy lips with his fingers as if to open a present.

Renardo feasts even more, his tongue working even faster than before. He brings his tongue up and up until it is dancing on my clit, while his fingers continue to work my insides. At this point, I am far readier then I thought I had expected to want him inside of me.

"Aw shit! Baaaby...baaaaby...baaaby," I plead as this is driving me wild. My mind is running a million times faster than it had ever done before. I am stuck in pure ecstasy and I only want it to keep going.

He grabs onto my hips as he continues to suck on my clit. Pressure continues to build higher and higher. A steady stream of white cream covers his fingers as my whole body pulsates in a crescendo of orgasmic pleasure. He draws the orgasm out as he continues to eat my pussy and fingers me.

It takes a few minutes for this wave of pleasure to wash over me. I feel out of this world. My pussy throbs as I try to regain my energy. Gently, I drag my tongue to his ear, and mumble, "Tell me you want me."

"I want you," he says in the sexiest tone, his dick solid as steel.

I want to please him the way he just did with me, so I drop gracefully to my knees.

"I love you," he says, placing a kiss on my forehead.

My tongue plays over his sensitive inner thighs. I'm not exactly sure of what I am doing, but I must be doing something right because Renardo quivers as I lift his dick with the strength of my tongue. I look up and give him a knowing look as my dripping tongue caresses and strokes his shaft. He groans with his hand gently petting my hair.

"Yeah, baby, just like that," he mumbles.

I repeat the move because I am unsure of what to do, but I am gentle with my mouth as he instructs. One thing I do know is that I must stay consistent because I don't want to reset him. My lips kiss up and down his throbbing dick, teasing it, causing him to shudder and moan. To know that my tongue has this much power over him is exciting.

I follow his words precisely, learning what he wants and what he likes. Holding the back of my head, he slowly pushes his dick into my mouth. I gag as he slowly pushes his dick down my throat. His dick goes deeper and deeper down my throat, until I have trouble breathing. Pulling his dick from my mouth, I try to catch my breath.

"You okay, baby?"

"Yeah," I say in between coughs.

"You're doing a good job, baby," he says while he fingers me. "This time just take it slow."

Heeding his advice, I drag my tongue from his balls up to the tip of his dick. My mouth tantalizes and my tongue stimulates as I suck the pre-cum that covers it. I love the taste of my man.

My left-hand strokes his rock-hard dick, up and down, down and up, in slow teasing increments, being sure to get it sloppy wet. I take my time, not moving too fast, but in a sensual motion because I want to make love to him with my mouth.

"Damn, baby," Renardo groans.

My eyes meet his with anticipation for his next instructions. On spur of the moment, my intuition kicks in. Renardo's eyes twinkle as a conceited smile graces his face while my juicy mouth engulfs his dick. Completely taken by the situation, his eyes shutter as the suction from my mouth and the moist titillation from the swirl of my tongue roam over the tip of his dick.

"Ah, yes, ah yes…" he moans.

Never in a million years did I think I would enjoy sucking his dick, but he is transported and I love it. I love every sound he makes when I'm down. I want to suck him dry.

"I need my pussy right now, woman," he requests, his hands urging me upwards.

His request is urgent, he has to have me right this minute. He needs to be inside of my body. Joined. My mouth, as directed, follows the course of his defined abs and hard contours of his chest up to his lips.

After planting the sexiest kiss on my lips, Renardo lays me down gently on his bed. Laying on my back, my legs are open granting him all access.

"You're so tight," he says with a laugh as he tries to enter me for the first time.

The third time proves to be the charm. With one hard thrust I can feel his dick inside of me. I let out a yelp of pain as my eyes water. Flipping me on top of him, Renardo leans up and kisses me slowly, whispering the words, "I love you."

As I come down, on his big thick long black dick all I can think of is how this couldn't feel any better. I love the feel of his hands over my body. Feeling how he grips my breast.

"Ah, ah, ah," I let out a wincing moan as the rest of Renardo enters me. Even though it hurts, his dick is the perfect fit for my pussy as it reacts to the grasp of my internal muscles.

As my very moist pussy moves further down his dick, I give Renardo a look that says I want and need him all the way inside me. He is so damn sexy, it is unreal. Our eyes never leave one another. We've been waiting so long, anticipating, dreaming of this moment.

To keep my balance, I place the palm of my hands across his chest. Up and down I go. Up and down. White cream covers his dick. I love how he watches me as my breast bounce and jiggle. I love catching a glimpse of a smile as he looks down, spreading my ass in excitement.

His dick feels so good inside of me that I break eye

contact. I look up at the ceiling which causes Renardo to draw me downward, so we are face to face. My undivided attention is what he wants and I give it to him.

"This your dick baby… make your dick cum, baby," he commands.

Pulling me down by the shoulders, he drives his dick into. I love how he talks dirty as I ride his dick. It only makes me want him more as we give ourselves to each other.

Before I can get comfortable in this position, he suddenly flips me into a doggy style position. I can still feel how hard he is inside me. I love being bent over and spread.… knowing his dick is behind me, hard and eager. His dick is powerful, much powerful than I could have ever expected.V12!

My back arches and another set of inaudible moans escapes my lips as Renardo thrusts into me with such power, fucking me slowly, yet strongly. I hold onto the sheets tightly while my eyes roll to the back of my head. With each thrust, he kisses my back, intensifying everything. He knows exactly what he is doing.

Flipping me over on my back, Renardo slowly moves in and out of me. The tip of his dick drags inside of me which drives me wild. I can feel every curve, every vein. The faster he goes, the more I can feel his dick throbbing inside of me. It feels so good that I can't speak a word. He gets even more turned on by seeing my wet pussy wrapped around his dick, drenching it.

"Cum all over my dick. Cum all over this good dick, baby."

He makes my body ache for more. I wrap my left arm around him with the urgency of someone drowning in a sea - a sea of love. Tiny sweat beads drip from our foreheads. My body flows so freely with his aggressive touches.

In the throes of passion, he pins my arms down to the mattress, taking me faster and harder, just to feel my body clench in pleasure. From somewhere deep inside of me, I erupt in a moan, my fingernails dig into his back as he reaches his full depth. Feeling the pressure of his climax building, I deliberately tighten myself.

"I love you," he whispers while looking into my eyes.

"I love you," I say as our souls leave our bodies for a higher love.

"Can I cum baby?" He asks.

"Yes…baby!" I reply in a high whiny tone, trembling as the climax intensifies.

In such an indescribable way, we become one with one goal and purpose, each utterly drunk with love for the other. Right next to his ear, I let out groans of pleasure, "Mmmm…baby. Fuck me! Renardo… Renardo…Renardo…Oooo baby, I want to cum."

"Oh, shit," he groans, his feet stiffen as my pussy tenses and clenches. "Don't close your eyes, baby. Look at me as we cum together."

We see each other at our most vulnerable, and cum harder and longer than we ever have. Between our loving smiles we both breathe deep, easy breaths. After a few moments, Renardo collapses besides me.

"I love you," he says grabbing my hand.

It takes no time for Renardo to be ready for round 2. Still tapped out and on an orgasmic high, I say with a giggle, "Baby, wait, wait, wait. I have spaghetti legs."

My legs are no longer usable as the orgasm leaves them limp and shaking uncontrollably. Renardo leaves the bed, to go to the kitchen. I can hear *The George*

Lopez Show playing on the television in the living room. Within a few seconds, he returns with a can of Sprite for us to share. The love-making has us both thirsty.

As the night progresses, we go round after round. We both can't stop until we get enough. We put our mouth in places that no one sees, swallowing each other's sweetness. We do things we'll never forget and undoubtedly never regret. We connect mind, body, and soul.

———◆———

AWAKENING FROM THE BEST REST I'VE EVER had, my eyes grace Renardo's gorgeous face smiling down at me.

"Good morning, sleepyhead," he says greeting me.

"Good morning," I respond with a smile running my fingers through his dreads.

A quick second passes before I realize what time it is. "Ugh, good morning means that I have to go and I don't want to," I say with my smile turning into a pout.

"We'll have plenty of nights like this, baby," Renardo says, trying to ease my mind.

"I know," I reply. "It's just that I don't want to go. I love being here with you."

"And I love having you here. I love you," he says, tracing his fingers down my arm.

"I want this feeling to last forever. I mean, here I am an Empress, here with my Emperor. I feel so safe with you."

"You are safe," he says, wrapping his arms around me.

"I'm glad you feel that way, baby. I want you to know that I will always protect you."

"You can't foresee everything, baby," I respond.

"Even so, I just want you to know that I will always keep you safe. You're the center of my universe and you know that. Now, what do I have to do to turn that frown upside down?"

"Just continue to be your sweet wonderful self," I say, giving Renardo a kiss.

"Now, if you continue giving me kisses like that our day will never get started," he says, making us both laugh.

~ NARD ~

EMPRESS, EMPRESS, EMPRESS...DAMN, I CAN'T keep my mind off that sexy woman. After 6 long months I thought this day would never come, but my patience has been rewarded with pure bliss. I was transfixed the moment my eyes saw her naked petite stature. Her brown beautiful skin with her conical, firm C cup breasts that I love to bury my face in and tug on her brown nipples. Her stomach is flat with a hint of underlying abs and her waist is small just how I like. Her inner thighs are softer than rose petals, just like her entire skin. Her body in the complete nude is a piece of art. If I knew how to draw portraits, I would have drawn one last night. She is gorgeous - like no other woman.

The night I first saw her I knew she was special. I give her the utmost respect for not giving herself to me until she learned everything she needed to know about me because any other female would've been gave me the pussy. I took my time and was gentle because she is so sweet and pure.

If I didn't have to leave the warmth and tightness of her walls, I never would. I can still hear her deep breaths turnin' to moans creating the sweetest rhapsody I have ever heard. I still hear her beg, "Fuck me…please," as she spread her legs and angled her sweet pussy up towards me. I still hear the gasp and tremor she made as I increased pressure. The look of panic and satisfaction on her face as she convulsed when she experienced her first orgasm. It was funny to see her search for words and open her mouth, but no words would form because she was on an intense high.

I love being lost in her love, taking my time to learn her insides and feeling each inch of my dick making her pulse and tense. I love drownin' in her sweet scent. I love lickin' her ass and eating her phat pussy. I love her sweet taste on my lips. My tongue into her opening and feeling the softness within. My nose bumping against her clit as my breathing began to rasp as it was cut off by her folds, which blocked my breath intakes. Tracing my tongue on her clit and being rewarded with her cries of, "Yes, baby, don't stop." My taste buds have never been more excited than when my tongue explored her skin. I never want to erase the taste of her out of my mouth.

I can close my eyes and visualize our night to remember. Empress lying on the bed. My hands massaging her beautiful brown titties. Me grabbin' her ass cheeks, or as she says the 'cakes', and spreadin' them apart so I could choose where to start. Grippin' her hair and poundin' into her and watchin' her full titties bounce wildly as she cried out my name. Her eyes never breakin' contact with mines as she sucked my dick was one of the sexiest things I have ever seen. Watchin' her beautiful face glow after she came all over my dick. I wanted all of her. Running my hands up and down her body and feeling the inside of her with my dick. My goal was to please her like no other man has and show her how I deeply I crave her.

I was in heaven. I could rest in her tight pussy forever. Feelin' the warmth of my skin against hers. Melting together was indefinable. I wish I could stay there, existing in her love until the end of time. I know the passionate love we made together united our souls. I loved taking in her beauty and the afterglow on her skin. When I entered her, and gazed into her eyes, I knew she loved no other man but me, and I knew she could see the same thing in my eyes. I loved the smile of discovery, of knowing, of awakening that graced her face. I'm deeply in love with this woman and she's deeply in love with me.

I don't want this to never end. I see so much with her by my side. She has given me purpose to want to change for the better. I've got to make a change or else all this bullshit I'm in will become a never-ending cycle until I'm dead or I've got life in prison. This shit crazy because I see this shit, but I still do things that will bring chaos in my life. I've got to go ahead and take care of that nigga Jaz and Heard's broad before shit gets even worse than it already is. Then I can hang up my guns for good.

Chapter Forty-two

~ NARD ~

"I REALLY CAN'T BELIEVE WE ARE FISHING right now. It's so different," Empress remarks as I am baiting her fishing rod.

"It's chill, right? I love the serenity and calmness of being out on the water," I comment, smiling because I love that Empress is enjoying a hobby of mine.

"It's so beautiful out here," Empress says admiring the surroundings.

Beautiful is the exact word to describe Empress, the moment, and the environment. This spring day is postcard perfect. The weather is gorgeous today. Blue skies, soft winds, and a sun that shines bright, yet not burn the skin. The sweet smell of jasmine fills the lakeside air.

Due to the little time I've been spending with Empress, I decided that coming to Lake Lanier would be a great way to make it up to her and so far, my choice has been correct.

Lake Lanier spans five Georgia counties and is full of gated communities that sit on the water. There are waterfront homes with individual docks and lakefront homes with community docks. Winding streets and bike paths are lined with tall, tulip poplar trees.

It is a nice, safe, clean and friendly place to live - the opposite of Rockdale. People wave at us as they are on boat tours, kayaking, and paddle boarding. The community looks like a picture out of a storybook. It's the type of place I would love to settle down with Empress.

"Baby, we're losing more bait than we are catchin' fish," I say casting my line.

"Hahaha, I know," Empress laughs. "We totally suck at this fishing thing."

"Speak for yourself," I say with a smirk as I reel in a bass.

"Oh wow, baby," Empress says watching me bring the bass up. "You caught a fish! I've got to capture this moment with a picture."

Empress pulls out her phone and snaps pictures of me in action. "Baby, you know I don't like takin' pictures."

"I know, but you're too cute not to," Empress says before giving me a short, sweet kiss. "Plus, I want to always remember today. What better way to do that than takin' pictures? Life is all about moments."

"Before I met you, I never knew what it was like to look at someone and smile for no reason," I say to Empress as she takes a selfie of us holding the fish.

"Looks like you've got sumthin to cook tonite," I tease.

"Um, me in a kitchen? Yeah, right," she says and we both laugh.

"Baby, that's sumthin we've got to change. You can't have me out here starvin'," I say in a joking manner. "You know they say the way to a man's heart is through his stomach."

"One, you will always have sumthin to eat, if you

know what I mean and two I already have your heart, so that lil sayin' does not apply to me," she responds in a joking manner.

"That's right," I add with a smile.

"Do you think I will catch one?" Empress innocently asks.

"Sure, baby," I say in an upbeat manner to give her motivation. "But it's goin' to take time and you have to develop a technique. Remember, fishing is a process and the better your technique, the more you'll catch."

"I would never have put Renardo Wade and fishing together," Empress says. "How did you learn to fish?"

"My grandfather used to take me from time to time when I was a little boy. He used to say many men go fishin' all of their lives without knowin' that it is not fish they are after."

"Is that where my Booskie Wooskie gets all of his wisdom from?"

"Some of it," I reply with a smile. "He was a man of principle."

"Just like you," she says in an adoring manner. "I'm so glad that your granddaddy taught you how to fish cause at least I know if we were lost at sea, you could catch us some supper."

"Baby, he taught me more than just a survival skill set. When we were out here on the water, my grandfather taught me something much more valuable."

"What was that, baby?"

"He taught me to observe the ways of nature and people."

Empress nods her head understandingly with her eyes smiling at me. "Well, I may not have any fishing experience, but I know I made the biggest catch out here," she says with a smirk.

"Booskie, how can you say that? You haven't caught nothin' out here."

"Tsk tsk tsk," she playfully says. "I caught you, didn't I?"

"My woman," I say blowing her an air kiss. "Tell me sumthin that I would never imagine Empress Cunningham doin' as a little girl."

For a second, Empress looks across the lake and smiles as she says, "Hmmmm... Hockey. I used to play street hockey."

"Baby, black people don't play hockey," I joke. "Now, I definitely can't see you playin' hockey, let alone on a street."

"It was no joke in my neighborhood," she says, continuing to giggle. "We started out with golf clubs and tennis balls. Then we upgraded to real hockey sticks and hockey pucks. I was the truth out there. I was the smoothest and the fastest with my inline skates. I had a mouth guard and knee pads because we were playin' on the streets - real hard concrete. I was gonna go pro, baby."

"Yeah, I bet," I say, making us both laugh. "I wish I had a time machine, so I could see you."

"Do you think we would have liked each as kids?"

"No doubt about it," I reply.

Empress is so sweet. She completes me in ways I never knew were possible. She is more than I could have ever asked for. When she smiles and laughs, I can't help but smile along too, even if it is just on the inside. Happiness with her is automatic. She exudes affection and warmth. Maybe it is the reason her beautiful brown skin glows. Inner beauty lights her eyes. I am captivated by her presence, and submerged in her aura of love and beauty.

As the sun falls, we head back to the dock. The sun

seems to set perfectly on Empress' face. Her eyelashes flutter like the wings of a butterfly as the sun seeps into her eyes.

"Sexy Lady," I call out with a smirk while observing her.

"Yes," she answers seductively.

"Do you know how the Italian painter, Carlotti, defined beauty?"

"No."

"Well," I say with a smile. "According to the Nicolas Cage movie, *Next*, Carlotti defined beauty as the sum of all parts working together in such a way that nothing needed to be added, taken away or altered. You fit that description, baby. You are beautiful."

"Aw, baby, you're going to make me start crying out here. That was so sweet," she says wiping the corners of her eyes.

"I love you," I state looking directly into her beautiful eyes.

"I love you, too," she replies with the most gorgeous smile. "You wanna know sumthin?"

"What?"

"You loved me before you knew it," she says with her smile still radiating from the sunlight.

"And why do you think that?"

"Cause I just know," she confidently answers. "As you always tell me, actions speak louder than words."

"Well, I did tell you that I love you first," I say teasing Empress.

"Yeah, yeah," she says. "But, don't forget that I saw you first, which is how our whole love story began."

I love playfully going back and forth with Empress about who loves who more, rather than argue about petty, childish drama.

"Baby, I need you to listen to what I'm about to tell you."

Hearing these words, Empress sits up straight. "What is it, baby?"

"It's nothin' bad, baby. It's just that I appreciate your love because I've never had anyone love me the way that you do. And I thank you. I know you've noticed I've been busy lately and have had little time on my hands. I can't tell you what I've been doin' but it's almost over. Then it's just you and me. I'll be completely done with the streets. Sometimes holdin' on to certain things causes more damage than letting go."

"You are right, baby," Empress says. "I just wish you could enlighten me on what you are saying because I'm lost. Is there something I can possibly help you with?"

"Baby doll, just know I love you dearly. You hold the keys to my success and my destruction. I've never given anyone that much control over me but I can't help it. I trust you and know you'll never betray me."

"You know more than anything that I just want you to be okay," Empress says, concerned.

"I am, baby. The last thing I want or need is you stressin' and worrying. Everything will work itself out, baby."

~ EMPRESS ~

OUR FISHING TRIP EARLIER TODAY WAS SO much fun. It feels so good to receive Renardo's love. He is so thoughtful and caring. I feel like melting when he looks at me in that special way…when we touch…mmmm. Electricity is what I feel when an unexpected expression of love from him comes my way. What a feeling it is to know he's in my corner and he won't let me go. We have such a strong bond. I will do anything for Renardo and I know he will do anything for me. Yet, at times, loving him can be upsetting because I don't know exactly what he is keepin' from me. I wish he would open up and tell me what is troubling him.

Wanting to curl up into the curve of his body, I stretch my arms out to wrap them around him. But, to my surprise, the only thing I feel is the crisp cotton sheets.

Partially opening my eyes, the bright red numbers on Renardo's alarm clock reads 3:14 a.m.

"Baby," I call out rolling over on my back, wrapping the sheets around my nude body.

My sleep-filled eyes scan the room, only to find Renardo sitting in the alpha brass chair I picked out for his bedroom. The moonlight creeping in through the blinds reveals his brows slouched down, leaving three lines across his forehead.

"What's wrong, baby?" I ask letting out a low moan as I climb further into alertness. "Can't you sleep?"

"Yeah, baby. I'm good," he says. "Larosa texted me and woke me up. Go back to sleep, baby."

"No, I can't sleep if you can't," I reply, sitting up.

"You were just sound asleep, baby," he says with a hint of humor.

"Yeah, but that was before I knew you were up," I remark.

Renardo is definitely trying to have his way, but I will not let him suffer through whatever he is dealing with alone. What kind of girlfriend would that make me?

"What's wrong, baby?" I ask again, this time more sternly.

"Now, why do you assume sumthin is wrong?" He asks, walking over to the bed.

"Well, maybe because you are sittin' in the dark at three sumthin in the morning," I throw at him.

"Well, maybe because I've been waitin' for my sexy lady to wake up, so I can do some things to her," he says with a smirk.

"Things like what?" I question with a smile.

"Things like this," he says, biting my neck.

Obviously, Renardo does not want to talk about whatever is on his mind. I'll let him have his way this early morning for I cannot resist his touch. Besides, whatever is troubling him will reveal itself in due time.

Chapter Forty-three

~ EMPRESS ~

TODAY I GOT TO SCHOOL EXTREMELY EARLY. The smell of cooked sausage, golden pancakes, and maple syrup woke me. Since Renardo could not sleep, he decided to cook breakfast. To my surprise, he is a pretty good chef. I enjoyed our weekend together and I wish it could have lasted forever. But here it is, just another manic Monday - back to school and work.

Since I am here so early, I work out in the gym. As I do my daily 100 crunches, Fallon walks into the workout room. I see her lips moving but I am deaf to the sound.

"What did you say?" I ask, taking off my ear buds.

"I was just sayin' hey and that I haven't seen you since the sleepover at Chante's house a few months back," Fallon says as she gets on the elliptical machine.

"Oh wow. Has it been that long?!" I say, trying to recall the last time we saw one another.

"Yep," she confirms. "I meant to drive out to Rockdale to see if you were okay after that shooting at your job, but I never found the time. You know how it is," she adds with a fake smile.

"No worries," I say in between crunches. "It's all good. I am fine and life couldn't be better."

"Oh really?" She says with a smile. "I do see a glow around you... either you're using really good moisturizer or you're fuckin'. Which one is it?"

"It is the latter," I say, blushing with a smile.

"What!?!?" Fallon says in the middle of her steps on the elliptical machine. "I can't believe it. Who met your standards?" She asks sarcastically. "I haven't heard any mention of you being linked to anyone at the school."

"Like I would really talk to any of the lame, nasty ass boys here," I say, wiping my forehead with my white towel.

"So, he doesn't go here? Oh, wait a minute," she says, looking into space trying to replay our last time together. "You were really feelin' some guy who worked at your job or something. Is it him?"

"He doesn't work with me, but yes, it is him," I say with a giggle correcting her.

"Cool," she says with a smile. "Have I met him?"

"No, but you will when we show up at the Lady of Brook soiree this weekend."

"Finally, the wait is over," she says with a giggle. "I don't see how you waited that long. One week without some play and even the most ugliest nigga looks good to me."

"You don't have no standards," I say while laughing and shaking my head.

"A dick is a dick. Niggas these days don't be talkin 'bout nothin' anyways."

"Well, I hope you being safe out here in these streets," I say, disagreeing with her statement.

"I'm just doing what niggas have done for centuries. Sowing my wild oats. Don't slut shame me, Empress."

"It's nothing like that," I say trying to avoid confrontation. "I'm just sayin' while you're out here doin' you, just remember what they taught us in health class."

"Yeah okay. Soooo…how was it?"

"Amazing doesn't even capture how great it is," I say with the broadest of smiles.

"Okay, then," she says, giving me a high five.

"Hey look, I gotta go shower so I can get to class on time. I will see you on Saturday."

"Alrite, just make sure you and your nigga come correct. Cause me and one of my boos is goin' to be on point," she says as I walk out the door.

"Come on now," I say. "You know me better than that. We gon dress to impress."

"My girl," Fallon says with a smile.

"Do you know what will be on the menu?"

"Girl, wack finger foods, like cucumber sandwiches with cream cheese
  and cheese blocks."

"Oh no!" I say. "All the money we pay in dues and we can never get a decent meal."

"You know we are a first-class club, darling, so we only eat foofoo food," Fallon jokingly says.

"Since we're so first class, how about adding filet mignon to the menu," I add. "Me and my baby will have to stop and get something to eat before we get there."

"Oh, for sure," she agrees.

"Okay, girl I'll talk to you later," I say heading to the showers.

CHAPTER FORTY-FOUR

~ NARD ~

THINGS COULDN'T BE BETTER FOR ME AND Empress. It seems like for the first time in my life, God is giving me favor because I did not have to take care of Bianca after all. She died in a coma two weeks after the shootin'. That is one less problem I have to worry about.

As I drive my Monte Carlo SS with Empress in the passenger seat, I glance at her, and she catches me and smiles.

"What, baby?" She asks.

"Baby, you have literally brought joy into my life. Never in a million years would I have ever thought I would be this happy," I say with a smirk placing my hand on her thigh.

Empress cannot hide her joy because she feels the same way about me. We are soulmates and we know it.

"Baby, I'm starving," she tells me.

"I am too baby."

"What do you want to eat?"

"You," I reply.

Caught off guard, she blushes. "Baby, I'm serious."

"I'm dead serious," I say with a grin.

"Baaaby, stop," she says teasingly. "You're making me wet."

"I love it when you're wet," I say with a smirk as I rub the front of her thong feeling the dampness.

"Baaaby…that's gonna have to wait until later," she says after letting me rub that phat pussy for a minute.

"Let's get sumthin to eat at Popeyes."

"Popeyes? You sure you want that, baby?"

"Yes, baby," she says with a smile. "I know this is goin' to sound so stereotypical, but I just love chicken."

"There's nothin' wrong with that. If that's what my baby wants, then that is what she will get," I say, giving her a kiss. "After all, I am wearing this preppy boy shit for you."

Of all places, she wants to eat at damn Popeyes. I drive to Popeyes despite my spirit tellin' me to choose another restaurant. I feel this way due to the fact that it is on the other side of town, just where Jaz and his YGC crew usually roam. But, my baby will always get what she wants as long as I can give it to her.

We enter Popeyes and order to dine-in. As we wait on our order, we sit in a booth and talk about our future and our plans. Empress talks about school, something I don't see in my future. *After I get my GED, I will strive to have my own business. I'm tired of school and I'm glad Empress understands how I feel. Her going to school is a plus, and as long as I have breath in my body, I won't deter her from that direction.*

"Oh yeah, baby, I meant to tell you that I booked some studio time for you to record a demo on your song, 'In the Stars'," I tell Empress as we wait on our food.

"Forreal???" She says, nearly choking on her sweet tea.

"Yes, baby. I'm forreal," I say with a smile.

"Oh, wow Renardo! This is so sweet of you. Nobody has ever been this kind to me. Ever. You don't know what this means to me," she says, wrapping her arms around me, giving me kisses and hugs.

"Well, baby, I'm not just anybody," I reply. "Remember that. I love you."

"I love you, too," she says, giving me a kiss.

I knew the studio time would make Empress happy, but I didn't expect her to be this excited. I love being able to bring this kind of joy to my woman.

Finally, our food arrives. As the waitress sits our food on the table, I hear a voice in my head telling me to look up. What I see makes my heart drop.

God…not tonight.

CHAPTER FORTY-FIVE

~ NARD ~

AS JAZ AND FOUR OF THE YGC NIGGAS WALK into Popeyes, I tense. Naturally, Empress notices the change in my disposition and immediately searches my eyes with her own.

"What's wrong, baby?" She asks with a worried tone and a concerned look.

Damn! My spirit told me to choose another place to eat. It's only a matter of time before they spot us.

"Baby, I need you to go get in the car and I'll follow you after," I instruct her, handing her the car keys.

Before Empress can question me, I give her a look of urgency. Without hesitation, she gets up and walks towards the front door. Of all the YGC niggas, Jaz is the first to look at Empress, just like I knew he would. Immediately, he tries to talk to her.

"What's good, pretty lady?" Jaz asks.

Empress gives him a look of disgust, which causes me to smirk. Damn, I wish I can dead this nigga right now! This is not the right time or place. I can't let them niggas know Empress is my woman. That's why I had her walk out ahead of me. I just hope I can get out of here without being seen, so

Empress remains safe.

Stepping in front of Empress, Jaz tries even harder to spit his wack ass game to get my baby's number. Seeing she can't get around him, Empress stops and literally screams, "Look, I've got a man!"

She then does the unbelievable and points in my direction. The world seems to slow down. With all eyes on me, I stand up and walk in the direction where everyone is standing.

"Well, you have some nerve to be in my hood on my side of town!" Jaz states firmly with animosity in his voice.

"Nigga, I have the green light to go wherever I please, so don't get this shit twisted", I respond, meeting him with the same aggression, positioning my body in front of Empress.

"You aren't about to just walk up out of here. You know that, right?" Jaz says, looking directly in my eyes taking a step towards me.

I look at him like he is crazy. For a second, we have a frozen standoff. Each disrespectful word only adds fuel to my fire. My fist clenches and my jaw tightens. I almost lose it, but Empress' soft hands bring me back to reality. Because I know I can't put her in harm's way.

"Jaz," I say harshly, yet coolly, as I try to maintain my temper for the sake of my woman. "Now, you know there are rules to this shit. If this shit go down right now, that's violating me in the worst way, especially if you don't kill me. Let your next move be a wise one and your best one," I state, clutchin' my .38 snub nose.

While in deep thought, Jaz looks at me through narrowed eyes. Looking around, I notice KG and another YGC nigga clutchin'. I know they will have to be the first niggas I take out. I wish Empress would just walk out, but I know I can't allow them niggas to make a move first or else we won't make it out.

Brrring!

The sound of the bell from the front door causes me to flinch. I draw my pistol while I have the chance. Now those short ass legs of Empress start moving. She takes off before the first shot lets out. Hoppin' in the driver's seat she cranks up my car.

Letting out four quick shots, I hit KG twice in the chest, the other YGC nigga once in the leg, and barely miss Jaz. I back up out of Popeyes, letting off my final shot, shattering the window just in case Jaz and the other two niggas come after us. Quickly, I hop in the passenger seat and Empress drives off into the night. The sirens in the distance do not escape our ears.

Chapter Forty-Six

~ NARD ~

THE CRAZY THING IS, I KNOW I HAVE FUCKED up, but I don't care. Empress is safe, and that is all that matters. I would be a fool to go to my apartment. Once the police review the camera footage, they will be knockin' on my door in just a matter of time.

Empress is driving and I can tell she is shook. She doesn't even have on her seatbelt, which is unlike her because she is a great believer in car safety. She's the type of person who does not crank up the car until all the passengers have their seatbelts on.

Damn, I never meant for her to see that shit, but she got to understand it had to go down.

"Empress, baby, are you ok?"

The look she gives me brings pain to my heart. "Is this the shit you were tryin' to tell me about on the boat!?!"

"Calm down, baby," I say, hoping to get her to slow down and calm down.

She may be a little woman, but she has a heavy ass foot. She has to be doing close to 90 mph.

"Don't tell me to calm down! Can you answer my

muthafuckin' question!?!" She yells.

"Whoa, baby, why are you talkin' to me like that?" I respond, shocked by her tone and language.

"You've got to be joking, Renardo! I've been asking you what is goin' on for the longest time and now this bullshit happens!!!" She screams hitting her hand on the steering wheel with every word she speaks. She rolls down the window and tosses her phone out.

"Now why the fuck did you just do that?"

"Since I don't keep secrets from you, I will tell you," she says sarcastically. "Everyone keeps blowin' my fuckin' phone up wondering why the fuck I am not at the Lady of Brook soiree. Fuck them!"

Empress is so wrapped up in her thoughts, she doesn't even hear me. I can't blame her, though. I hate she saw me blow up and I hate she was exposed to this side of me.

"Baby, turn right here," I say, pointing to the bright yellow and red Super 8 Motel sign.

"Here?" She questions with an attitude.

"Yes, baby."

"Are we seriously stayin' at this dusty ass 'pull up to your room' motel???"

"Baby, please. After what happened, we can't risk goin' back to Rockdale right now. Plus, they don't require ID here. Just sit tight. I'm goin' to get a room key."

~ EMPRESS ~

I CAN'T BELIEVE HOW QUICKLY CHAOS ENSUED at Popeyes. One minute, Renardo and I are waiting for our meal, the next minute, a shootout is happening. I'm scared, uneasy, nervous, and upset. Why did this happen? What if those guys want revenge? This is too much!!!

Renardo grabs me to stop me from pacing the floor. "Listen, baby," he says, sitting me at the foot of the bed. Talking very slowly he continues, "I'm about to tell you some things that are extremely confidential. I know I can trust you, but you have to promise me you will never tell another living soul."

"Okay, baby," I say while preparing myself for whatever it is he is about to tell me.

Taking a long, deep breath, he begins, "A few days or so before we met, me and Larosa robbed some niggas."

Looking into his eyes, I calmly reply, "Let me guess… the guys at Popeyes were those niggas."

"Yes," he slowly says in an ashamed manner. "Remember shawty who was eyein' me at Krystal's?"

My heart beats even faster. What kind of question is this??? Of course, I remember her ass. Slowly, I nod my head.

"Well…she is one of those nigga's wife and she recognized me from the robbery that night at Krystal's. That's why she kept lookin' at me."

Shocked by Renardo's revelation, but putting all the scattered pieces in my mind together, it all makes sense. Stacks…the shooting at Krystal's…the shooting at Popeyes.

"Time and time again I asked you what was going on!!! You could have just told me then!!!" I yell out in frustration.

"I know baby, I know," he says, looking down at the floor.

Renardo's words pass through me like a tornado as I stare at the horrible 1970s theme wallpaper that is peeling off the walls. My mind is on idle, trying to digest his words and my feelings.

"I'm so sorry baby...I never meant for you to get involved," he sorrowfully apologizes.

Silence looms as our eyes study each other. We both seemed to be paralyzed out of fear. Fear of what the other might say. Fear of what is to come. Waiting and anticipating the other's next move. After a minute or so passes, hugging is my way of saying all the things I cannot in the moment.

"I know this is a lot, baby. But, I need to know you're okay. I love you and I pray to God this won't affect our relationship," he says with his arms wrapped so tight around me that I can barely breathe.

"It is a lot to take in, but I will be okay. This does not change my love for you. I love you. I will always love you," I reply, my eyes becoming watery.

"My woman," Renardo says, taking a sigh of relief.

"Not so fast!" I say rejecting his kiss and ending our hug. "All this shit you are into is fucked up, but we can't change the past," I add, pacing the floor. "I don't like what you're telling me at all and the fact you hid this from me doesn't make it any better. No secrets, remember?"

"I know baby, I know. And again, I am sorry. It really hurt me keepin' all this away from you...but to be honest, I wish you never had to witness what you saw today. I don't want you to have that image of me in your mind and I just didn't know how to tell you some shit like this, especially, when we first started dating. And even now I don't like talkin' about it."

"I know," I whisper.

The 'I know' means so many things. It is knowing it is painful for Renardo to reveal the truth, yet it is knowing he is only revealing certain truths and not the whole truth. It is understanding even though I don't like it.

Taking a deep breath, I run my hand across Renardo's face and say, "I love you, baby. You know I will keep this between us."

"My only priority right now is your safety. You mean the world to me. It's no secret what we mean to one another. I will protect you. I just need for you to stay cool, baby," he says. "I will never intentionally bring harm your way or do things that hurt you. You've got to know and believe that."

"I do, baby. But I can't deny…I am so afraid for you," my voice trembles as I fight back tears.

"Don't cry," Renardo says as he hands me a tissue. "I love you so much. I'll be fine, baby."

Chapter Forty-Seven

~ NARD ~

"SAY, FAM? WAT'S GOOD, BRUH?" LAROSA answers the phone.

"I got into a shootout with Jaz and his niggas at Popeyes."

"Say what!!!" Larosa yells into the phone. "Wat the hell you doin' on that side of town?"

"Listen, FAM. I'm not tryin' to hear this shit you talkin', but if you really need to know, I was with Empress," I say in an annoyed tone.

"Did you get him???"

"I know I shot two of his niggas. I'm not sure about him, though. As you know, I'm on the run. Once they look over the cameras, which I'm quite sure they already have, it will be a wrap for me. So, I'm goin' to need you to go to Vee and get some money for me, so I can get out of town."

"I got you bruh, but where you headed to?"

"I'm not sure yet. I've got to make some calls. Oh, yea, tell Vee that Michael Jackson is moonwalking and she will give you the package. That's the code we use," I instruct Larosa. "Call me once you get it."

"Why don't you just call and tell her I'm comin'?".

"FAM, just follow instructions," I reply, short on patience.

"I got you," Larosa quickly says, sensing I am about to blow a fuse.

"Get at me when it's done," I add.

"Love," we both say, ending the phone call.

"I couldn't help but overhear you say that you are leaving," Empress immediately says.

"Baby, I've just shot two niggas, possibly three. Hell, I don't even know if them niggas dead or alive."

Instantly, I notice that my statement hits Empress hard.

Fuck!!!

Why did I just say that?

"Baby, why did you do that?" Empress whimpers with her eyes watering and lips quivering.

I walk over to her and place my arms around her trying to comfort her.

God, why did this have to happen while she was with me?

"Baby, I had no other choice," I say. "I couldn't risk them niggas pullin' first and you get hurt or even worse, die. I would stop living if sumthin was to happen to you. I love you more than my life itself. I will make any sacrifice for you if it means keeping you safe."

Empress pulls away slightly while looking directly into my eyes and asks a question I've yet to sit down to ask myself. "What happens from here? How long do you plan on running?"

When she asks me these questions, something else hits me. When the police review those cameras, they will see Empress in Popeyes and will want to question her. No doubt, they will be at her school or both of her jobs tomorrow.

"Baby, you've got to listen carefully," I say, grabbing

her hands. "You've got to do everything I tell you to do. The police are probably goin' to bring you in for questioning. Tell them that you want to speak with an attorney. They may try to arrest you and if they do, you won't be in there for long."

"Say what!?!" Empress screams, looking at me like I am speaking in tongues.

"Baby, calm down," I say, trying to get a hold of her.

"So, you tellin' me I may get arrested for that bull-shit?!?" She questions, pointing at the door as though it is the "bullshit" she is referring to.

Not wanting to answer, I say nothing at all.

"I can't believe you!!!" She screams as she throws a pillow at me. "This the shit you are supposed to pro-tect me from! Everyone tried to warn me about you but I didn't listen."

"What the fuck you mean?" I snap. "Hell, what the fuck is 72 hours of lock up compared to 20 years to life for tryin' to protect your ungrateful ass?"

"Baby, I didn't –"

"No, you meant exactly what the fuck you said! You wouldn't have said it if you didn't mean it," I respond cutting her off.

"Baby, but I –"

"Here," I pull out 3 twenty-dollar bills and give them to her, "I'm leaving so take an Uber."

"What?" She says in a confused, whiny tone.

"I will contact you through Larosa," I say, writing Larosa's number down. "I'm about to get rid of my phone, so wait for my call. If anything, unexpected happens, contact him."

"Baby," Empress yells as I walk towards the door.

I stop dead in my tracks because I can't resist her. She runs over and gives me the most heavenly kiss.

Through this burst of emotion, our connection shows the strength of our love, the mutual need we have for one another. Feeling starts, thinking stops. She weakens me in the way that only she does and causes me to become disoriented. I am struggling with my brain and my heart. My heart obviously is winning out. This is the most intense and passionate kiss I have ever had. I have to get out of here because I want to be with her forever.

"Take me with you," she repeats so softly in between our kisses. "Take me with you."

"I can't be selfish, baby. I love you, Empress. I love you more than anyone and anything in this life. I want nothin' more than to take you with me, but I can't, baby."

"Yes, you can, baby. I don't care where we go as long as we're together," she says with tears streaming down her beautiful face.

"I love you more than my life itself, baby," I say, wiping some of her tears away with my thumb.

Heading for the door, my heart aches as I hear my soul mate cry. I turn around and the look in my eyes tells her everything she needs to know.

"There is no love lost, and there never will be," I say. "I love you dearly, but I've got to remain focused, baby."

"I know, baby. I just hate this. I wish there was another way," she says.

"There is no other way. Never doubt my love baby. We will be together soon," I say, walking towards her to give her one last embrace and a kiss which seems to last forever.

Chapter Forty-Eight

~ EMPRESS ~

AS I SIT IN THIS TIRED, BAD-SMELLING MOTEL ROOM, I can't believe all of this is happening right now. I still have not fully wrapped my head around all this chaos. Just when everything is so beautiful for us, something so ugly has to happen. I do not know if I can do this without him. I miss him already. I love Renardo so much that I can't think straight. We have formed a bond that will bind us together forever. Still, I'm so worried. The mere thought of being without him crushes me. Why did this have to happen, God?

I do not understand the purpose of God bringing the guy who is my soulmate only to remove him out of my life. I'm dealing with so many emotions right now. Initially, I was outraged and somewhat angry at Renardo for hiding things from me and for putting me in danger, but now the feeling has changed to sympathy and support because I realize that he risked his life and freedom to protect me and now who knows what the future holds for him…for me…for us.

They say everyone who falls in love will have one chance where they can turn around and walk away from it all. At that moment, you still have the power to decide whether you will keep your heart solely for yourself or give someone the sole power to do what they wish with it. I had that moment, and I literally ran to it. How could I not? The angels were telling me Renardo was the one.

We are two soulmates wanting to be with each other more than anything, but tragic circumstances are pulling us apart. We have the right love at the wrong time.

My body literally aches. I try crying because I know tears have a magical way of permitting people to feel a little better. This is useless. In an almost second nature way, I pull a tissue from the Kleenex box and begin scribbling lyrics to a melody that forms in my head:

If home is where his heart is
His home is in the streets
We are where heaven and hell meet
I don't care what they say
Cause he's my baby
Each night we kiss, kiss
Kiss goodnight
I say a prayer for him

CHAPTER FORTY-NINE

~ NARD ~

CLOSING THAT MOTEL DOOR WAS THE HARDEST thing I have ever had to do. My consciousness tells me to turn around and get my woman, but I know I can't take her with me. God, why??? When everything was going good for once in my life, I managed to fuck it all up.

As I sit in the driver's seat, I stare out the door. It feels as if my soul is leaving me. My heart is aching and longing to be by Empress' side. My heart knows everything will be OK if I'm with her. I need her. I've got to -

My phone rings and brings me out of the daze. Without looking at the phone screen, I answer, "Wat's up?"

"Now, that's no way to answer no phone, baby. Especially when talkin' to me," says the affectionate, shaky voice on the other end of the phone line.

"I apologize, Mrs. Vee. I'm under a lot of stress right now," I regrettably respond.

"I can see you had a certain individual come pick up that package. Will an old lady like myself be intruding too much if I asked why?" She asks.

Mrs. Vee is probably the only mother figure I have and I can confide in her about anything, but some things are best left unsaid.

"You wouldn't, Mrs. Vee. But, I don't have the time to explain. Did you give FAM that package?"

"I'm handing it over as we speak," she responds.

"Thank you, Mrs. Vee. I will contact you once I reach my destination, but lose this number because I'm about to get rid of this phone."

"OK, baby," she says lovingly, adding a cautious, "Be careful, baby."

I smile to myself because I know she means it. "Oh yea, tell FAM to just meet me at the Greyhound," I request.

"OK, baby," she says for the final time.

Hanging up the phone, I open my car door and slam the phone on the concrete, shattering the screen into tiny pieces. I roll over the frame to ensure there are no traces left.

Driving off, I head towards the Atlanta Greyhound station.

Chapter Fifty

~ NARD ~

STARS IN THE SKY ARE NONEXISTENT. IT IS funny how things change throughout the course of the day. Just a few hours ago, the sun radiated across me and Empress' face as we laughed. Now there is no sunlight and I am alone. The sky is moonless and clear. If only my future were this clear.

Reaching my destination, I quickly spot Larosa's cocaine-white Charger in the Magic City parking lot, despite the large crowd. He hops out of the Charger when he sees me pull in. With a worried look on his face, he opens the passenger door of my Monte Carlo SS and takes a seat.

"What the fuck is in that shit?" He asks, tossing me the package.

Opening the package, I reveal $10,000 in cash and a .357 magnum I stashed away two years ago. I knew there would come a time when I would need to unexpectedly leave. And that time is now.

"Where do you plan on goin', FAM?" Larosa asks.

"B-more," I respond. "Look into what happened to those niggas, so I will know what charges I will face and who to retain as my attorney."

"Damn, my nigga, why the fuck you had to go on that side of town by yourself?!?!?" Larosa screams, his emotions pouring out.

I can't even get mad because I know he is only venting since he won't see me for a while.

"FAM," I dolefully say. "I can't turn back the hands of time, so there is no need to dwell on that shit. It's done."

"You right, bruh, just make sure you hit me up as soon as you get up there, and be safe," he says in a big brother manner. "I will clean up the rest of this shit."

"That's love, FAM."

"Naw, nigga, I love you, my nigga. We brothers for life. Loyalty over everything," he says.

"I love you too, bruh. Know that," I reply. "Make sure you look after Empress. I gave her your number just in case anything happens. If the police pick her up to question her, call Vee and let her know. If they hold her, call Karen and leave a voicemail. If that happens, I'll be down to turn myself in, so I can free her."

"Wat if them niggas dead, FAM?" Larosa asks, alarmed by my statement.

"That's just sumthin I will have to deal with when that time comes," I respond. "I can't live with myself if Empress is locked up, and I am free."

Larosa shakes his head, not believing the words that are coming out of my mouth.

"I forgot to tell you to have someone drive with you so they can drive my car back, so here," I say as I peel off 3 hundred-dollar bills from the stack of money and hand it to him.

Larosa looks at me like I'm crazy and pushes my hand back towards me. "You will need it more than me, bruh. I will take care of everything."

Handing Larosa my .38, I ask him to get rid of it. Once I step out of the car, I hand him the keys. "I've got a bus to catch," I remark.

With each step I take towards the ran-downed, cramped bus station, something doesn't feel right and my spirit tells me to get back in my car. Crossing the street, I look over my shoulder, just in time to see Larosa drive off. Walking closer to the front door of the Greyhound station, the voice in my head screams louder, trying to plead with me to turn around.

I don't know if it is her walk or her slight smile that tells me that I am walking into a trap, but it is too late. As soon as I turn around and focus my eyes across the street, all I hear vehemently is "FREEZE!!!" and "GET ON THE DAMN GROUND!!!"

The flashing lights, the voices of the police, and the bodies of the bystanders all seem to blend into each other. Kneeling on the pavement and putting my hands up, my chest constricts, my breathing becomes shorter and everything becomes a blur because all I can think about are three individuals. The only three who knew I was coming to the Greyhound station, the three who I love the most in this world, the only three who could have set me up…Empress, Larosa, and Vee.

ACKNOWLEDGMENTS

Through God all things are possible and we thank you heavenly Father for allowing our minds, bodies, and spirits to unite and keeping us covered in your grace. This book was born on that kismet night in October of 2007 and realized later as a different project than this one. This book is the result. (P & E)

A thank you to my husband, for putting my pretty little hands in yours. Your focus, insight, and persistence has made this collaboration process easy. Thank you, baby! (E)

Shout out to my big brothers, Larry Rhodes aka Savage, Willie McLaughlin aka J ROC, and Donald Forte aka G. Thank you all for your support and never doubting me or my wife. (P)

Thank you to my mother, Simmona, for your continued support and encouragement of my artistic growth. (E)

Curtis Suber aka CJ and Ralpheal Petite aka Doughboy Rashaud Uptner aka Shotgun Shawty, even though y'all make me mad at times, I still have love for you both. (P)

Love and gratitude to my sister, Lxy. Thanks for generously donating your time and energy with your efforts of proofreading and providing feedback. "These are the moments…" lol. (E)

Marcus Porter aka Dirt and Varico Odari Williams aka Rico, men with a heart like mine - what's understood doesn't have to be explained. Our bond is unbreakable. (P)

For everyone who I've forgotten to mention, please don't be in your feelings because it's nothing but Love for my family and friends, even if we don't speak. We must bridge the gap that we have that is separating our people from striving together as one. Let's try something new. Love and Loyalty. (P)

54325700R00168

Made in the USA
Middletown, DE
13 July 2019